DIRTY
DEEDS

Squeaky Clean Mysteries, Book 4

By Christy Barritt

DIRTY DEEDS
By Christy Barritt

Dirty Deeds: A Novel
Copyright 2013 by Christy Barritt

Published by River Heights

Cover design by The Killion Group

The persons and events portrayed in this work are the
creation of the author, and any resemblance to persons
living or dead is purely coincidental.

Acclaim for the Squeaky Clean series:

Christy Barritt's novel, *Hazardous Duty*, is a delightful read from beginning to end. The story's fresh, engaging heroine with an unusual occupation hooked me, and I couldn't put it down. I highly recommend *Hazardous Duty*. ~ Colleen Coble, bestselling author

The next time you're tempted to watch CSI reruns, read this book instead! Spunky, sassy Gabby St. Claire sparkles in this new series. She'll keep you turning the pages. ~ Siri Mitchell, INSPY award-winning author

With Gabby St. Claire, Christy Barritt has created a fun sleuth in a unique profession. *Hazardous Duty* provides both humor and an engaging mystery. The twists and turns of the whodunit are matched only by the surprises of Gabby's spiritual growth and romantic entanglements. ~ Sharon Dunn, multi-published mystery and suspense author

Stay tuned and watch for more from this gifted, talented author. You'll love it. ~ Cheryl Wolverton, multi-published author

Crime scene cleanup should be a safe enough occupation, right? It comes after the crime is over. Not necessarily! Come enjoy this fun romp through the complications . . . men, mold, mayhem and murder . . . in Gabby St. Claire's rollercoaster life. ~ Lorena McCourtney, author of the Ivy Malone mysteries

Crime scene cleaning is dirty job, but Christy Barritt has made it hilarious. Amateur sleuth Gabby St. Claire is back, and in trouble again! *Suspicious Minds* delivers a riveting mystery, but it's Gabby's irrepressible charm as she engages

3

a zany cast of characters that keeps readers turning pages. Put this series on your must read list! ~ Claudia Mair Burney, author of the Amanda Bell Brown Mysteries

Suspicious Minds is witty, punchy and fast-paced. Kudos to Christy Barritt for an entertaining and intriguing read! ~ Janice Thompson, award-winning author

Suspicious Minds plays havoc on the nerves and the funny bone as crime scene cleaner Gabby St. Claire wisecracks her way between dead bodies and flying bullets. A treat not to be missed! ~ Jill Elizabeth Nelson, author of the To Catch a Thief series

DEDICATION:

This book is dedicated to all of my readers who keep asking for more. Those are the words a novelist loves to hear!

A special thank you to Kathy, Janet, Carolyn, and Shannon for your help with this book.

DIRTY DEEDS

CHAPTER 1

"I only have one request this week." Riley Thomas snuck a glance at me from the driver's seat of his beat up old Toyota Camry as we climbed the mountain road.

"You name it," I told him.

"No snooping. No following your curiosity wherever it leads. No sticking your nose into other people's business. No almost getting yourself killed. For once, I just want us to have fun."

I glanced over at my fiancé and nodded, as if he'd just asked me to do something ordinary and mundane, like cooking his favorite meal. "Of course. No following, sticking, or getting killed on my part. I can totally handle that."

This was going to be a long week. Just having fun? When did I ever do that? Fun *was* following leads and being nosy. The "almost being killed" part was debatable. I'd earned a bit of a reputation in the past for my work as a crime scene cleaner.

Riley's hands were casually draped through the steering wheel, despite the fact that even an Indy car driver might be stressed out right now with all of these twists and turns through the Virginia mountains. Steep drop offs threatened us on one side and looming cliffs on the other.

Before we'd turned off the main highway, I'd seen a sign declaring "Treacherous Road. Remain cautious." But our GPS led us onward and upward. And who were we to argue with the GPS?

Instead of stressing, I turned up the radio. I'd plugged in my smart phone, and an MP3 of *My Fair Lady* swooned through the car. "Wouldn't It Be Loverly" to be exact. For a moment before embarking on this trip, I'd been tempted to practice my Cockney accent, then I decided against it.

This was the first time Riley and I had taken a trip together. Ever. And this was my first trip out of my hometown of Norfolk, Virginia in ages. We were meeting some of Riley's friends from law school for some kind of attorney conference. During the day, he and his friends would go to their workshops. I, on the other hand, would relax and do things like swim in the pool, play tennis, take golf lessons, or get a massage.

I would not—I repeat would *not*—snoop, as per my recent promise to Riley.

As we rounded another sharp curve, sweat broke out across my forehead. I lifted my red hair from my neck to cool off. Normally I wore my hair curly and down to my shoulders. But we were going to this fancy resort with his fancy friends, so I'd decided to straighten it. I'd traded my normal jeans and T-shirt for some nicer jeans and a nicer T-shirt.

Sacrifices. That's what relationships were about.

Riley, on the other hand, looked the part of a prep school boy in his neatly pressed khaki shorts, a royal blue, V-neck shirt that matched his eyes, and some loafers. His thick dark hair was just tousled enough to show that he wasn't totally uptight, and he'd decided to forgo shaving for the week, so stubble lined his chin and the edges of his cheeks.

I grasped the armrest as another blind curve appeared in front of us on the snaky, desolate mountain byway. "This road is a death trap. Are you sure this is the right way to Wealthy Springs?"

"It's Healthy Springs," he corrected. "And this is a fun ride, isn't it? It gets your adrenaline pumping."

I looked out my window at the nearly endless drop into the valley below. My ears chose to pop, like they didn't want me to forget the thinning altitude. "Fun wouldn't exactly be my word of choice."

But *Wealthy* Springs would be exactly what I meant to say.

I thought my word choice fit the whole resort persona better, at least from what I'd read about the place online. The resort, called Allendale Acres, had once been a playground for the country's wealthiest, including more than twenty presidents, who all came here to enjoy the resort's natural springs. My previous idea of a nice hotel meant staying at a Holiday Inn instead of a Super 8.

Riley jerked the steering wheel to the left as he rounded a U-shaped bend. I could picture us flying off the road and remaining suspended in the air, much like Wile E. Coyote in one of those old cartoons, until the imaginary bottom disappeared, and we crashed to our deaths.

I swallowed and closed my eyes. I had to take my mind off this road before I lost it. "So, all of your college buddies are going to be here this weekend, huh?"

"That's right." Riley glanced over at me, a hint of a smile on his lips.

"Eyes on the road!" I instructed, pointing straight ahead. "There'll be plenty of time for you to stare at me and tell me how beautiful I am later."

"I can think of nothing else I'd rather do."

My cheeks actually reddened for a moment. How did Riley still have that effect on me? I sucked in a deep breath, realizing that between the road, Riley's pure and perfect chivalry, and this reunion, I was jumpier than popcorn in a frying pan.

Still, I was excited to see a different side of Riley. Since we were getting married in six months, I thought this weekend trip could be really interesting. It could also be painful because the likelihood that I would fit in with his law school friends was slim to nothing. No, my chances were better for fitting in with the inmates at a local correctional facility, and I'd put quite a few of them behind the bars there, if that told you anything.

Riley's friend Derek had called him a couple of months ago and suggested having a reunion, going as far as to say they could combine business with pleasure, because there was going to be this professional development conference going on at Allendale. According to Riley, there would be six of his old friends from Georgetown School of Law there.

As if he could read my mind, Riley said, "I think you'll really like them, Gabby."

I nodded, absorbing his quick words and tight voice. Very unlike my confident, levelheaded fiancé. "You're uncomfortable about something. What? Are you afraid your friends won't like me?"

I wasn't sure I really wanted to know the answer to that question, but it was too late. My inquiry was already out there, hanging suspended, much like I imagined this car after just one wrong turn.

Riley's face softened, and he threw a quick glance my way. "No, not at all. It's not like that. I know they'll love you."

"So why are you tugging at your shirt collar like you suddenly can't breathe?" I was an investigator—I'd been an official, respectable one for a whole month, at least—so I felt like the power of observation was on my side.

He finally sighed and raked a hand through his thick brown hair. "My friends are . . . my friends are different, Gabby. I know I don't talk about this very much, but I'm not the same person as I was back then."

Now I was curious. Were his friends part of a secret lawyer-by-day/motorcycle-gang-by-night group? Or maybe they all had dreads and listened to reggae, specializing in law cases involving voodoo and marijuana? Or maybe they'd all banded together because before law school they'd had aspirations of joining the circus? My imagination could make this far worse than reality. "What does that mean, exactly?"

"It's just that—" Before Riley could finish his sentence, the car hit a patch of gravel and skidded. The vehicle fishtailed, veering left, then right. The edge of the mountain loomed precariously close.

I grabbed the dashboard, bracing myself for either a harsh collision with the rock wall beside us or a free fall down the steep cliff on the other side. This was not how I saw my life ending.

At the hands of a vicious killer? Maybe.

In the middle of a gang fight? Perhaps.

Heck, I could even see my life ending because I'd breathed an airborne pathogen. But not in a car accident. Especially not in a car accident with no one chasing us, hanging out of the window with a gun in hand.

The car careened, the back tires edging dangerously close to the drop off. Those flimsy pine trees below wouldn't be any match for the furor of this chunk of metal tumbling toward them with endless momentum. No, those trees would snap in half like pencils. So would my neck for that matter. And Riley's.

Riley jerked the wheel again. The car spun and spun. My life flashed before my eyes.

This trip was supposed to end with "I've Had the Time of My Life," complete with Riley and I dancing on stage at a talent show like Patrick Swayze and Jennifer Grey in *Dirty Dancing*. Instead, it was looking more like the trip would start with R.E.M.'s "It's the End of the World as We Know It."

I screamed and braced myself.

CHAPTER 2

The car continued to spin and screech until finally colliding with the wall of rock beside us. My head jutted forward on the impact, before being stopped by a spray of white powder and a huge balloon.

That would be the air bag, I supposed. I'd never had an up close and personal encounter with one before.

As all went silent, I punched the cushiony material away, coughing the powder out of my lungs.

I craned my neck to check on Riley. My heart pounded in my chest at a steady staccato as I wondered what I'd see. Blood? A lifeless body?

Please, let him be okay.

"Riley?"

The airbag disappeared, and his face came into view. He was scowling but appeared uninjured. "Gabby? Are you okay?"

"I'm fine. You?"

He drew in a deep breath. "Yeah, I'm okay. Not so much the car, though." He shoved the deflated airbag out of the way and tried the ignition. It moaned and groaned before going silent. "We're not driving away from this one."

"I'm happy just to be *walking* away."

My phone must have come unplugged because, at that moment, "Staying Alive" by the BeeGees blared from my tiny speakers. Appropriate. Somehow my playlist had switched to "Oldies."

"Let's get out of the car before someone rams us." Riley pushed himself out and then reached his hand in to help me.

I would have to climb through his door since mine was crushed against the mountain. Still, that could have been much, much worse. *We* could have been crushed.

Riley's hand wrapped around mine, and he helped me maneuver over the center console. My flip-flop nearly slipped off as I pulled my leg over the steering wheel. They were my favorite pair—they had black sequins on the straps—so there was no way I was leaving these in the wreckage. I quickly grabbed it, slipped it on, and then hopped out onto the asphalt. Despite the towering trees, the sun hit my shoulders, reminding me that everything would be just fine.

Riley led me down the road in search of safety. We found a little nook in the side of the mountain. We pressed ourselves there, into the craggy rock, drawing as far away from the road as possible. The stone was cool and moist. When I looked up, I saw a small trickle of water coming down from above.

Riley pulled out his cell phone and held it in the air. "No reception. Go figure."

"Certainly someone will come past . . . eventually," I offered.

Riley pulled me toward him and kissed the top of my head. Whenever he did that, it made me feel tiny and protected. Though I usually prided myself in being independent, I actually liked the warmth that spread through me at his affection.

"I'm glad you're okay," he mumbled.

"That was some scary stuff. Sorry about your car."

His hand traveled down to caress my cheek. "Cars can be replaced. I was just worried about you. This is not, however, how I wanted to start this trip."

"Well, our plans take other paths sometimes. Isn't that what you always say? We plot our course all we want, but the Big Guy upstairs sometimes has different ideas."

"You know it." He shifted, tugging me back farther from the road. "You do realize that this is the first trip we've taken together?" He sent a sharp glance my way. "It will be a good chance for us just to have fun together like a normal couple."

I jerked up one eyebrow, making my doubt evident. "I don't think we're ever going to be a normal couple, Riley. You do realize that, don't you?"

His blue eyes sparkled. "Who wants to be normal? But you know what I mean. Ever since we've known each other, we've just been caught up in some type of investigation, it seems. It will be good for us just to chill out and relax."

Chilling out and relaxing seemed so unnatural. Would this be a good time to tell him about the news I'd received right before we left? That due to state budget cuts my position with the Medical Examiner's Office had been eliminated? My heart lurched at the thought. My dreams had been within my grasp, only to be snatched away. That seemed to be the story of my life.

Riley had sounded surprised I'd managed to get the time off so quickly for this trip, especially since I'd only worked at my new job for a month. But I did tell him only two weeks ago that, due to budget cuts, my hours had been taken back to part time, so he knew that much. He just didn't know that I'd received confirmation that money woes were striking budgets everywhere, and my career had effectively died before it began.

Now I was going to have to beg Chad Davis to let me come back to my crime scene cleaning business. Truth be told, I'd kind of missed the job, anyway. At least I'd had freedom and flexibility. I'd set my own hours, dressed however I wanted, and answered to no one but myself.

Somehow, being introduced to Riley's friends as a Medical Legal Death Investigator had a better ring to it than being introduced as a crime scene cleaner, though. Medical Legal Death Investigator made people nod with curiosity and admiration. Crime scene cleaner made people flinch.

Hence my hesitation.

Still, I had to tell Riley the whole story. I'd been waiting for the right time. I supposed I could have spilled the beans on the way here. We'd gone to church, grabbed some lunch, and then hit the road for a four-hour drive.

By that time, I'd been too preoccupied with singing along to my favorite hits from the 80s. "Eternal Flame," "I Think We're Alone Now," and "How Will I Know." Speaking of "How Will I Know," Riley had to love me, because he'd gone along with it. Any sane person would have asked me to turn the radio down and not to sing so loud.

I'd only switched to *My Fair Lady* in the last twenty minutes. I'd waited to see if Riley made the connection between the movie and my feelings about this trip, but he gave no indication he did.

Right now, we were stuck on the side of the mountain with nothing but time to kill. I suppose I could mention the job situation now.

"So, Riley. There's something I've been meaning to

talk to you—"

A car zoomed down the road toward us. Riley waved them down. Of course, my mind, being what it was, imagined Riley flagging down a serial killer. Maybe that's what too many brushes with death did to a person.

A pale blue Mercedes pulled to a stop by us. The passenger side window came down, and a man with gelled blond hair and a pressed white shirt came into sight.

"Everything okay—?" A smile suddenly cracked his face. "Riley Thomas? I can't believe it. Is that you, man?"

The tension suddenly left Riley's shoulders. He reached for the man's outstretched hand and did some kind of exaggerated handshake. "Derek Waters! Am I ever glad to see you."

A chorus of other voices sounded in the car. The best I could make out, there was one other man driving in the front seat, and one woman in the back. As more windows came down, I spotted highlighted hair, fake tans, and expensive clothes.

Just how I imagined Riley's old friends.

Riley looked back at me. "Gabby, come here. There are some people I want you to meet."

I forced on a smile, one I'd been practicing ever since Riley invited me on the trip. I stepped forward, trying to look regal and graceful instead of like someone who'd grown up on the wrong side of the tracks. "Everyone, this is my fiancée Gabby St. Claire. Gabby, this is, well . . . everyone!"

I pulled a hair behind my ear and offered a small wave. They politely reciprocated. Thankfully, their attention quickly turned from me back to Riley.

"What happened?" Derek—the one in the front passenger's seat—pointed to Riley's car. "That's messed up!"

"Just a little accident. These mountain roads are crazy, and I don't have a cell phone signal out here to boot."

"Glad you're both okay. I know a great malpractice attorney, if you need one." Derek grinned.

Riley laughed. "I'm sure you do."

Derek nodded toward the backseat. "We can give you a ride. Hop in!"

"Great." Riley tugged me forward. I saw the cramped quarters inside that car and put the brakes on. There was no room for both of us. And I was pretty sure my deodorant was nearly depleted after that car ride. That was not the impression I wanted to make with Riley's friends. No. Way.

"You go ahead," I insisted as Riley started to climb in.

He paused, raised his head, and brought his eyebrows together. "What?"

I pointed to the car. "We're both not going to fit. You should go."

He stood, an incredulous look on his face. "That's ridiculous. I can't leave you here."

I shook my head, acting tougher than I felt. "I'll be fine."

He looked flabbergasted. "On the side of a mountain road by yourself? I don't think so. What kind of fiancé would I be if I left you here?"

I shrugged. "I've survived worse. You just get there, check in, and call a tow truck. I'll only be here for what? Thirty minutes max?"

He shook his head. "I seriously can't do that."

"I insist. They're your friends. You should totally catch up with them." I dropped my voice and muttered, "Please."

A moment of uncertainty crossed his features. "Are you sure?"

I nodded. "Positive."

He hesitated another moment, stared at me, and finally nodded. Then he kissed my cheek and climbed into the car, amidst the laughter and chatter of his friends. Two minutes later, they pulled away, reminding me of college fraternity brothers driving off to a wild party. I sighed and leaned against the car.

I'd gotten myself out of one awkward situation. But how was I going to survive a whole week of this?

***

An hour later, a tow truck pulled up. A middle-aged man with a brittle reddish-brown beard hopped out, grunted a few times, and examined the car. Finally, he hitched Riley's sedan and threw his thumb over his shoulder, motioning for me to climb into the cab of his truck.

I ignored the stench of old fast food and auto exhaust, resisting the urge to give the man some tips on how he could get those grease stains from his upholstered seats. I did have a few tricks up my sleeve from all of my years as a crime scene cleaner. What worked on blood would work on automotive fluids also.

"Lots of accidents on this road," the driver mumbled, rubbing his beard before putting the truck into drive and rumbling down the road.

"I can see why." I glanced over at the steep drop only mere feet away. Riley and I had been lucky. Very lucky.

"Those new fangled GPS units," he enunciated each letter of "GPS" with the emphasis of someone spitting, "always lead people this way. There's an easier route. A few miles longer but much safer." He shrugged. "At least this road keeps me in business."

"You have a lot of accidents down this way, huh?"

"At least a few a week. And since we're the only tow company in the county, I can't say I mind. As long as no one gets hurt, mind you."

"Of course."

Silence stretched for a moment. As the truck bumped down the road, I reviewed what Riley had told me about his friends.

Derek Waters was a malpractice attorney now living in Boston. Apparently, he was also the king of TV commercials advertising his law firm. Based on the stories Riley told me about him, I'd already nicknamed him Derek "Playboy" Waters.

Jackie Harrington was an assistant D.A. in Georgia, came from old money, and loved jelly beans. She was the sweet one of the group, always smiling and laughing.

Jackie was bringing her boyfriend with her. No one knew his name yet or anything else about him.

Lillian Berkhead was a divorce lawyer who was also known as a shark in the courtroom and a cougar in the dating game. She was only a part of the group because she and Jackie had been best friends. Riley had even mumbled something about "Ice Queen" in one of our conversations.

Jack Lemur was the quiet member of the group. He was a financial attorney, married with two kids. His family wasn't taking this trip with him. Riley had warned me that he had a tendency to double-dip, which meant his new name, in my book at least, was "Jack the Dipper."

Then there was Lane Rosenblum. He was a tax lawyer in Washington D.C. He was also the newest addition to their group, only joining the rest of them during their senior year after transferring from some school out West.

Apparently, most of the gang hadn't seen each other for nearly six years since they graduated from law school and entered the real world.

"So, you from this area?" I remembered there was someone in the vehicle with me and turned to better face Grizzly Adams.

The tow truck driver grunted and shrugged. "Yeah, you could say that."

"Seems . . . " I glanced at the mountainside as it blurred by the window. " . . . pretty."

"This fancy resort you're going to employs nearly seventy percent of the county. There aren't many opportunities for other people."

"At least there are opportunities." I tried to sound optimistic. Based on the scowl the tow truck driver gave me, he didn't appreciate my insight.

I went back into quiet mode. Which meant I went back to thinking about Riley's friends and just how the social dynamic this weekend would play out.

Aside from Riley's parents, I'd only met one other person from his past life, and that was his ex-fiancée Veronica Laskin. She'd been thin, beautiful, and rich. She'd come from a family of wealth and power.

How Riley had ended up with me was a mystery that I just didn't understand sometimes. But I wasn't complaining. As the song "Bless the Broken Road" said, hard times could often lead us into the arms of the person we were meant to be with.

Except when they didn't.

A huge, historic-looking building appeared out the front window. And when I said huge, I meant *huge*. Its exterior was all red brick. Massive columns stood probably six stories high. It was bigger than the White House. Bigger than my high school. Maybe even bigger than my local mall.

Lush green grass stretched in front of the circular drive. A pond with a gazebo was to one side. Old, grand homes could be seen lining the surrounding streets. A fancy golf course teased behind the building.

The tow truck stopped. I hadn't even stepped out when Riley appeared by my side. His hand grasped mine. "You okay?"

"Of course. I'm fine. You think I'm going to let a mountain road defeat me?"

"If a mob boss can't defeat you, then I don't know what I was thinking." A hint of a smile pulled at his lips, even though I knew he was worried about me.

The tow truck driver grunted beside us. "You should probably unload your bags unless you want me to take them with me to the repair shop." He nodded toward Riley's car as he extended Riley's no-frills key chain. I'd recently added a flip-flop and crime scene tape lanyard to mine.

"You need to call your insurance company?" the driver continued.

Riley took his keys and stepped toward his mangled mess of a car. "I only have liability. Calling them won't do me any good."

No sooner had Riley opened the trunk than did a swarm of uniformed men surround the car and begin pulling luggage from it. I stepped in to help.

"Let them get it, Gabby," Riley whispered.

I grabbed my suitcase. "That's ridiculous. I can help." I placed my luggage on the little brass cart beside me, which caused one of the valets to scowl.

Riley leaned closer and lowered his voice. "Gabby, really. Let them do their job. You can just relax."

Relaxing was not something I was good at. "But, I'm perfectly capable of—"

I stopped talking as Riley shook his head and shoved some bills into the valet's hand. That's when I resigned myself to step back and relinquish my control of the situation. There were worse things than being waited on hand and foot.

A moment later, Riley had his arm around my waist and was leading me inside. There was no going back now. We climbed extravagant, stately steps and stepped into one of the fanciest lobbies I'd ever seen.

When I was a kid, my mom had made me dresses that mimicked the ones from the movie *Annie*. So, it only seemed appropriate as I stepped onto the rich marble floors of the building that I mumbled, "I think I'm going to like it here."

Yes, I was like the Little Orphan Annie stepping into Daddy Warbuck's mansion—a person coming from nothing stepping into extravagance like I'd never known or dreamed of. The only thing that would make it more perfect was if the entire staff burst out into song and dance.

I paused for a moment, half expecting it to happen, before releasing my breath and resisting my urge to tap dance. That was a good thing because I *couldn't* tap dance.

We only made it two steps when a scruffy-looking man in a flannel shirt came running through the front door. There was something urgent, maybe slightly crazy, in his eyes.

"You're Riley?" His voice sounded breathless, frantic.

"That's right." Riley nodded.

"I recognized you from the picture Jackie has on her bookshelf. Have you seen her since you arrived?"

Riley shook his head. "No, we just walked in, though. Why?"

"She's missing." Panic laced the man's voice.

Riley's hands went to his hips. "What do you mean missing? How long has it been since you saw her?"

The man ran a hand through his unruly, thick brown hair. "Three hours. She took a hike. She was supposed to be back by now."

"Maybe she ran into someone she knows?" I suggested

The man shook his head. "No, something's happened to her. I'm sure of it. She's in trouble."

"*Trouble* trouble?" I asked. My pulse sped.

The man's eyes met mine. "Yeah, *trouble* trouble. You've got to help me find her."

I glanced at Riley. So much for acting like a normal couple.

And so much for minding my own business too, for that matter.

CHAPTER 3

"Jackie!" I yelled. I stood at the edge of a massive boulder. Below me was a streaming river that made my head spin for a moment. Still, I didn't move. There was something I kind of liked about living on the edge.

Riley grabbed my hand and tugged me back. "Careful."

"Always." I grinned.

The rest of Riley's friends had been gathered, and we'd divided up into groups to search for Jackie. The man who'd run inside to find us was Clint, Jackie's boyfriend, apparently. Riley and I had decided to take one of the longer trails that looped around the resort's property. Summer was in full bloom around us with vibrant green leaves filling out the oak and maple trees. The sky overhead was a brilliant blue and the air felt crisp.

Maybe I *would* like it here.

I expected Riley to urge me down the trail again, but instead he pulled me forward and wrapped his arms around me.

I raised my face, realizing that Riley was one of the nicest views around here, and he had a lot to compete with. "What are you doing?"

"I told you I had all week to tell you how pretty you were. I wanted to take my first opportunity now." The pupils of his eyes swirled with emotion that made my stomach burn.

I was one lucky girl. I told myself that all the time because it was true. Riley was the man of my dreams. "You're making me blush."

"I want to make you blush for a long time." He lowered his head, and his lips came down on mine. When he pulled away, he brushed a hair out of my face. "I love you, Gabby."

I let my head rest on his chest for a moment, comforted by the sound of his steady heartbeat. Steady . . . that's what Riley was. I needed that characteristic in my life. "I love you, too, Riley."

He stepped back but kept his fingers intertwined with mine. "We should keep looking, huh?"

"You don't seem worried." Which was strange. It wasn't that Riley worried a lot; it was simply that he had a heart for justice and helping those in need, which was just one more reason we were so perfect together.

He'd just opened his own law firm several months ago, and he only took cases that were socially driven. He'd given up a job as a hotshot prosecutor in L.A. and decided to follow his dreams of making the world a better place instead. That said a lot about him.

He shrugged. "I guess I'm worried. It's just that Jackie has always had a habit of not thinking things through very well. I suspect she got distracted by something. Maybe she went off on a different trail. Maybe she lost track of time. I don't know."

I tried to compute what he was saying as we started down the trail again. "Can people in law school afford not to think things through?"

"Jackie's always been a bit spacey."

"But she's an assistant district attorney."

Riley shrugged. "I don't know what to say. I realize this won't sound very nice, but we were all a little surprised that she actually made it through law school. I don't think being a lawyer was ever her dream. It was more of her mom's plan for her life."

"Do you have a picture of her? It helps me to put a face to the name."

He pulled out his phone, swept his fingers over the screen, and then showed me a picture. Jackie Harrington looked an awful lot like a young Jackie Kennedy. She had the same bobbed brown hair and petite build. Only Jackie Harrington had a slight sparkle in her eyes, a sparkle that belied her otherwise sophisticated demeanor.

"Pretty," I mumbled. My gaze scanned the area around me, looking for a sign of something out of place. "Her boyfriend looked awfully upset. Beside himself, for that matter."

Riley helped me over a tree that had fallen in our path. "He did."

"You said you'd never met him before?" I landed with a thump on the rocky ground below.

"No, he wasn't in school with us. I think they've been dating a year or so. Not really sure. I know from a couple of posts she's put on her social media sites that her mom doesn't really approve of the relationship."

"Why?"

"Jackie comes from old money. Her boyfriend . . . well, he's a construction worker. Sure, he has big plans to start his own company one day, but he hasn't yet. Jackie's mom doesn't think he's good enough for her."

I liked Jackie's boyfriend already. This was great. There was at least one person here I could relate with. But the rest of the people, the ones who came from old money? I had no idea what to do with them.

We continued to walk. My mind wandered to my last trip to the mountains. It had been a long time. I wasn't exactly a world-traveler kind of girl. No, my family's idea of a vacation when I was growing up was heading to the beach for a day. Once, my dad had set up a tent in our backyard, and my brother and I had spent the night there, eating gummy worms until our stomachs hurt and telling scary stories with a flashlight. Tim had probably been too young to stay outside without any adults, but we'd made out just fine. I smiled at the memory.

The last time I'd been to Virginia's mountains, my dad had brought me. I'd probably only been seven. It was one of the few times in my childhood that I could remember my dad being sober. After one of his friends died of a heart attack before reaching 40, my dad had been determined for two whole weeks to turn his life around, so he'd quit drinking and tried to be the father he'd always wanted to be. Those two weeks had been great, and I remember as a little girl I'd prayed they wouldn't just be a phase. I wanted a family like those happy ones I'd seen on TV.

That weekend in the mountains with my dad had been fun. We hadn't stayed in a place like Allendale, but my aunt had let us use an old fishing cabin. The place was a dump and hadn't been used in years. I still remember the smell of dead fish and rotting leaves.

My dad had made a campfire, and we'd roasted hot dogs and marshmallows. We'd explored trails through woods so deserted that we didn't see another soul. He'd told me stories about when he'd learned to surf as a kid and how he'd gone out to win a championship competition on the East Coast. The honor had gotten him endorsement deals and, he hadn't said it, but probably tons of women.

My mom had been the one who'd caught his eye. In her younger days, before cancer ravaged her body, she'd been a real looker. Life had worn her down well before the cancer, truth be told.

"Your dream vacation? What would it be?"

Riley's voice pulled me from my thoughts, and I shrugged. I never spent a lot of time thinking about traveling, actually. My life seemed to be my friends and my work. I was always on call as a crime scene cleaner and had no vacation days or even sick days, for that matter. If I wanted to get paid, I had to work. In fact, I couldn't even remember the last time I'd been out of town.

In college, my friends and I had driven down to the Outer Banks of North Carolina for a weekend trip. That had been probably eight years ago. The thought made me want to put an "L" on my forehead. I really needed to get out more.

Before going on this trip, Riley and I had sold some stuff online in order to raise the cash. Riley could have used his law firm money, but he said he didn't feel right using people's donations to fund a class reunion, even if there were workshops tied with it. That was Riley for you. Since he took on a lot of cases pro-bono, people and organizations often donated to help keep the firm going. He'd gotten some pretty big endorsements from some national faith-based organizations.

"My dream vacation." I closed my eyes but only for a moment. "I guess I'd want to go on a cruise to somewhere tropical and warm."

"A cruise, huh?"

"I want ocean water so warm it feels like a bath and sand so soft it's like a cushion under my feet. Nothing fancy, but definitely clean. It has to have good seafood and maybe a place to catch a show."

"Good to know."

I stole a glance at him. "How about you?"

He shrugged, a grin tugging at his lips. "Anywhere with you."

I squeezed his arm. "And that is just one more thing to love about you. But let me guess—you've already traveled the world."

"I've been a few places. It's not so much where you go as it is whom you're with."

"Have you been practicing your one liners or something?" Don't get me wrong. Riley was incredibly sweet and sincere, while still being masculine, smart, and even a little tough when times called for it. But the one thing he wasn't was smooth. He was too into being authentic to be the type to have lines he used.

"No, maybe this is just what getting away from it all does to me."

I tucked away that information for later and glanced at my watch. "We've been looking for an hour. I wonder if anyone else has had any luck finding Jackie."

He pulled out his cell phone, squinted at it, and then held it in the air. "I don't have a good signal out here, but they said they'd call if there's news. Let's walk a little bit more."

The woods were pretty desolate, probably not a good place for a woman to be hiking alone, even at a fancy resort. I could easily imagine being out here on an early morning walk where I'd have some uninterrupted time with God. We could talk about Him dangling my dreams in front of me and then snatching them away. And I could tell Him how, despite that, I was so grateful for His forgiveness and mercy in my life.

I hadn't been a Christian for long, but living for someone outside of myself was a life-changing thing. I still had rough days, and I still had days when doubt crept into my psyche, at least for a few dwindling moments. But most days I felt new and alive, and I wondered how I ever lived before without the hope I had now.

Riley was a big part of that.

Riley sighed and turned toward me. "We should head back. Maybe someone else has heard something."

I nodded. "Sounds like a plan." Part of me would much rather remain on this hiking trail with Riley than go back and mingle with his friends. I don't know why the thought of hanging out with them had me in knots like it did. Feeling like the outsider of the group was never my first choice, I supposed.

This was a part of the give and take of being a couple. Besides, once we got married, I was going to have to get used to this kind of thing. I'd be terrible at it, but I'd have to persevere.

As silence stretched on the trail, I wondered if this would be a good time to tell Riley about my job situation. I just couldn't seem to open my mouth to do so, however. For just a short period, I'd had a job that matched his: I'd been a professional with a respectable career—a career fit for a lawyer.

Now I was back to cleaning up guts and gore.

I had to tell him the truth, though. I knew Riley would still love me. Despite that, there was a part of me that wondered if he'd be disappointed. There was a part of me that wanted to hold on to the illusion that I'd pushed past all of the obstacles in my life and become the girl everyone had underestimated.

But being dishonest only led to trouble.

I sucked in a deep breath and squeezed his hand.

"So, there's something I've been meaning to tell you—"

Before I could finish, a figure darted out into the trail. Clint. Where had he come from? His eyes were wide and dazed, and his breathing was labored as if he'd been running maniacally. "Did you find her?"

Riley shook his head. "No, man. We didn't pass anyone on the trail. No one else had luck either?"

Clint moaned and put his head in his hands. "No. It's been four hours now. She was supposed to be back two hours ago."

"Maybe you should call the police if you're this worried," I offered. "They know how to handle situations like this."

He shook his head. "What is it they say for adults? Don't they have to be missing for twenty-four hours or something? She could be dead by then." He moaned and looked to the sky. Strain was obvious in the bulging muscles at his throat and neck.

"Dead?" I mumbled. I'd been trying to take a backseat in this, to not get too involved. But . . . "You've tried her cell phone?"

His head flipped down, and bloodshot eyes met mine. "It goes right to voicemail."

"Has she ever wandered away like this before?"

"No, never. But she's not a mountain girl. She's more of a Macy's girl. What if she took a wrong turn? Wandered off a path? Hit her head?" He jerked his head back and forth as if he couldn't stand the thought of it. "What if she needs her inhaler?"

I stepped forward. "Let's go back to the hotel. Let's make sure no one else has seen her. Have you checked her room?"

Clint shook his head, the setting sun bathing him in an eerie orange glow. "No, not yet. I mean, I knocked at the door and all, but no one answered. I don't have a key."

"We should do that, also," I told him. "Just in case. Maybe she got back early, turned off her cell, and took a nap."

Hope lit his eyes. "Now that sounds like something she might do."

We all began walking back toward the resort together. Clint walked fast enough that I had to hurry to keep up. I could understand his anxiety. I'd be the same way if I thought one of my loved ones was in trouble.

"You seem pretty good at this," Clint mumbled over his shoulder.

I started to say something when Riley beat me to the punch. "She does work for the Medical Examiner's Office."

Guilt pressed in on me. But now didn't seem like the ideal time to say anything. I mean, we should have the conversation in private. Out of respect for Riley, if nothing else.

Clint glanced back again. "Oh yeah? That seems pretty cool. Dead people and all." He seemed to realize what he said and shuddered. I wondered if he'd thought about Jackie and what it would be like for her to be laying on a table in a sterile room with strangers examining her most inward parts. It didn't seem like a very graceful way for life to end. But, I supposed by that point, modesty didn't matter anymore.

We scurried into the lobby of the resort, and Clint took off in a jog toward the elevator. "I'm going to check her room."

"Do you have a key?"

Clint put the brakes on. "No, who is her roommate again?"

"Gabby," Riley said.

I was? I was rooming with a girl who was potentially missing. It was like the world was just *begging* me to get involved.

I'd agreed to have a roommate in order to save money, which was the same reason why Riley was rooming with Lane. Derek and Jack the Dipper were staying together, and Lillian was staying with a colleague from work.

Riley slid a key card into my hand. "I didn't have a chance to give this to you yet. I checked us in when I got here."

I raised it in the air. "Let's go."

Clint repeatedly hit the UP button on the elevator. "Come on, come on, come on!"

Finally, he sprinted toward the broad, winding staircase only a few feet away. Just as everything else in the hotel, the stairs were grand and ornate with velvety red carpet, which was the color of blood.

I'd been around too many crime scenes.

Riley and I looked at each other before sprinting after him. We made it up three flights of stairs—but the place had high ceilings, so these weren't just normal stairs. The ceilings in this place had to be at least 15 feet high.

I hated to admit it, but I was huffing and puffing by the time I reached room 3412. With a steady hand, I pushed the card into the little slot on the front of the door. The light turned green. I twisted the knob and nudged the door until it swung out.

I stood there a moment staring at the room, waiting to hear a sound indicating someone was there. As of now, all I could see were some high-back chairs and a built-in bookcase.

Clint darted ahead of us. "Jackie? Are you there? Jackie?" He ran from door to door, frantically jerking open each one. I assumed those were closets, a bathroom, and two bedrooms. I'd never stayed in a hotel suite like this one before.

Clint opened the last door and moaned.

Riley and I rushed toward him. I had to blink several times before everything came into focus.

Clothes were littered all over the bed. The TV had been smashed. Cosmetics dotted the floor.

Someone had been in here. Looking for something or trying to send a message? I wasn't sure.

"Jackie . . . " Clint muttered. He fell back into a chair, almost as if everything overwhelmed him to the point where he couldn't hold himself up. "What happened?"

I surveyed the room, looking for something—anything—that would give me a clue as to what was going on. Had there been a struggle? My gut told me no.

If you asked me, someone was trying to make a statement.

I stepped over a gutted bag of cosmetics and paused by the dresser. What I saw there made my blood freeze.

"Uh, guys. You're going to want to see this."

I pointed to a note left on the wood there.

CHAPTER 4

Clint buried his face. His body language screamed "distressed" as he sat on the couch in the living area of my suite. The rest of Riley's friends had been called, and now they stood in a semi-circle around Clint.

He raised his head, nearly crumpling the note in his hand. A couple of tears splotched the words. "A ransom note? A ransom note! Why?"

I tiptoed closer and tried to take the note from him before he destroyed any evidence with his tears. Insensitive? Perhaps. But I really only wanted what was best.

I carefully plucked the note from his hand and slid it into a plastic bag that was supposed to be used for laundry. I caught Lillian staring at me like I was stealing tissues from a grieving man.

"There could be prints," I explained.

Shouldn't she know that? I was pretty sure lawyers had a grasp on these things. According to Riley, Lillian didn't let many things get past her.

The note had informed Clint that Jackie had been abducted and that unless a $200,000 ransom was paid, she'd be killed. And, of course, it ended with the infamous warning not to get the police involved.

How many lawyers would it take to figure out the best method of getting her back?

They all discussed their different ideas, talking on a totally different level than me. Apparently, they were talking on a different level than the commoner Clint as well, because he looked equally as perplexed.

I got my first good look at Riley's friends and quickly assessed them. Derek "Playboy" Waters had a fake tan, highlighted blond hair, and teeth so white I needed sunglasses. He carried himself like he owned the world.

Lillian "The Shark" Berkhead was tall, big boned, and seemed to love power suits. Her blonde hair was cut in a sharp wedge, her eyes small, her lips thin, and her smiles infrequent.

Lane Rosenblum was only a couple of inches taller than my 5'4". He had an oversized head topped with thick brown hair. Based on how he was dressed tonight, he liked khaki shorts that were too tight and too short to be stylish.

Jack the Dipper looked the most normal of the group. He was as large as a bear, had close-cropped light brown hair, a round face, and hardly said a word.

As everyone else continued to discuss the best way to handle the situation, I leaned closer to Clint. "What they're saying is that you should call the police, even though the note says not to," I explained.

Understanding finally settled in his gaze but only for a second. He shook his head. "I can't do that. I'm not going to do anything to put her in danger. I've got to get my hands on that money somehow."

"How do you plan on doing that?"

He stared at the wall a moment. Finally, he nodded. "I'm going to call her mom. Her mom is loaded, and Jackie is her only daughter. She'll do whatever she can to get her back."

Riley pulled away from the other conversation and stepped closer. "I don't know if that's a good idea."

Clint shook his head. "That's what I'm doing. No one's going to convince me otherwise. I've got to get my girl back."

Everyone else's conversation stopped as Clint pulled his phone out and dialed. A moment later, he stepped toward the corner and mumbled something into the mouthpiece. Even from where I stood, I could hear the sobs on the other end of the phone. The sound made a weight press on my chest.

Grief.

I hoped I never became immune to how painful it was. I never wanted to brush off someone else's hurt simply because I'd seen so much of it. I never wanted the loss of life to not affect me, even when I was acting as a professional.

A moment later, Clint turned back to the group. "Carol's working on getting the money now. She should be here by mid-morning."

"When did the note say you needed to leave the cash?" Even as I asked the question, I glanced down at the bag in my hands, the bag where the note now was. I quickly took in the ragged edges of the yellow legal paper. The horizontal lines were blue, the vertical lines pink, and the handwriting probably done with a black marker. The tear on the left side of the page was deeper than the one on the opposite side. I tucked those observations away.

Clint began pacing. "Tomorrow at four. I'm supposed to leave it by the trash can at the overlook near Glass Falls." He pulled his hand over his face, but his eyes still looked dull; his skin lifeless and pale. "I hope she's okay. What if . . . ?"

I squeezed his shoulder. "Sometimes it's better if you don't ask yourself those questions. Just hold on to hope."

He nodded. "You're probably right. I just don't know what I'd do without her in my life." He sucked in a breath and buried his face. "Oh, no."

I put my hand on his arm. "What is it?"

Clint raised his head. "She didn't take her inhaler with her. She has asthma, and it can be triggered by stress." New lines of worry appeared.

My throat got drier. "Are you sure?"

He pulled a small canister out of his pocket. "I'm sure. She asked me to hold it for her. Said it bulked up her pockets, and she wasn't taking her purse." He looked at each of us. "Guys, if she has an asthma attack, it's all over. She'll never survive."

***

After everyone else had called it a night, I sat in my bed in a suite that I was supposed to share with a woman who was missing. I leaned against the headboard and let the quiet absorb me for a moment.

Riley had been hesitant to leave me here, in the place where Jackie had stayed and where her abductors had been while leaving the note. His friends had mumbled something about catching up to the twenty-first century, which pretty much meant they thought I should just stay with Riley.

No, that would have been the old me. The new me had standards. As part of those standards, I was going to stay in my room tonight by myself. I'd locked my door and put on the security chain and deadbolt and anything else I could find, just to be safe. I saw no reason for the kidnappers to come back, though.

When Riley had told me good night, he'd echoed his words from earlier. *Remember, you promised not to get involved.* I'd forced a smile and nodded.

Why had I ever made that promise?

I pushed that thought aside, closed my eyes, and reflected on what Clint was probably going through right now. I couldn't imagine. He had to be beside himself. What had started as his girlfriend going on a walk had turned into a nightmare.

I began developing a timeline in my head—not because I was getting involved. Just because I was curious.

Of course.

According to Clint, Jackie had gone on a walk at 3:30. Riley and I had arrived here at 6:30, which meant she'd been gone three hours. We'd searched for her an hour and gotten back to the hotel by 8:30.

Somewhere in the middle of all of that, someone had gotten into this room and left the note. That left a five-hour window for them to get in, but assuming that Jackie hadn't been snatched right away, it was more likely a three or four-hour window.

How had someone gotten into the room? Risky move considering someone else could have been here or seen them coming and going.

My gut told me there had to be more than one person involved, just based solely on the note. Someone would have to snatch Jackie and take her somewhere, while someone else wrote the note and left it.

The front desk should have a keycard entry record. If they did, I wondered if they'd give it to me. It was my room, after all. Didn't I have the right to know?

Who came and went from this room could be an important clue.

I knew that Clint wanted to handle things his way. The last thing I wanted to do was interfere and somehow mess things up. But the more information a person was armed with, the better. That was my theory at least. It had worked for me so far. I hadn't gotten anyone killed . . . yet.

I sat upright, not even a hint of exhaustion taunting me. I couldn't sleep. *Of course* I couldn't sleep. There was a mystery at hand. I was here. I couldn't simply sit idly by. I was Gabby St. Claire, after all. I could just poke around without really investigating. There was a difference. At least, I convinced myself that was true.

I climbed out of bed, just for a moment relishing the lush feel of the white coverlet underneath my fingers. The bedspread had probably cost more than my entire bed at home did. That did not deter me from wanting to jump up and down on it, however.

I crept out of my room, into the living area, and stood in front of Jackie's door. The woman was missing. I had no business looking at her things.

But I was going to anyway.

I turned the doorknob. Slowly, the door swung outward, and her room came into view. The place was still a mess.

Did the person behind this intend for it to look like there was a struggle? Somehow, I just didn't buy that. Everything was too strewn, as if it had been done on purpose. A couple of pictures on the wall had been broken. A bottle of perfume had been smashed. There wasn't a clear path of destruction or point of ground zero. The mess was an equal opportunity offender.

Then there was the note.

I slowly walked into the room. I tried to be careful not to touch or move too much. You know, just in case the police ever did show up. The last thing I wanted them finding were my fingerprints.

Something on the nightstand caught my eye. Jackie's phone.

Why would she go on a hike alone without a cell phone? Even if the signal was spotty, I'd still think she'd want to have it with her. I would.

I picked it up. The screen showed several missed calls. I'd bet the number that kept reappearing was Clint's. Spontaneously, I slid the phone into my pocket. Someone needed to monitor the device, just in case someone of significance called. Until the police were pulled into this, that person would be me.

It was just out of consideration, I reminded myself. Because I was Gabby "Most Considerate Woman of the Year" St. Claire.

Yeah, right.

CHAPTER 5

Since I felt wide-awake, I went back to my room and threw on some jeans, a red sweatshirt, and flip-flops, and pulled my hair back into a ponytail.

I slipped my keycard into my pocket, grabbed my purse, and stepped into the hallway. I didn't even know where I was going. I just knew I had to go somewhere. My brain was too active to sleep.

I bypassed the elevator again and took the stairs down to the first floor. One lone attendant stood behind the check-in counter. I moseyed up to her and plastered on my brightest smile.

"I was hoping you could help me," I started. "I need to find out if someone other than me has been into my room today. Do you have that information?"

The woman, probably in her early twenties, nodded. Her sleek blond hair bobbed with the movement. "We do. Is everything okay?"

"Someone said they saw a man leaving my room. It was probably a member of your staff, but my work has a very high security clearance, so I want to make sure that's correct." I leaned closer. "I'd tell you what I do but then, you know, I'd have to . . . "

The check-in clerk's eyes widened, before she nodded quickly and began tapping away at the computer. "Of course, ma'am."

Ma'am? It wasn't every day I got called that.

"I need your name and ID and room number."

I pulled out my driver's license and slid it across the granite countertop toward her. As she typed, I marveled at the massive columns making up the inside of this room. The marble structures had to stretch at least four stories high. Twenty of my apartments could fit inside the entryway of this place alone—maybe more.

"It looks like a key assigned to a Jackie Harrington was used at 9:42, 1:12, 3:15, and 7:05 today. You also had maid service come at 12:30. It appears you used your key at 8:41. Does that help?"

I nodded. "Immensely. Thank you."

Had whoever kidnapped Jackie taken her keycard and used it to break into the room? That was my best theory.

I started to wander the downstairs level. Past the grand entryway, there was a little café and marketplace, a huge dining room, rows of shops, and every other thing a person of means could imagine. And this was just in the East Wing. Apparently, the West Wing had a spa, swimming pool, bowling alley and movie theater.

I took another hallway, one that led away from the social hub of the hotel. Based on the signs I was seeing and the sheets of plastic, this area was under construction. That didn't stop me from wandering deeper and deeper down the wing.

I stopped wandering when I spotted someone familiar in the distance.

Clint.

He was in the corner, whispering to a rough-looking man in dirty jeans and a flannel shirt. Another man was also there. He was painfully tall, and his back had a curve to it. He stood away from the other two men, seeming to observe them. The conversation looked rather heated.

What exactly was going on?

Who were those men? Definitely not people here with Riley's group. Clint didn't seem like the type who'd know other people who vacationed here. Just like I didn't seem like that type.

I hoped that Clint wasn't doing something foolish, something like trying to hire someone other than me to find Jackie. Or maybe Clint had called a brother or friend to come here and be with him in his time of need. Face it—the man probably didn't relate to Riley's friends, nor did they relate to him. And I wasn't judging. I'd rather hang out with Clint.

As Clint turned, I stepped behind an ornate column that decorated a doorframe behind me. I didn't know why, but I didn't want him to see me. The man deserved his privacy, especially in light of what had happened.

I looked up and saw a sign on the door that said library. I pushed it open and quietly slipped inside, just as Clint started down the hallway.

I stood there, my heart beating double-time in my ears. An unsettled feeling sloshed in my gut. I didn't know what it was or why it was there. I'd have to figure that out later.

"I'm sorry, ma'am. The library is closed."

I nearly screeched at the voice behind me. I twirled around, my hand over my heart. A maid stood there, duster in hand, and a perplexed look on her face.

The woman was probably in her mid-twenties

with dark hair and a figure that neared the plump side. Her hair was curly and stretched halfway down her back.

She continued to stare at me as if I was crazy.

And she'd called me "ma'am."

This was the second time tonight I'd been addressed that way. The first time I'd felt semi-honored. This time I felt old.

I pointed toward the door behind me. "I didn't know. Sorry about that."

"It's no problem. I just have to get this cleaned. Including that wine stain on the carpet." She pointed to a purple area beside a wingback chair and shook her head. "Some people. I'm not supposed to say that, so please forgive me. It's not professional. But why would someone spill their wine and not clean it up? Don't they know it stains?"

I leaned down by the mark. "No, people don't care. In fact, I'm convinced that people are perfectly content to have other people clean up the disasters they've made."

The maid nodded. "Me too! I just don't get it. I've scrubbed at that stain for fifteen minutes. Now I'm just letting the solution soak in. I'm hoping that will do the trick." Her accent had a hint of a mountain drawl that sounded charming and colorful.

"I know of a formula you can use. It will come right up. I use it all the time on—" I stopped mid-sentence. I almost said, "on blood at crime scenes." Most people just didn't know how to handle statements like that, though, so I kept it quiet. Maybe I was maturing after all.

"Do you own a cleaning company?"

I shrugged, not sure how to answer that question. "In a manner of speaking, I suppose."

She chuckled and waved a finger in the air. "I

knew you just couldn't *work* for one. Otherwise, this place would be way out of your price range. I know firsthand. That would be like me actually being able to afford a weekend here. Not happening."

I glanced around the ornate room and was again reminded that I was so out of my element. Mahogany wood, shiny and lemon-scented, stretched floor to ceiling. Brass fixtures and lamps. Furniture upholstered in the finest fabrics. Volumes upon volumes of astute looking hardbacks. "It is expensive here."

"You're telling me. I've never seen such hoity-toity people in my life." She stopped and shook her head, fluttering her feather duster in the air. "I'm sorry. I don't know what's gotten into me. I've never spouted off like this to a guest before. Please forgive me."

"There's nothing to forgive."

A look of worry crossed her face. "If the executive housekeeper finds out, she'll fire me."

I raised my hand. "Really, I find your honesty refreshing. I'm not reporting anyone."

The maid put a hand over her heart. "Thank you. I think it's just that I work this shift by myself. I mean, there are others working as well, but they're all on different floors on different wings. Only four of us work the nightshift. It's hard to vacuum when guests are sleeping and all, but we clean the spa and take linens to guests who need them in the middle of the night." She shook her head. "Believe me, I don't even ask. Anyway, I get so tired of being alone with my thoughts."

I smiled. "I'm Gabby, by the way."

"I'm Deanna."

"You work here long?"

"Five years. They recruited people from all the counties around Healthy Springs to work here. It turned out my deadbeat boyfriend had just left me, and I was looking for a change. And some money. I'm from a coal-mining town, and all the jobs there dried up when they closed up the mines. Allendale Acres provides housing for its staff and a decent pay, so I grabbed up the job. I can't complain."

I shoved my hands into my jean pockets, not in a hurry. "I bet you get to meet some interesting people here."

She raised her eyebrows and kept dusting. "You better believe it. We've had movie stars and politicians and everyone in between. We have a dignitary staying here now, for that matter." She paused. "Of course, I wasn't supposed to say that. Privacy and all."

"I won't tell." The woman was seriously making me chuckle. On the inside. But a silent chuckle was still a chuckle. I raised a hand, as if taking an oath.

"Thank you. Again, I'm running off at the mouth. I probably wouldn't have said anything, but I can't get the man out of my mind. He's so handsome." Her hand went over her heart and a dreamy look filled her gaze. "And rich."

"Does he speak English?"

Deanna burst into laughter. "Does he speak English? Of course. He's from some country in the Middle East. Or was it Asia? I can't remember. But he's hot."

"Dignitary just makes him sound so . . . foreign."

Deanna laughed again, much louder than I expected. "You are so funny. I like you already. You're different from a lot of people I meet here."

I'd never been insulted at the thought of being different. In fact, I took it as a compliment. Why would I want to be like everyone else?

"Is he single?"

Deanna shrugged. "No idea."

"Why don't you ask him?"

Her mouth gaped. "I could never do that, for more than one reason. Staff is not supposed to ask anything personal of the guests here."

I leaned back onto the arm of an ornate couch and crossed my arms. "Is this a nice place to work?"

"They're pretty good to their employees. I mean, Mr. Allen is kind of uptight and nitpicky, but I guess you're supposed to be like that if you run a place like this. I've only seen him lose his cool one time, and that was because he saw a snake. I guess he's kinda terrified of them. Besides, after you've been here a while, everyone starts to feel like family." She sobered. "We were all heartbroken last week when we heard about Maurice. I felt like I'd lost a brother."

"Maurice?"

"Oh, you must have just gotten here, otherwise you would have already heard. One of our bellhops died last week. It was so sad. He was one of the nicest guys. He was always cracking jokes and talking about all the places he wanted to visit. Top of list? Detroit. Who wants to visit Detroit?"

I pushed myself up straighter. "What happened to him?"

"It was just terrible. He went kayaking. His boat must have hit a rock and flipped over. The police found his body washed up in the river. It was so strange because he knew better than to go kayaking alone. Anyway, it won't be the same without him around here."

"I'm sure that's hard."

"He was the best fake person around here."

"Fake person?"

She nodded. "Let's face it. Most of us are from the

mountains. Knowing how to act at a fancy resort like this doesn't come natural. We have to take all of these classes on how to be proper and how to treat our guests, etc. You would think he was born with a silver spoon in his mouth the way he acted around here, all suave and gentleman-like."

"And when he was away?"

"He tricked out his car, cussed like a sailor, and liked nothing better than to drink some moonshine." She waved her hand in the air. "Listen to me. I'm sure you don't want to know all of this."

I leaned forward. "Deanna, I know this is a strange question, but do you know if this place has security cameras?"

She stopped dusting for long enough to snort. "You're joking, right?"

Right . . . I nodded. "I mean, *of course* they have cameras. Every establishment like this does. But who monitors them?"

"Security, of course." She picked up a stack of books and twirled her duster. Fine particles flew into the air.

I stood and joined her. I picked up the books so she could dust under them, and then moved them back to their rightful place. "Do you know anyone who works in security here?"

"Ricky works security."

"Do you think he'd let me take a look at some tapes?"

She stopped again, her eyes wide. "Are you serious? That's, like, a major no-no."

"I'm serious. Unfortunately. I can't tell you why, but it's majorly important."

She shook her head. "I couldn't do that . . . "

I put my hand over her duster for a moment, knowing that's what I had to do to get her attention. "Listen, I know it's a no-no, but it's important. What if I found out if that dignitary you were gushing about is single or not . . . "

She stared at me a moment. "Really? You could do that?"

"I could do it more easily than you. I'm sure you're not supposed to ask personal questions like that. There's nothing stopping me."

"If he were single . . . " She looked up at the ceiling and twirled around. "It could be my very own Cinderella story. I haven't given up hope yet, you know."

"Hope is always good."

She continued staring for a moment before nodding. "Okay. You promise not to get me in trouble? You can't tell anyone I put you up to this or tell anyone that I'm letting you into a secure part of the hotel."

"Understood. You have my word."

"I'll try and help you out, then. Ricky doesn't start his shift until tomorrow. Meet me in the lobby at one, and I'll introduce you. Okay?"

I nodded. "That sounds perfect." I knelt beside her on the floor. "Now, let me give you that top secret formula to get out wine stains. You'll be the talk of the housekeeping staff for this one."

CHAPTER 6

Just as I put the final touch of concealer under my eyes the next morning, someone knocked at the door. My heart rate sped when I pulled it open and spotted Riley there. I hoped that quickening of my pulse never stopped happening when I looked at him.

"Morning, sunshine," he mumbled. He stood there, his hands stuffed into the pockets of his khaki pants and wearing a neat, pressed button up shirt. Business casual, I realized. Just as his conference required. The soft grin on his face captured my heart.

I leaned up and gave him a quick kiss. "Come in a minute. I've just got to put my shoes on."

He stepped inside, shut the door, and glanced around as if expecting to see that I'd strung up crime scene tape or something. Finally, he bobbed his head up and down as if pleasantly surprised. "How are you this morning?"

Dog tired, more curious than ever, and anxious about my meeting with Ricky from security.

"Same old, same old, I guess." I grabbed some ballet flats and slipped them on.

"No flip-flops?" he asked, his eyebrows raised.

"I decided to step it up a notch. Ballet flats somehow seem classier than my normal flip flops." So did the nautical wear I'd seen on sale downstairs, but a girl had to have some standards.

"You look cute in either."

"I knew there was a reason I wanted to marry you." I grabbed my purse. "Let's go."

We started down the hallway. I tried to remember my posture and to keep my chin up. I'd been perfecting the act of drinking with my pinky in the air, so I'd be all set come breakfast this morning. Hoity-toity, as Deanna the maid had said.

"So, what's the update on Jackie?" I asked. "Have you heard anything?"

"Her mom is on her way into town early this morning, and two of Clint's friends are here for him."

His friends? Were they the guys I'd seen him with last night?

Riley continued. "I think they all want their privacy. Derek and I stopped by to see Clint this morning, and he said they didn't need anything. They were going to follow the kidnapper's instructions, and he'd let us know what happened."

"And that's that? It just seems like we should be doing something."

Riley shook his head. "That's your modus operandi. Speaking of which, I'm proud of you. I half expected you to be out all night looking for answers."

I pointed to myself, guilt pounding at me. "Me? I'm a changed person. What can I say?"

By all definitions, I wasn't searching for answers. I was just asking questions. There was a difference.

Riley squeezed my hand. "I'll check in on them later today, but there's not much I can do. They're just waiting all of this out. None of us really know Clint."

"What was Jackie like? I mean, what *is* Jackie like?" I corrected myself.

"She's a great girl. I hate to think of her going through this nightmare. She's a bit of a space cadet, almost made it to pro tennis status, and her family has more homes than I can count."

"Must be nice."

He cast a lingering glance my way, slowing his pace for a moment. "How are you doing? I know this is probably bringing up bad memories for you."

Leave it to Riley to be the thoughtful one. My brother had been kidnapped when I was a child. My family had never gotten a ransom note or any contact with his abductors, for that matter. We went years with nothing, and that very *nothing* had torn my family apart. Just within the past couple of months, my brother had shown back up in my life.

"I'm doing okay. I'm grateful, grateful that I got a happy ending after all of those years." Tim had turned out just fine, despite the trauma in his life. I was happy to have him living only fifteen minutes from me now and to be able to reconnect.

We stopped in front of a dining room. My eyebrows took on a mind of their own and shot up toward the ceiling. Wow. My jeans and ballet flats just didn't seem sufficient for the linen tablecloths, tuxedoed wait staff, and multiple pieces of silverware.

"You're going to love this," Riley insisted. He squeezed my hand and pulled me inside.

I'd been joking about raising my pinky while drinking, but maybe it was no laughing matter. This was just the type of place where I was bound to trip into a vat full of sugary strawberries or accidentally knock the candle over and catch a tablecloth on fire.

The maître d' led us to a group of Riley's friends. Derek and Lillian were sitting with Jack at a table for four. Instead, Riley and I sat at a table beside them.

I overheard Derek bragging to Lillian and Jack about how he got a car thief off on charges because the police had mishandled his arrest.

I was really glad I wasn't sitting with them because I might not be able to bite my tongue. I was so glad that Riley didn't defend scumbags. The whole "true love conquers all" thing would be invalid if he did. True love did not conquer unscrupulous behavior.

Besides, I was grateful to have a moment alone with Riley. But no sooner had we sat down than someone pulled out a seat between us. Lane "Big Head" Rosenblum.

"Any updates?" Lane shook out his napkin and placed it across his lap.

Riley shook his head.

"I just want to jump in and stop Clint from all of these bad decisions he's making. He should call the police." Lane signaled for the waiter to fill his coffee mug.

The man looked so at ease with people waiting on him, like he'd done this a million times before. Was he used to having people wipe his mouth and feed him grapes as well? Too bad he wasn't quite as experienced when it came to picking out his clothes.

"Jackie was . . . " Lane shook his head, his cup of coffee suspended mid-air. "I don't know. She was always a dreamer, you know? Nothing ever got in the way of her getting what she wanted." He paused. "I can't believe I almost married her. That seems like another lifetime ago."

"Speaking of which, I thought you were bringing some new girl you met." Riley took a sip of his coffee.

I, in the meantime, watched the conversation like

a ping-pong game. Back and forth. Back and forth. I thought it was safer this way. I'd rather Riley's friends think of me as quiet than as an idiot. I knew I wasn't an idiot, but other people did accuse me at times of being opinionated, headstrong, and persistent.

Lane grinned. "I am. She should be here tonight."

Riley slathered some butter on a biscuit he pulled from the basket on the table. "Aren't you going to tell us about her?"

"I thought I'd just wait until she got here and introduce you. She's incredible. The total package, from her looks to her brains. You're going to really love her."

Before Lane could gush anymore, a man approached our table. He wore a business suit, not one of the standard-issue formalwear pieces that the rest of the staff did. He had a wide forehead, thinning hair, and wire-framed glasses. "Good morning. I do hope you're enjoying your stay here at Allendale Acres. Your satisfaction is our top priority."

Riley nodded. "Absolutely."

"If there's anything we can do for you, please let us know. I do hope you enjoy your visit." He hurried to the next table. I wondered what his persona was outside of the hotel, just as Deanna had talked to me about last night. Did he make stills of moonshine? Trick out his car?

Nah, I just couldn't see it.

As the man recited his same spiel at the next table, I wanted to raise my eyebrows at the over-the-top customer service, but I didn't. Score one for Gabby. I could perhaps go this whole week without mocking rich, affluent people once. It wasn't likely, but it could happen.

Just then, I noticed a man walk past the table. His skin was dark, his hair darker, and he had a colorful silk sash around his midsection. I knew exactly who he was.

Deanna's dream man.

I stood, regretfully jostling the table as I did. "I've got to find out if that man is single."

Riley's eyebrows knotted together, and his head lurched forward in confusion. "Say what?"

I shook my head, my cheeks warming. "That's not how it sounded. It's a long story, actually. I'll be right back."

Before anyone could object, I started after the Middle Eastern/Indian man the maid had talked about last night. I'd told her I'd find out if he was single. She said that if I did, she'd find a way to show me the security footage. This sounded like a win-win to me.

How exactly I was going to do this, I had no idea. But I'd find a way. Somehow.

I walked at a quick clip behind the man, my mind racing, when I heard someone hiss, "Gabby!"

I jerked my gaze to the side. Deanna stood there, in an alcove where no one else would spot her. She'd changed into jeans and a sweatshirt, so obviously her shift was over. I glanced around to make sure no one was watching before slipping beside her. "What's going on?"

She pointed toward the distance. "That's him!"

"I know! The hot dignitary." I leaned closer. "So, you just think he's hot or you really like him?"

She sighed and put a hand over her heart. "He's like a Casanova. You don't understand. He picked up my feather duster when I dropped it. He smiles and it melts my heart. He actually sees me, a member of the cleaning staff . . . " She shook her head, seeming to snap back to reality. "It's like we're invisible sometimes."

My heart panged. I could understand that. That fact often helped me in my investigations, though. "He sounds like a winner."

"None of the maids can figure out his status. Believe me, they've tried. Do you really think you can?"

I shrugged casually, trying to ignore the scent of bacon and my stomach's Pavlovian response of growling with hunger. "I can find out a lot of things."

She glanced to the side and nibbled on her fingernail a moment before looking back at me. "I could get in so much trouble for this."

"I won't tell." She was awfully concerned about getting in trouble, yet that didn't seem to deter her. I knew there was a reason I liked Deanna.

She leaned closer. "And that solution you gave me for wine? Brilliant. Worked like a charm. I'm like the superhero housecleaner of my shift."

I straightened my shirt and emerged, trying to look like I was supposed to be hiding in a nook talking to one of the maids, like this was nothing unusual. A quick perusal of the room, and I spotted the Mr. Hottie in the corner, tapping away at a computer while eating a muffin . . . with his pinky raised. I almost wanted to snicker, but I didn't.

I took a step forward. *Here goes nothing.*

I "accidentally" knocked into his chair with my purse. My purse, then in response, fell to the floor. Out rolled my lip balm, wallet, my cell phone, a sheet of fake mustaches, and . . . a book called *Guide to Poisons*. I'd forgotten that was in there. You never knew when I might have a free moment to read up on deadly substances, though. It was only for my job.

Of course.

I squatted down. "I'm so sorry. I didn't spill your coffee, did I?"

The man's eyes widened, and he reached for the floor. "No, not at all."

I grabbed the book and shoved it to the bottom of my purse, hoping that I didn't seem too creepy by carrying the guide. "I'm so clumsy sometimes."

"It is busy in here. Understandable." He handed me my wallet. His words were clipped with an accent I couldn't quite identify.

I finished gathering everything, heaved my purse onto my shoulder, and stood. I extended my hand. "I'm Gabby, by the way. Gabby St. Claire."

"I am Ajay." His accent was thick, but understandable, and he certainly was handsome, just as Deanna had said.

"Love the accent. Where are you from?"

"India."

"I've heard it's beautiful there."

He smiled. "It is unmatched. But this Virginia in the United States is nice as well."

"What brings you here?" I pulled my purse up tighter, trying to appear casual. I was not someone who instantly made friends wherever I went or who didn't know a stranger. But, at times when life demanded it, I reached deep down inside myself and made it happen. For the sake of truth.

He stared at me a moment. "You ask a lot of questions."

I waved my hand in the air as if trying to brush away his uncertainties. "I'm sorry. I'm a little too talkative for my own good."

He stared at me a moment, that same small smile on his face. "Do not apologize. Your kindness is refreshing. I am here to get away from it all, as you Americans say."

"By yourself?"

He chuckled again. "Yes, by myself."

"Sounds relaxing, but don't you miss your family?"

I tugged at my collar as I realized I was pushing a little too hard. But in the distance, I could see Deanna nodding at me from behind the alcove. She was counting on me. And, though I didn't know the woman, I didn't want to let her down.

It was twisted logic. I knew that. But it was all I had at the moment.

He offered a sad smile before shaking his head. "I am what you call unattached. So, no, there is no one to miss me. Not really."

I nodded. The grief and melancholy in his eyes made my guilt pound even harder. "I'm sorry to hear that. I know you'll have a wonderful stay here, though."

He nodded crisply and stared into the distance a moment. "I hope I will Miss St. Claire. If I meet more people like you, I am sure I will."

I nearly blushed. Which wasn't good, because I was engaged. Happily engaged at that. Just because this man had a rockin' accent and a tragic past didn't mean I was attracted to him.

It did, however, mean that he should apply to be on *The Bachelor* or one of those other reality dating shows. Those bachelorettes would swoon all over him. It would be ratings gold.

I cleared my throat. "I should go."

He nodded slightly, almost like a mini-bow. "Take care."

I released a deep breath as I walked away. Okay, I had Deanna's answer. Now I hoped that Deanna would help find one for me as well.

CHAPTER 7

Riley disappeared to his conference, and I still had four hours to kill before I met Deanna and her friend from security. I'd been surprised at his lack of questioning to what I'd been up to, but maybe that just went to show how much he trusted me now. Our relationship had come a long way.

Riley had told me on the way here that I should go down to the spa and utilize some of the services there. Or maybe get some sun or play in the pool. You know, things that normal people did on vacation.

But I was still thinking about Jackie-O and Clint.

I was thinking about Riley's friends and how different they seemed than him. I wasn't sure what I'd expected. But not the group of people I'd met here.

Riley's friends, in the brief amount of time I'd been around them, seemed so into themselves and money and titles. Riley had given up what most people considered "the good life" in order to help people. I'd imagined him hanging out with other do-gooders, not people who seemed so . . . I'd never used this word before—and a part of me inwardly rebelled against it—but "worldly."

I glanced around at the people passing by. Some

were well dressed. Some were eccentric. I wasn't sure what it was that screamed "rich" when I looked at them. Maybe it was just the way they carried themselves. I couldn't pinpoint the exact differences.

Just for the record, I really didn't have anything against rich people. If someone who was a part of the "One Percent" wanted to come to my house for dinner, then they were more than welcome.

Maybe there was just a part of me who was more Robin Hood than James Bond. I liked helping commoners who had little resources at their disposal. The rich had so many advantages just because they had money.

Or maybe I was uncomfortable around wealth because of Carina Armstrong. Carina had gone to high school with me and never missed an opportunity to remind me that she thought she was better than I was. Truth be told, I didn't really care. I was happy with myself, so that was all that mattered. That's not to say that I wasn't at fault for that science experiment that went wrong, resulting in Carina's hands being stained green for two weeks.

I paused in the lobby, near the concierge. I took a step toward her, ready to ask about something asinine like how to sign up for a falconry course. Before I could, a deep voice sounded behind me.

"You've really done a number on Riley, haven't you?"

I turned and spotted Derek "Playboy" Waters. He stood behind me with a twinkle in his overly confident eyes. He stood close—too close—with his hands stuffed casually into his pockets.

I raised my eyebrows and tilted my head, certain I hadn't heard correctly. "What was that?"

He shrugged, that same satisfied smirk on his face.

"Riley. He's . . . he's different. He's changed since I saw him last."

I shrugged, really not sure what to say, which was unusual for me. "People do change." I certainly had. In fact, I'd changed mostly since I'd met Riley, and it was all for the best. He'd shown me how empty my life was before. Not before him, but before I understood how desperately I needed Jesus.

There was a time when I'd never thought I'd say those words. Now I couldn't imagine not saying them.

"All right." Derek looked me up and down like I'd just offended him. "I'm just saying I never thought I'd see the day when Riley Thomas would turn down a party."

I nearly choked. Thankfully I didn't have anything in my mouth or it would have been ugly. I tapped my chest just to make sure I hadn't gone into shock. "We must be talking about the wrong person."

Derek grinned, his eyes lighting with amusement. "He didn't tell you?"

"Tell me what?"

He nodded in that very urban, uppity manner that seemed to fit him so well. "You'll have to ask him about it."

My brain whirled faster than a computer at NASA. "I will. Believe me."

Just then, Ajay rounded the corner. "Miss St. Claire!"

I caught a quick glimpse of Derek. Why were his eyes dancing in amusement? It almost seemed like he was making assumptions that he shouldn't be making. The little turd.

Ajay held out something in his hands. "You left this." He handed me some lip balm I'd left at his table.

I blushed as I took it from him, which was

ridiculous. There was just something so chivalrous about the man, something that time seemed to leave behind as a relic of the past. Even Riley, who was extremely considerate, didn't seem quite as charming when he treated me like a lady. "Thanks. Sorry about that."

"No, really, it was my pleasure." He offered a slight bow before continuing on his way.

When I looked up, Derek's eyebrows were suspended and a sly grin stretched across his lips. "Interesting."

My hands went to my hips. "What's interesting?"

"This can be our secret, Gabby."

My eyes widened, and I shook my head. "It's not like that." I was going to have to pull out some crime scene stories here soon, just to horrify him enough to change the subject. It worked every time.

He nodded, appearing unconvinced and as smug as ever. "It's okay. I get it. Now I know where you were sneaking off in the middle of the night." He flashed another grin.

I forgot about my crime scene story strategy. "You saw me last night?" My mouth gaped wider.

"I'm a bit of an insomniac. But it's like I said. You don't have to worry." He straightened the starchy white collar of his shirt. "I make a living keeping secrets."

I stepped close enough that I could hiss and still be heard. "I'm not worried about you keeping any secrets, because you have no idea what you're talking about. You're full of hot air."

"Feisty." His raised eyebrows clearly showed that he didn't believe me. "I look forward to getting to know you this week, Gabby." He snapped his arm up and glanced at his watch. "Now, I've gotta say that I'm late for my workshop. Don't tell my boss. Oh right, that's me!"

I let out a fake laugh, one that quickly ended as soon as Derek walked away.

Our conversation wouldn't leave my thoughts quite as easily. Riley? A partier? Those words didn't compute together in my brain.

Riley was the good boy who always went to church every Sunday. Who read his Bible every morning. Who turned to prayer right away when things got tough—and even when they didn't.

Riley was not a partier. Certainly he would have mentioned that at some point during one of our conversations.

But now that I thought about it, we didn't really talk much about his past. I knew he'd grown up in a Christian home, so I just assumed he'd always stayed on the straight and narrow. He just seemed like the type to never wander off that path.

Oh yes, Riley and I were going to have to have a talk. There were more layers to that man than I'd guessed. In all of my investigations, there was one person whose background I'd never thought about looking into.

Thankfully, I had a lifetime to investigate this case.

CHAPTER 8

"Are you here for the tour, ma'am?"

I swung my head toward the concierge, a woman who was probably in her early thirties and wore her dark hair pulled back into a tight bun, a look that didn't in any way compliment the unflattering, standard-issue suit. She stood behind a desk with a granite-countertop that came to her chest and had numerous brochures neatly organized on top.

"The tour?"

She nodded. "Of Allendale. One of our historians will walk you through the property and explain the historical significance of each section of the building. Most find it enlightening."

The tour sounded downright boring to me. But maybe it would give me some insight to the place and wouldn't look as weird as me wandering around aimlessly. "I'd love to go."

A group of seven other people joined us at the desk. Then a man with a monocle and a tweed suit called for our attention. A monocle? I had no idea people used those anymore. All he needed was a pipe and he'd fit my every stereotype of the type of person who frequented places like this.

"I'm Jefferson Willis." He tugged at his jacket lapel and addressed everyone pensively. "My family has worked at Allendale for three generations. It's my pleasure to guide you through our wonderful facilities."

We began our tour at a brisk pace. The guide rambled about how more than one-hundred years ago a man named James Allen, who'd at one time owned a coal mine, had forever changed the fate of Healthy Springs when he opened a resort here that soon became a playground for the rich.

The resort fell into some hard times around the Great Depression, and the family lost ownership. Twenty years ago, it was sold to some big corporation who still owned it to this day. The Allens, however, like many other families, still worked here at the resort.

The natural springs were said to have healing properties that lured the "who's who" of the world here. Presidents had campaigned from the porch. Generals had taken breaks from battles in the springs. The rich had bought rooms so they could stay year-round. Blah, blah, blah.

We passed ballrooms, one of the original horse and buggies that had carried dignitaries, and shrines with pictures of the place when it had first begun.

My mind was not on anything the historian was saying, though.

No, my thoughts were on Jackie-O.

For her to have been kidnapped here, only hours after arriving, someone would have to plan very carefully. The kidnapper would have had to know about this trip, when Jackie was arriving, that she'd go hiking, and that she'd go hiking alone.

They'd had to know that no one was in her room

when they ventured inside to leave the ransom note.

They'd had to know that she was loaded and that one day's time was adequate for getting a large amount of cash like the ransom had demanded.

There were a lot of variables in that scenario that could have easily gone wrong, I mused as we started upstairs, passing some of the guest suites.

What had Riley said? That Jackie was an Assistant District Attorney. She was the one who put the bad guys behind bars. Had someone she'd put behind bars been stalking her, waiting for just the right minute to exact their revenge? Perhaps her abductor was someone who wanted to teach the family a lesson?

I shook my head. Something just didn't seem quite right about the situation to me.

What if one of Riley's old law school buddies was somehow involved in this whole fiasco? Lane had been engaged to her. What if he didn't like seeing her with someone new? Derek was a self-proclaimed playboy. Those malpractice attorneys seemed like they could twist and turn anything to get what they wanted. Would he have gone as far as to kidnap an old classmate?

None of my theories made sense. Not yet. First, I needed more information.

I heard the door open not far away and someone say, "I'm just going to go on a walk and stretch my legs some."

I glanced back, and Clint appeared in my view.
Clint.

He was leaving his hotel room and walking in the opposite direction.

I made a split-second decision and slipped away from the tour group to run after him. "Clint!"

He slowed and turned to face me. Grief lined his

eyes, as well as uncertainty.

I sucked in a deep breath, trying to regain my composure. "I'm not sure if you remember me. Gabby St. Claire."

He nodded, glancing behind me before meeting my gaze again. "Yeah, I remember."

I pulled a hair behind my ear, trying to collect my thoughts. "How are you?" I fell in step beside him as he started down the hallway at a lazy pace.

He shrugged. "As well as you can imagine."

"Anything new on Jackie?"

He shook his head. "We're just counting down the time."

"In case I haven't said this, I'm really sorry."

He nodded and stuffed his hands deeper into his pockets. "Thanks."

"Look, I know this sounds weird, but can I ask you a few questions?"

He stopped and stared at me. "About?"

"About Jackie." I locked gazes with him, hoping he could see the sincerity in my eyes. He stared at me as if trying to determine if I was trustworthy or not. When I thought he was going to refuse, I offered, "I was a professional investigator for a while. I may be able to help."

Finally, he nodded. "I guess."

We started walking again, though I had no idea where we were going. We were ambling aimlessly, I supposed, but that was okay with me. "Who knew she was coming here this week?"

"Everyone in her office back in Atlanta, I suppose."

"Was there anyone in particular she was having trouble with? Maybe someone she argued with? Someone who threatened her?" We reached the stairs and started down them.

"What are you getting at?"

"I was just thinking about it, and someone had to know she was going to be here. They had to follow her from her home."

He glanced at me and squinted. "So, you think someone from Atlanta is behind this?"

I shrugged. "I think it's someone who knew her."

He stayed quiet for a moment. "One of her colleagues is here this week. His name is Doug Matthews, I think."

We reached the lobby and kept walking until we were outside. Warm sunlight hit us. Clint threw his head back and soaked it in for a moment, looking desperate for some sort of relief from the agony he had to be experiencing.

"Did she ever have any problems with Doug?"

Clint shook his head. "I don't know. She didn't talk about work a lot, especially not with me."

"When did you guys get here?"

"Me and Jackie? We got here Saturday evening. Why?"

I ignored his question. "How about the rest of the Georgetown gang? When did they arrive?"

He rubbed his chin. "Derek and Lillian got here at lunchtime yesterday. That Jack guy probably came an hour later. Then you and your guy. Lane must have come when we were looking for Jackie."

"Did you talk to anyone yesterday? Have lunch together?"

He stared at me a moment. "Do you think one of her friends is behind this?"

"I'm not thinking anything. I'm just asking questions."

His hand moved from his chin to his cheek, the rubbing motion becoming more vigorous. "We chatted with Derek and Lillian in the lobby. That's when Jackie said she wanted to go on a hike."

"She didn't invite her friends with her? They haven't seen each other in years."

"I dunno, man. They'd just gotten here and hadn't even unpacked. That Lillian lady was wearing a suit—on a Sunday, and she hadn't been to church."

"Why didn't you go with Jackie on the hike?"

"I fell from a ladder three months ago and broke my ankle. It hasn't been the same since. Besides, there was a race on TV. I hung out at the bar to watch it."

It sounded like he had an alibi. But what about Derek, Lillian, and Jack?

"What do you do for a living, Clint?" I leaned against one of the massive columns and watched as the valets scurried to help people arriving for their stay.

"I work construction." He snorted. "I know. I'm terribly out of place here. I almost didn't come. Now I kind of wish I hadn't, and that I'd tried to convince Jackie to do the same. Maybe none of this would have happened then."

"How'd you meet?"

"I was installing a new tennis court in her backyard. She thought I owned the company, but I was really just a peon." He chuckled. "When she found out the truth, she forgave me. We were inseparable after that."

"I know this must be hard on you."

He picked up a rebellious piece of grass that had sprung up between the bricks and tossed it into a nearby rose bush. "Jackie's mom doesn't exactly like me. I just had to get out of that room with her and her new 'man friend' for a while. They're driving me crazy, and they keep looking at me like I'm second-class. I've never exactly had their approval."

"That's hard. I can understand where you're coming from." I could. Maybe no one had ever said that to my face, but I still felt it. Riley always said it was only in my mind, but I didn't one hundred percent believe him.

Clint looked at me and raised his chin, as if I passed some kind of brotherhood test. "At least there's one person here this week who doesn't think I'm no good because I get my hands dirty for a living."

"People who get their hands dirty for a living are some of the best people I know. Honest, hardworking, bone tired at the end of the day. That's nothing to be ashamed of."

He scuffed his feet against the bricks for a moment before looking up. "Thanks for listening, Gabby. I've got to get back to the firing squad inside, though." He found a gum wrapper in his pocket, pulled out a pen, and jotted something down. "Here's my phone number. If you hear anything, let me know."

I shoved the paper in my pocket. "Is there anything else I can do?"

He frowned. "Just wait."

"I'll pray also."

He nodded. "I'm not so sure God wants to do anything for me. I've messed up pretty bad."

"You might be surprised. I know I was." There couldn't ever be truer words spoken.

He pointed inside. "I'm going to get back now. Thanks again for the talk."

I watched him shuffle back inside.

I prayed this all would turn out well. But I had a strange feeling it wouldn't.

CHAPTER 9

I grabbed lunch at the little market, having no desire to sit by myself in the massive, swanky dining hall. Riley had a lunchtime workshop today and couldn't meet me, so I was on my own. I found a little wrought-iron table outside overlooking the pool area and sat down with my ham salad sandwich, some chunks of cantaloupe, and a bottle of water.

I could have seen a movie and bought a round of coffee for all of my friends for the amount this meal cost me. At least at breakfast you just signed this little paper, and the hotel charged your meal to your room bill. It was a lot less painful that way.

At least, until you got the bill.

Something jabbed me in the rear, so I reached into my back pocket, and pulled out Jackie's phone. I'd forgotten I'd stuck it in there.

I hit the button and the screen lit. Several missed phone calls caught my eye. I pulled out my purse, found some paper and a pen, and jotted the numbers down. I really needed to return this to Clint, but I wanted to get some information first.

I tried to figure out Jackie's code, so I could see

what other interesting information might be on her phone. I couldn't crack it, though.

I sighed and stared at the numbers instead. There were three that repeated several times. One had to be Clint's, the other Jackie's mom, and the third . . . I wasn't sure.

I found the scrap of paper where Clint had jotted down his digits, and I compared it to my list. Interesting. I saw his number listed there twice.

Twice?

I'd expected him to try to call her uncountable times. Like, every five minutes or something.

But, no, he'd tried to call at 6 and then again at 7.

If I was worried about someone, I wouldn't be able to stop myself from calling as much as I could.

Out of curiosity, I pulled my own phone out and dialed the other number. The phone rang and rang. No answer. No machine. No voicemail.

Interesting.

I dialed the third number. Before the first ring was finished, a woman answered. Breathless. Hopeful. Strained.

I knew whose number this was.

Mrs. Harrington's.

I mumbled that I had the wrong number, apologized, and hung up.

So, whose number was this third one? Whoever it was had tried to call at 1:30—that would be before Jackie left—and then again at 2 and 2:30.

Using my smartphone, I did a quick search on the area code. I blinked at what I saw. Healthy Springs.

Someone local had tried to call Jackie. Or what if it was . . . someone here at the hotel?

I gulped down the rest of my lunch, stuffed

Jackie's phone back in my pocket, threw away my trash, and hurried inside. I was going on a hunch and a prayer.

I approached the concierge. "Excuse me, I'm trying to figure out who's been trying to call me from extension," I glanced at the paper in my purse, "1241. Do you have a list of extensions?"

"I don't even have to look that one up. That's the extension of our courtesy phone." She pointed to a lone phone nestling on an intricate shelf on the other side of the lobby.

I tapped the marble-topped desk. "Excellent. Thank you."

The information wasn't really excellent, though, because that courtesy phone number meant that anyone could have been trying to call Jackie.

***

After I freshened up, I went back downstairs to meet Deanna. She waited for me in one of the chairs in the grand entryway. She said nothing when she saw me, and instead stood and nodded for me to follow. I quietly did just that. She was probably worried about getting in trouble because, in the short time since I'd known her, that was all she'd worried about. Finally, we turned off from the main hallway into a quieter one in the West Wing of the facility.

I looked behind me. It was just us. No witnesses.

"If anyone asks, you're a friend," she mumbled. "The management doesn't exactly smile on the staff mingling with the patrons, if you know what I mean. It's more like the peons mingling with royalty. It's not supposed to happen."

"Understood." I hurried to keep pace with her.

"Did you find out the information?"

"I did. Ajay is single. Definitely."

She let out a little squeal before quickly composing herself. "That makes my day. My week. My year!"

"So, are you going to approach him now? What's your grand plan?"

Deanna gasped and threw a glance behind her. "Are you crazy? I could never do that. I'm not that kind of woman."

I didn't even bother to ask what the point of finding out his status was then. Maybe she just needed the information to feed her crush. I'd done some crazy things under the influence of infatuation before. "Did you get any sleep? You were wide awake only five hours ago at breakfast when I saw you."

"I've learned to live on four hours."

I did a double take and quickened my steps. "Four hours? Are you crazy?"

She shrugged and threw a long curl over her shoulder. "I'm used to it by now." She stopped by a door and locked gazes with me. I half expected to need a retinal scan to get into the room. "In here."

I slipped inside. Floor to ceiling monitors and computers filled the room on two walls. A security guard sat behind the desk, staring at the screens and looking bored to tears.

He looked our way as Deanna approached. "Ricky, this is my friend I told you about."

The man, who was probably in his late-twenties with thinning blond hair, raised his chin in hello. "Wassup?"

Deanna nodded toward me. "Someone's causing her trouble, and we're hoping you can help." She paused and cocked her head as if reenacting a Sunday night crime drama. "Off the record, that is."

When Ricky glanced at me, I shrugged. "It's a long confusing story. Believe me. But I can't get the hotel involved. Not yet, at least. Not until I have more proof."

"Trouble with your ex?" Ricky asked.

"Just trouble. I'll leave it at that."

He stared me down. "I'm not supposed to do this."

"Remember when I didn't tell anyone when you and that valet wrecked a car you took for a joyride?" Deanna zigzagged her chin, hand on hip, and full-blown sassiness on display.

His eyes widened. "You weren't ever supposed to bring that up."

Deanna raised her eyebrows. "I'm cashing in on that favor you owe me."

Ricky stared at Deanna, then me, and then the door before sighing. "Be my lookout," he told Deanna. "And after this, we're even."

"Done."

As Deanna scurried away, Ricky sat up straighter. "All right. What time and what location do you need to see?" He pushed out a chair, and I lowered myself there.

"I need the camera that shows everyone coming and going out of room 3412. The time would be between 4 and 7."

He hit some buttons, and a few seconds later, my hallway came onto the screen. He pointed to a door in the center. "That should be the room you're looking at."

I nodded and leaned closer. "Perfect."

Several people walked up and down the hallway. No one I recognized, though.

Finally, someone paused at my door. "Stop right

there!"

He slowed the tape. I leaned closer. That was Jackie-O leaving the room. She stepped out and looked both ways down the hall. Strange initial reaction for someone stepping out.

Unless she suspected that someone might be watching her.

My back muscles pinched tighter.

The woman was beautiful. She wore jeans, a sweatshirt and hiking boots, so she had planned on going hiking apparently. I was struck again by just how much she did look like Jackie Kennedy.

What kind of trouble had she gotten herself caught up in?

In my mind, I figured that if Jackie-O had just left to go hiking, it would at least be two hours until her kidnapper came back with the ransom note. "Fast forward a bit."

Only thirty minutes later, a man stopped outside the door to her room.

Thirty minutes? That wasn't enough time to kidnap Jackie, write the note, and make it back to the room.

I squinted, trying to soak in the figure. He wore a flannel shirt and baseball cap. He was so tall that his body seemed to arch forward like a stick with too much weight on it. Where had I seen that man before? He looked vaguely familiar.

He kept his head low, inserted the key card, and slipped inside. Ten minutes later, he stepped out. He didn't bother to look around for witnesses. He simply walked away with his head down and his hands stuffed into his pockets.

I sucked in a deep breath as realization hit. I knew

where I'd seen that man before.

That was the man who'd been talking to Clint in the hallway last night.

CHAPTER 10

By three o'clock, I'd composed myself. Riley and I were supposed to meet, but I was still shaken at seeing Clint's friend leave Jackie's room.

Ricky and I had scrolled through the rest of the tape, just to make sure no one else had stopped by in the time between Clint's friend leaving until the entire gang arrived, me included, a little after dinnertime. They hadn't. That left us with one clear answer.

Clint's friend had left that note.

Did Clint know? Was his friend so desperate for money that he'd abducted a pal's girlfriend? What had he told Clint as his excuse for being here?

The even bigger question for me, at the moment, was whether or not I should share the information. Clint had asked us not to get involved. If I admitted I'd seen the video, there would be no denying that I'd done some research. If I didn't admit to my involvement, Jackie might be killed.

I sighed, the weight of the decision pressing on me. I would wait until Clint dropped off the money today, I decided. I'd see if Jackie was returned safe and sound. Then I'd figure out the best plan of action.

I attempted to look casual as I lounged in an upright chair in the lobby. I tried not to pace or twist my fingers or mumble aloud. I tried not to show any evidence that I'd been anything but a concerned citizen as I'd asked questions and looked at videotapes today. Definitely not nosy. I wasn't sticking or following or nearly getting killed.

Not yet, at least.

The original plan was for Riley and his friends to play golf this afternoon. That meant that *I* was supposed to play golf this afternoon as well. The closest I'd ever come to a golf course was playing putt-putt down at the beach, and I hadn't even enjoyed that.

Every time I thought about being on the green, I frowned. Was there ever a more wretched sport? I was not looking forward to going and chasing after some ball. I'd much rather be chasing a bad guy.

But now that Jackie was missing, I wondered how the gang's plan would change. Certainly they couldn't go out and have fun while their friend was abducted. They would be voted the most insensitive group of classmates *ever* if they did.

"Riley told me to tell you that he should be here any minute."

I looked up and saw Lillian. From what I'd observed so far, the woman was my polar opposite. I was emotional and excitable and passionate. She was logical, thought-out, and non-emotive. She wore a navy blue power suit. Last night, she'd worn a white one.

"Great," I mumbled. "Thanks for letting me know."

She paused by my chair. "Terrible about Jackie, isn't it?"

"I heard you were best friends."

She nodded. "Were. I mean, don't get me wrong. We're still friends. But you do lose touch with people after a while, you know? We emailed on occasion, but I haven't seen her since graduation."

"What do you think of her boyfriend?"

Lillian turned her nose up. "She could do better. But Jackie always surprised us."

"How?"

"You know, I think she hated to do what was expected of her. Her mom put a lot of pressure on her. So Jackie was kind of sneaky. She'd take these weekend trips without telling anyone. She got a job as a waitress just for the fun of it. She got a tattoo somewhere it'll never see the light of day. Just small acts of rebellion."

"What's her story? Where's Jackie's dad?"

"Her parents divorced when Jackie was young. Her dad was considerably older than her mom, and he had a heart attack and died when Jackie was only eight. Mrs. Harrington never remarried. She was too afraid someone would be after her money and find some way to scam the prenuptial agreement. According to Jackie, she's always had 'man friends' who wanted to marry her. Mrs. Harrington will never go for it, though."

"All because of money?"

Lillian nodded. "Their money all comes from her side of the family, and her reputation is very important to her. Mrs. Harrington won't let anyone make her look like a fool again."

I let the new information sink in. I had no more questions at the moment, not until I swallowed what I'd just learned. Instead, I strayed to a more neutral subject. "I heard you were a divorce lawyer?"

She sneered. "It's the reason I'll never get married. Relationships just get so ugly. All of them."

Not all of them, I wanted to argue.

She snickered. "I know that look. You think you're

immune."

"I've had my fair share of ugly relationships. Riley's different." I glanced down at my princess-cut diamond and smiled. I never wanted to take this ring off.

"Any relationship can turn sour. Any one. I hate to be the bearer of bad news."

What did she know? I shrugged.

"That said, you've got yourself a good one," Lillian continued. "I always wondered what kind of girl would finally snag Riley."

"Snagging's one of my many specialties." I realized how lame that sounded and decided to not be cute. "I'm really thankful to have him in my life, actually. Sometimes I still pinch myself."

She rested a well-manicured hand on the chair. "He was a hot commodity in law school."

I raised my eyebrows, not in surprise of the fact that Riley had been desirable, as much as I was shocked by this conversation. "What was he like?"

She stepped closer. "Let me put it this way. Derek is handsome and he knows it. Lane is smart but kind of nerdy. Jack was . . . well, he was Jack. Riley was a perfect mix. He was handsome like Derek, but smart like Lane, and minus all of their bad qualities."

I nodded. "He's a catch." *A catch?* Did anyone say that anymore?

She crossed her arms and leaned against the chair, as if she was ready to settle in for a long talk. "He had this wild streak that made him interesting, too."

I nearly choked on my spit for the second time today. "Wild streak?" Of all the things I would call Riley, wild was not one of them. Ever. By any stretch of the imagination. In my craziest dreams. Not even after what Derek had said earlier.

"He was always the one planning our outlandish excursions. Spring break trips. Backpacking adventures. We all went to Europe one summer and stayed at hostels. We knew if Riley were there, we'd have a good time. He liked living on the edge."

"Riley?" I had to stop repeating things. But I felt certain she was talking about someone else and not my fiancé.

She seemed to be on a roll as she waved her hand in the air and settled in for the conversation. "He was the king of drinking games. He could come up with some outrageous ones."

I leaned forward to get a better look at her face. Certainly there was a twinkle in her eyes that would let me know she was joking. Nope, there wasn't even a sparkle. "Drinking games?"

She straightened, crossed her arms, and shook her head. "It was such a tragedy about his best friend . . . "

I wanted to ask, but just then I saw Riley approaching. Lillian waved and scurried off, mumbling something about giving us some time alone.

I forced a smile as Riley got closer. I was so not good at this whole being fake thing. In other words, I could never work at this hotel. I'd be fired in a day.

I wanted to tell Riley about Jackie. I wanted to ask him about his drinking games. I wouldn't do either. At least, I wouldn't do either right now. There was a time and a place for everything. I often forgot that rule, especially when I was looking for answers.

But my goal was to be prim and proper this week. That meant abiding by certain rules of social etiquette.

He leaned down and kissed my cheek, the scent of his leathery aftershave filling my senses. "How was your day? Did you visit the spa?"

I shook my head. "No, but I did take a tour of the building." At least, I'd taken half a tour. "A historian led it. It was interesting. And the guide had a monocle. If he'd had a cane and a top hat, he would have reminded me of Mr. Peanut. That made it all worth it."

Riley chuckled under his breath. He took my hand and pulled me to my feet. His hand went to my waist, sending flutters up my spine. "Good. I'm glad you found something to amuse yourself. I don't want you to feel bad about taking time for yourself. Sign up for some lessons. Enjoy the pool or soak in the springs. You've been busy lately. You deserve to relax some."

I nodded as we started walking across the lobby at a leisurely pace. "I appreciate that. I'll talk to the concierge." I said the word in a nasal tone, my best imitation of a French accent. It wasn't pretty.

The rain in Spain . . .

Sally sells seashells . . .

Peter Piper picked . . .

I had to work on my speech, not because I spoke Cockney, but because mastering accents could be a great pastime. First, I needed to master the tongue twisters, though.

Riley's lip curled. "You don't have to say concierge with an accent, you know."

I nodded. "I know. I just like to."

"Then by all means, do." His smile slipped, and his steps slowed. "Any word on Jackie?"

"I ran into Clint earlier. He said the plan was still the same. He wants to keep everything low key. They're intending to drop off the money at Glass Falls in," I glanced at my watch, "fifty minutes."

"I hope it all works out like he wants it to." Riley let out a long breath.

"You would have called the police?"

He shrugged. "It's hard to know exactly what you'd do until you're in that situation. I can't help but think the police would know what they're doing better than I would. Still, it's one stressful position I wouldn't wish on anyone."

"I'm surprised the whole gang isn't more upset by this. It just seems like life keeps going on. Is that weird to you?" When my friend Sierra had gone missing, I'd stopped everything until I knew she was okay.

"What are we supposed to do? Just sit around all day and wait? Clint has pretty much told us he doesn't want us around. We can't tell the police. We have no idea where to search and doing that could just get Jackie killed."

I nodded. He sounded just like a lawyer, but he had some good points. "I can't argue with that." I stopped walking, unsure where we were even heading. "What now? Do we stay here and wait while they drop off the money?"

"What else are we supposed to do?" Riley's crystal blue eyes connected with mine.

I shrugged, trying to look innocent. "Someone needs to keep their eyes open for the person who picks up the stash. What if they don't deliver Jackie? What if following them is the only hope for finding Jackie when this whole thing blows up?"

Riley's hands went to his hips, and his chin jutted out in thought. "I'm assuming Glass Falls is a pretty public area. I can't imagine that they'd request somewhere too secluded."

"I did a little research." I treaded carefully, remembering my promise not to get involved.

"Okay . . . " His expression remained neutral. As

hard as I tried to read it, I couldn't.

Instead, I pulled out a map of the resort and pointed to a little dotted line on the outskirts of the hotel. "There's another hiking trail that runs above the falls. If we could hike there, Clint wouldn't see us. We could hang out and see who picks up the bag of money."

He squeezed my shoulder. "I know this is hard for you to stay away from, Gabby."

I shrugged. "I just don't want to see this end poorly."

Riley stared at me a moment before nodding. "How long does it take to get there?"

Hope soared in my chest. Maybe Riley understood me better than I thought. "About forty-five minutes, if I read the map correctly."

"Let me get changed. We can make it in forty."

CHAPTER 11

As Riley gripped my hand, I realized how grateful I was to have him with me on this search. I liked being independent and all, but there was something comforting about someone having your back.

I glanced at my watch one more time, wishing I had the chance to admire the scenery around me. Instead, we'd moved quickly to get to the area where we could overlook the falls.

Only five more minutes, and Clint was supposed to leave the money.

I saw a railing ahead and figured we were almost there. Thank goodness. My lungs were screaming for air. I hadn't adjusted to the altitude change yet and my body was letting me know.

We paused at the railing to catch our breath.

"You okay?" Riley asked. He didn't look winded at all, which prompted a dirty look from me as I nodded.

"Just fine."

He pointed to the falls. "Just across there is the overview. There's a trashcan off to the side. That's where Clint is supposed to leave the cash."

I pulled up my binoculars. The overview was busy

with various hikers. Apparently, one could drive there as well or take the longer hike through the mountains to get to this astonishing view of the waterfall.

Through my lens, I saw Clint approaching. His gaze skittered from side to side. He was nervous—obviously. He had a black backpack slung over his arm as he paused by the railing.

Then he walked to the trashcan, put the bag down, and threw away a wrapper of some sort. His gaze traveled from side to side another moment before he stepped away.

He walked back to the parking lot, got in his car, and drove away.

I blinked in surprise.

That had been easy. He hadn't tried to be a hero. He hadn't veered off plan.

That was a good thing, right?

For some reason, it felt all wrong.

If I'd been in his shoes, I would have waited in my car to see if someone got the money. I would have set up friends on the perimeter to catch a glimpse of the person who picked up the book bag. I would have put some kind of tracking device in the lining of the bag so I could trace it.

"Well?"

"He left the bag." I sighed. "I wonder how long it will take for someone to get it." I wondered if he had any idea his friends might be involved.

"Your guess is as good as mine."

"I wonder if the kidnappers have made any contact by phone at all? Jackie could have told them Clint's number. Even her mom's cell phone number." I sighed again. "This whole situation is just disturbing, to say the least."

"I'm proud of you. You haven't gotten involved

like I thought you would. You're actually taking this vacation thing seriously."

Guilt crept in. Should I tell him about the security tapes? How I checked the keycard? Nah. Those were just small little details. Really, for the most part, I'd kept my nose out of things.

I twisted my lips as I pondered the truth of my thought.

Just then, I spotted someone approaching the bag. "Someone's walking toward it!"

A baseball cap concealed his hair and an oversized sweatshirt didn't help with additional details. The person looked around before swooping down to grab the bag. As he turned, I caught a glimpse of his face . . . or, should I say, her face?

A woman? A woman was behind this? Was she in on this with Clint's pal?

I expected her to walk toward the parking lot, which would be the quickest getaway route. Instead, she started down the trail.

"Come on! Maybe we can follow her." I had a sudden burst of energy as I hurried back from the direction we'd come. I didn't bother to look back and see if Riley was following. Instead I kept my eyes on the woman.

She moved with a bounce in her step, as if she were just out taking a stroll. If that was part of her cover-up, she was good. Really good. No one would suspect she was guilty of anything looking as casual as she did.

"Wait up, Gabby," Riley called behind me. "If you fall and twist your ankle, we'll never get to her in time. The rate you're going, you're going to hurt yourself."

I slowed my pace some. "You're right." I dodged a tree root. "I just don't want to lose her." The trees thickened on the other side of me, and I couldn't see the woman for a moment.

We kept that pace for the rest of the hike back, all forty or so minutes, until we reached the clearing, and Allendale came into view in all of its majesty. I stopped, searching for the woman with the backpack.

"There!" I pointed to her as she climbed the steps leading inside.

I quickened my steps again, knowing that once she got inside, it would be easy to lose her. I couldn't do that. This could be Clint's only hope of finding Jackie.

Who knows? That woman with the ball cap may have gone in with Clint's friend to arrange all of this. People had done things more twisted before. I'd seen it firsthand.

My pace quickened to a jog. I reached the grand entryway, flew by bewildered looking valets, and stopped dead in my tracks atop of the marble floors inside.

Where had she gone?

Riley stopped behind me. "There!" He pointed toward the distance.

I followed his outstretched finger and saw the woman. She stood at the check-in counter . . . handing the bag to the clerk there?

No . . .

I sighed and hurried to catch up. "Excuse me. Did you find that bag somewhere?"

The woman quickly assessed me before nodding curtly. "Someone left it on the trail. It feels heavy, but I don't know what's inside. I just know they probably didn't want to lose it. Is it yours?"

I shook my head. "No, but I think it's a friend of mine's. I'll let him know it's here."

I could have taken the bag, but I wanted to let Clint handle this. Besides, showing up with 200k in my possession could quite possibly make me look guilty.

I glanced up at Riley. "I guess we should go tell Clint."

CHAPTER 12

We'd found Clint in his room, pacing frantically, along with Mrs. Harrington and her "man friend." At some point, Derek and Lane had joined us. Riley and I updated them about what had happened.

"Now, of all times, someone decides to be a Good Samaritan!" Clint muttered, still pacing. Sweat beaded on his forehead.

Jackie's mom looked like an older version of her daughter. Her hair was dark and bobbed. Her petite figure had put on a few well-distributed pounds over the years. Even in her distressed state, she still looked neat and prim.

Her man friend just sat in a chair looking lost. My guess was that he was whipped and knew his opinion wouldn't matter a lick here.

"What do I do now?" Clint asked.

Derek and Lane lounged in chairs at the other end of the room. Lillian and Jack the Dipper stood in the corner. Riley and I found a spot by the door.

Tension stretched in the room, and it almost seemed like one wrong move—or word—would cause the whole place to shatter into a frenzy of name calling, finger pointing, and accusation.

And I'd been the one who was the bearer of this bad news, so I feared a lot of that heat would come my way.

Clint and Mrs. Harrington hadn't looked too happy that I'd gone hiking and spied on the transaction. I'd told them that if I hadn't, they might not know any of this.

"Have you tried her cell phone?" Derek asked.

"Of course I've tried her cell phone. She doesn't answer." Clint ran a hand through his hair.

"When was the last time you tried?" Riley asked.

Heat rose through me. Her cell phone. It was in my pocket. If someone called it, and the ringer was still on . . . I had to put an end to this.

I opened my mouth, trying to divert the subject, but Derek and Clint kept going back and forth. In the meantime, Clint had pulled out his own cell phone and started dialing.

"I tried her last night. No answer. You think the kidnapper will spontaneously let her have her phone, just in case I call?" Clint stabbed another button.

"I—" I held up a hand.

"I would think if it was my girlfriend, I'd be trying every hour, just in case. I'd be doing whatever I could to help," Derek came back.

"Just because you have some law school education behind you doesn't mean you know everything," Clint retorted.

"You guys, really—" How was I going to explain this?

"I would have called the police," Derek said, standing now. "You're obviously doing a lousy job with this."

Clint stepped closer. "How are you—"

Just then, something jangled in my pocket. The

room went quiet and all eyes were on me. I swallowed my pride—and dared not look at Riley—as I reached into my pocket. I held out the cell phone and frowned.

"I found it in the room. When I realized that no one was monitoring it, I grabbed it, just in case Jackie called or someone called with a clue. I meant to give it to you earlier, Clint, but it slipped my mind."

The silence remained, as did everyone's piercing gazes. If only the floor would open up and swallow me whole. Instead, I did my best Lucille Ball imitation as I frowned and shrugged sheepishly.

Then Riley squeezed my shoulder. "You guys, she works for the State Medical Examiner. She knows her stuff, and she's gotten more than one person out of a tight spot before. She was just trying to help."

Clint stepped forward and snatched away the cell phone, the scowl never leaving his face.

I guess this would be a bad time to tell Riley that I'd lost my job?

The hole I was in just seemed to get deeper and deeper.

My gaze fell on Clint's friends who lingered in the background. I guess this would be a bad time to bring up that I'd looked through the security footage and seen one of them leaving Jackie's room, as well? No, I'd keep that to myself.

For now.

I needed more evidence first. More proof.

"All of you stop with this nonsense. My daughter is missing!" Mrs. Harrington stood, tears glimmering in her eyes. "All of this arguing is getting us nowhere. I need my daughter back, and I need her back now. Don't you understand? The kidnappers think we fell through with our end of the bargain. They said she'd die if we didn't leave the money or if we got the police involved."

Silence subdued everyone. I stepped back and forced myself to look away, as if not to invite a challenge with anyone. Riley's hand remained at my shoulder.

He was my rock. What could I say? He kept me grounded, and I desperately needed someone to keep me grounded.

"Maybe they'll try to contact us again," Clint finally said. "In the meantime, I need to think. So, thank you all for your help, but I want some time alone."

I nodded, along with the rest of the gang, and we plodded outside. I'm sure this was not the way any of them saw this little reunion going.

"I'm going to go down and grab a drink. Anyone want to come?" Derek asked.

"I'm down with that," Lane muttered.

Lillian and Jack the Dipper agreed.

Riley shook his head. "Go ahead without me. I need to check on my car."

"Oh, come on, man." Derek's hand clamped Riley's shoulder. "It could be like old times."

Riley shook his head. "I'll pass. I'll catch up with you guys later, though."

As soon as the gang walked away, I stared Riley down. "I'm in bizarro world. The conversation I just heard could not have possibly happened."

Riley let out a soft laugh. "There's a lot you don't know about me, Gabby."

"Why?"

"There are parts of my past I'd rather forget."

I shook my head. "I don't understand. For as long as I've known you, you've been this role model citizen and practically like one of the twelve disciples."

"Even the twelve disciples had their issues at some

points."

I shook my head. "I can't believe you haven't told me, though. I mean, we're getting married. Happily ever after and all that jazz."

"I'll tell you. Just not right now. Right now, I need some fresh air. I need to check on my car. And I need to get away from this craziness." He held out his hand. "Walk with me into town to visit the mechanic shop?"

I stared at his hand for a moment before lacing my fingers through his. I didn't care what his past held; I just wanted him to trust me enough to share it. But I had little room to talk when considering the things I'd been keeping from him. "Let's go."

CHAPTER 13

As we walked, I desperately wanted to ask Riley questions. A lot of people had garbage in their past. I certainly had my fair share. I just didn't understand why Riley had never talked about his. Especially to me, not only as his fiancée, but as someone who struggled big time with messing up. When Riley and I had met, I'd been unforgiving, I couldn't stand Christians, and my only hope was in the things of this world.

He'd played a big part in the changes in my life. He'd invited me to church. He hadn't given up on me. He'd been there when I needed him the most.

Most of all, he hadn't made me feel judged, for the most part, at least. He'd loved me when I was unlovable. He'd been patient with me when any normal person would have just slapped me silly.

So I'd discovered this week that Riley liked to drink and party at one time. What else didn't I know? What had caused the changes in him?

He didn't seem keen on talking about it at the moment, so I turned my focus on the buildings around me. Adjacent to Allendale was an old historic town with a few gift shops, the garage, two restaurants, a gas station and a general store.

An older, smaller hotel also rested on the corner, though it looked like it was no longer in use—as a hotel, at least. By other standards, the place had probably been grand at one time, but it dwarfed in comparison to Allendale Acres. It was four stories high, covered in whitewashed wood, and had quaint little balconies.

"Hi, Gabby!" someone yelled.

I looked up and saw Deanna leaning out from one of the windows. I smiled and waved back. This must be the apartment building where the employees lived.

"You know her?" Riley asked.

I shrugged. "What can I say? I'm a people magnet." I said it tongue in cheek. Of course, in one way it was true. On a purely scientific level, one side of a magnet attracted things while the other side repelled them. That sounded pretty true to my life. People either loved me or hated me. There wasn't much in between.

We walked into Buck's Garage just as a man walked out. I stared for a moment at the twenty-something man with a baby face. Where had I seen him before? He was definitely familiar, but I couldn't figure out why.

I shook my head. It probably didn't matter anyway. I simply had an insatiable curiosity that always wanted answers.

I glanced around the reception area of the garage. Cheaply framed photos of classic cars like Mustangs and Corvettes were placed around the room. Most had faded either with age, from the sun, or both. The front desk was made up of wood paneling straight from the seventies and an odd, purple stuffed bear held a "Welcome" sign on the counter.

Riley moseyed up to the desk, where a woman with streaked-blue hair and trendy glasses waited. As she pulled up Riley's information on a dinosaur of a computer, I peered through the doors leading into the bay area and spotted the same tow truck driver inside. He was working underneath another car, this one a sporty looking Porsche. Nice.

The woman tapped at the computer keys and finally looked up. "Says here that the damage on your vehicle is 'extensive.'" She made air quotes. "It's going to cost somewhere in the range of $7000 to get all of the body work done, not to mention that the engine block was cracked.

"Seven thousand dollars? Are you crazy?"

"I feel crazy sometimes. If I were you, I'd sell it for parts and buy you something new. I don't know how long you plan on being in town, but this work is going to take a minimum of a week, maybe longer. That means another trip out here to pick the car up, if you have to head out of town first."

"I had no idea the damage was that bad," I mumbled to Riley. I felt bad for him. He was always very careful with his money, and this new law firm he'd opened up operated a lot on grants and the goodwill of other people.

Riley sighed and ran his hand through his hair. "I've got to think this one through. I'll get back with you."

"The sooner, the better."

Riley nodded, tapped the counter with his fist, and then turned to leave.

This trip was not going exactly how I'd envisioned. Not even close for that matter, unless you included how totally uncomfortable I thought I'd feel around his friends. I'd hit the nail on the head with that prediction.

Riley sighed as we stepped outside, a sure sign that something was heavy on his mind. "I can't believe that."

"At least the car had a good life."

"A new car isn't in my budget."

"You could ask your parents for money."

He cut a glance at me. "You know I won't do that."

"They wouldn't mind."

"I'm well beyond the stage where I want to depend on them. No, I'll make my own way."

"I could ask Chad to drive my van out. He could pick us up."

"That's a possibility. I don't know how we're going to pay for the wedding if we keep having added expenses like this. At the rate we're going, it's going to be five years before we have enough money saved up."

We were paying for the wedding ourselves, even though Riley's parents had offered to help. We wanted this to be our day and not to be indebted to anyone else. "You know I don't want anything big. We could elope for all I care."

We'd planned for a Christmas wedding. In the evening. With lots of romantic lights dangling around us, creating a magical feel. I wanted candles and soft music and for all of my friends to be gathered around.

He shook his head. "No, I want our wedding to be nice. I know it's important to you."

I had always kind of wanted a big wedding. My version of nice was totally different than these people here at Allendale. I just wanted a warm church, a pretty dress, and a reception that offered a little more than cake, peanuts, and mints.

"It will all work out," I told him. "More important than the wedding is the marriage. Isn't that what you always say?"

He sighed again. Something was bothering him, but what? His car? The wedding? Or something else?

I squeezed his arm. "What are you thinking about? You're not acting like yourself."

He paused on the sidewalk and brushed a hair out of my face. "You know me well."

"I should hope so."

He looked in the distance a moment before making eye contact with me again. "I guess I just wanted this whole week to be fun, a chance for you and me to get away. It seems like it's turned into anything but that. Jackie is missing. My car is totaled. My friends haven't really grown up like I thought they would have. In my head, we were all tight. Now that I'm seeing them again, I feel like I hardly know them."

"People do change."

"I know they do. I just hoped that they'd changed for the better. You know, less of *The Breakfast Club* or *The Hangover*, and more of *Star Wars*."

"*Star Wars*?" I questioned.

He shrugged. "I was trying to think of some movie where the main characters grew up by the end. I was having a little trouble."

"Obviously." I winked.

He hooked a hair behind my ear. "I promise you, before we leave, we're going to have at least one night together to do something. Have a fancy dinner. Go to the spa. Something."

I grinned up at him, soaking in every wonderful angle of his face. "Promise, Luke Skywalker?"

"Promise." His lips grazed mine.

I fought a frown. I'd made a promise to Riley when we started this trip, and I was doing a lousy job keeping it.

I had to do a better job at minding my own business.

That just might be the biggest challenge of my life.

***

Back at Allendale, Riley headed to grab some sandwiches from the market downstairs. We decided to simply eat in my room and unwind a little, and that was fine with me. I hadn't even been here a day, and I was already craving cheap pizza and Chinese food.

I started back up to my suite to tidy up. I decided to take the elevator this time. I stepped inside, saw Jackie's mom, and realized it was too late to escape.

As soon as the doors closed, Jackie's mom reached for a button and held it. The elevator jerked to a halt.

I stared at the woman as if she might be a crazed killer. But, no, she was just a grieving mother. I tried to remember that and ignore the fear that started to rise in me. I cleared my throat, about to offer some platitude that I'd probably later regret. Before I had a chance to, she started.

"You're an investigator?"

I tried to step back but couldn't. "That's right." Again, not a good time to go into the details of it now. Po-ta-toe, po-tah-toe, right?

"I want to hire you to find Jacqueline."

"I'm not sure what I can do here." I practically stuttered as I said the words.

A promise is sacred. I think I'd just read that in my devotional last week. *It signifies trust.*

"You've got to be able to do more than what's currently being done. I'll pay whatever your cost. Money isn't a problem."

I had to get out of this somehow. "But Clint—"

Mrs. Harrington raised her index finger, one with a very pointy red fingernail, I might add, up in the air. "Clint is her boyfriend. I am her mother. I'm the one calling the shots here, no matter what that redneck thinks."

I sucked in a long, deep breath. "I see."

"Will you do it?"

How could I say no to someone in need? It wasn't like I needed to go undercover or anything. I could simply look around on the web, ask a few questions, keep my ears open. It wouldn't be investigating by the strictest definition.

I knew in my heart I was trying to justify things, though. I knew I should say no, or at least talk to Riley first about revising my promise.

But then a tear trickled down Jackie's mom's face.

I thought about my own brother who'd been kidnapped, only to reappear in my life nearly twenty years later. I remembered my family's grief, how his disappearance had torn us apart. We'd never been the same afterward.

My dad started drinking to drown his guilt. My mom worked two jobs to make up for my dad's bad decisions. I began the endless task of trying to right my mistakes since I'd been the one watching him when he was taken.

Mrs. Harrington grabbed my arm. "Please, Gabby. If it makes you feel better, we wouldn't have to tell anyone. It would just be between you and me."

Her words drove away my doubts. This could be our secret. No one would have to know except Mrs. Harrington and me. I could do this, and Riley would never have to know.

I nodded. "I'll do it."

She sniffled and wiped away her tear using a tissue she pulled from her purse. "Thank you. I can't tell you how much this means to me." She let go of the button long enough for the elevator to start its ascent, only to press it again. We jerked to a stop. "I've called the police, as well."

"You did?" I blinked in surprise. How did Clint feel about that? But she was right. This should be her call. She was Jackie's mom.

"So why do you need me?"

She raised her pointy little chin in what I would call defiance. "I trust you more than the police. Besides, my first husband used to always say two heads were better than one. Maybe between you and law enforcement officials, one of you will discover something."

"Sounds like a plan to me."

"If you find out any information, I'm in room 4561."

She let go of the button. We started moving. Until she pressed it again. My stomach dipped. We'd probably moved a whole four inches since I stepped foot inside this elevator.

That was getting really old.

"I should tell you that they're in your room right now."

"What was that?" I put my hand on the mirrored wall, trying to brace myself for any more sudden moves or stops.

"The police. They're searching your room. I thought you should know."

So much for that relaxing evening.

***

"I do apologize for this inconvenience, but since this room is now part of a potential crime scene, we're going to have to move you to a new room."

I stared at the man standing in my doorway. He was the same person who'd greeted us at our breakfast table our first morning here. I glanced at his nametag and read "Bentley Allen." I wondered if he was related to the Allens who'd founded Allendale.

Manners, Gabby. Manners. I sucked in a deep, calming breath. "It's no problem. I only want what's best for this investigation."

I just gave myself another mental point for letting courtesy win over snarkiness.

It was the small victories I'd learned to hold on to.

The police were all over my suite like ants on a slice of watermelon. They wanted me to leave everything until the scene was officially cleared. Thankfully, I had some makeup stashed away in my purse, but everything else I would have to do without.

That meant that in the morning, I could take my skinny little wallet down to one of the overpriced gift shops downstairs and pick out some nice nautical wear, which was all they seemed to sell here. Well, that and golf shirts. At least I'd fit in better if I dressed liked the masses.

Riley arrived just as Bentley was leading me to a new room, apparently the only open suite in the whole place. I filled Riley in on what had happened as we climbed the stairs. Bentley led me up one floor to a new suite that was nearly identical to my old one. Same couch, two wingback chairs, a coffee table, TV, and breakfast nook. It had two bedrooms, each with its own bathroom.

Riley and I ate our dinner while watching the news and then stepped out onto the balcony for some fresh air. The beautiful mountains were only shadows on the horizon since night had fallen. From behind me, Riley slipped his arms around my waist and rested his chin on my shoulder. For a moment, I felt blissful and safe. I forgot about everything else that was happening.

"So, Gabby, about my old life . . . "

I turned around, relieved that he might finally be opening up. Maybe that unsettled feeling would finally leave my gut. "Yes?"

"There are some things that I haven't told you. Mostly because I'm not proud of them."

"You can tell me anything, Riley."

He looked off in the distance. I could tell by the set of his shoulders, by the strain in his eyes, that he really felt burdened by whatever it was he had to share. "You know I grew up in a Christian home, right?"

I nodded. "Yeah, you've talked about that a lot."

"In college, I was determined to stay on the straight and narrow. I found an on-campus group for Christians. I attended a church that was close by."

Just as I'd imagined.

He drew in a deep breath. "But then I became friends with this guy named Scoggins."

"I've never heard you mention him before."

Riley rubbed a hand over his forehead. "Yeah, I don't talk about him a lot. Scoggins was a really fun guy. He was my roommate my junior year and was the 'life of the party' type of person."

I didn't miss the "was." I gripped the railing, a nudge of anxiety growing in my gut. Where was this conversation going? My anxiety didn't overshadow my curiosity. I really wanted to know about this part of Riley.

"Then there was—"

A rapping sound stopped him mid-sentence.

I wanted to strangle whoever was knocking at the door. "You didn't order room service, did you?"

He hung his head a moment, his gaze heavy. "We'll finish this later?"

I nodded, feeling equally as disappointed. "Yep."

I walked with Riley to open the door. Lane stood on

the other side, a wide, semi-goofy smile on his oversized head.

"Lane, what are you doing here?" Riley's eyebrows went together in confusion.

Lane's grin widened. "My fiancée just got here, but apparently there are no more rooms open at Allendale. She's never had a problem with that when she's stayed here before. Anyway, since we're doing this whole 'morality' thing and no one is living in sin, or whatever it's called nowadays, I was wondering if she could stay with Gabby?"

Riley glanced at me. That was my cue to take charge. I appreciated Riley not speaking for me.

"Of course that's fine," I told Lane. I hoped his fiancée would be quiet and mind her own business. I didn't need any more drama during my stay here.

He rubbed his hands together as if he was about to take a gamble. "Great. Because she's here. I can't wait for you to meet her." He reached toward the wall and pulled someone forward.

A blonde—tall, skinny, and gorgeous—appeared.

My mouth dropped open. This wasn't just any tall, skinny, gorgeous blonde.

This was Veronica Laskin. Riley's ex-fiancée.

You had to be kidding me.

CHAPTER 14

"Riley?" Veronica asked, her eyes widening.

"Veronica?" Riley just stared—like any male would do if they encountered someone who looked like Veronica.

"You guys know each other?" Lane asked, scratching his head. "What a small world."

"Yeah, you could say that," Riley mumbled. He took a step back, looking uncertain as to whether or not he should hug her or run the other way.

I voted for running the other way.

I thought back quickly, trying to remember what Riley had told me and do some quick calculations. He'd started dating Veronica after law school, I think. So how had Lane met the woman?

"It's been forever," Veronica purred. She glanced at me. "Gabby? What are you doing here?"

I almost muttered that I was part of the cleaning staff. Thankfully, Riley beat me to the start. "We're engaged," he explained.

Veronica's eyelashes fluttered. "Engaged? Well, well, well. What a surprise."

"Is it okay if we come in?" Lane asked.

I didn't want to move, but Riley nudged me back

some so Lane and Veronica could flood inside. Two bellhops, each tugging carts loaded with suitcases, came with them. Veronica strutted across the carpet, perched on the couch, and waited as Lane tipped them.

Thankfully, my views on God had changed recently, otherwise, I'd think He was like a cosmic joker the way He arranged things in my life sometimes. I couldn't think of one person I'd like to stay with less than this woman.

After Lane got all of the bags inside, he sat down beside his fiancée. His fingers intertwined with hers. I couldn't help but notice that he was a good two inches shorter than his future wife—not that there was anything wrong with that.

But there was something wrong with this whole scenario.

With the couch taken, that left Riley to sit in one wing back chair and me to sit in the other one halfway across the room.

"So, how do you all know each other?" Lane asked. "I had no idea."

Riley and Veronica glanced at each other. Could anyone say *awkward*?

Finally, Riley spoke. "We go way back. I actually worked at her father's law firm right out of college. We met over dinner at his house one night."

"No way! What a small world."

I waited for someone to say they'd been engaged at one time, but no one offered the information.

I cleared my throat, wishing I'd taken more time to do my makeup. "How about the two of you? How'd you and Lane meet?"

Veronica smiled at Lane. Was it my imagination, or did her grin not quite reach her eyes? "We met at a gala up in D.C. I like to call it love at first sight."

"We met over the punchbowl. I entranced her with my love of numbers."

Love of numbers? I doubted that. Maybe because Veronica had dollar signs in her eyes? She loved large numbers in banking accounts? That seemed more likely.

Veronica giggled. "I just thought he was cute as he stood there and started talking about all of his calculations of an upcoming election. I knew he had a good head on his shoulders."

"I couldn't believe she'd give me the time of day," Lane continued. "I mean, look at her. Do women get any more gorgeous than this?"

I felt liked chopped liver sitting over in my wingback chair—alone and obviously not as gorgeous as Veronica. I couldn't even bring myself to glance at Riley. Surely he'd see the resentment in my eyes.

"See, isn't he sweet?" Veronica crooned.

They rubbed noses and giggled for a moment until I thought I would barf.

I had to get out of here. I stood and yawned. "Man, as much as I'd love to stay out here and chat, I'm just exhausted. A long day at a resort will do that to you. Anyway, good to see everyone." I nodded toward my bedroom. "But I'm going to have to say goodnight."

I offered Riley a little wave before stepping inside my room. I didn't even bother turning on the lights. Instead, I closed the door and stood there for a moment, breathing in a moment of peace and tranquilly.

Until I heard the door open behind me. I twirled around, wondering who was interrupting my moment.

It was . . . Riley?

Being in a bedroom alone with me was definitely against his rules. He was all about being proper and pure and avoiding temptation, which I appreciated—and I needed.

"What are you doing?" I whispered.

He quietly closed the door behind him and stepped toward me. "I had no idea she was going to be here."

"I had no idea I was ever going to see her again." I'd *hoped* I'd never see her again.

"I'm sorry, Gabby. Just when I think things can't get worse, they do."

"Tell me about it."

His hand brushed my cheek. "This isn't going to change anything with us. We're just going to have to deal with this whole situation the best way we know how. That's all we can do."

I started to say something. Instead, I decided to rest my forehead against his chest and enjoy the feel of his arms around me. I soaked in his familiar scent, and I realized that I couldn't wait for the day when we didn't have to say goodnight and go our separate ways. I wanted to be Mrs. Riley Thomas.

I loved the way he wrapped his arms around my waist and pulled me close, and the way my skin tingled still like it was our first date. I loved that my heart still raced when he was near. Most of all, I loved the fact that he could so easily see through the me everyone else saw and see the real me—flaws and all.

Veronica was not going to ruin anything for me.

Like she'd almost done the first time we met. She'd shown up and somehow Veronica and Riley had decided to give their engagement another try, effectively becoming whom I called "Viley." It had taken a long time for me to get over the trust issues I'd had with Riley after that. I had trust issues *before* Veronica showed up the first time. Feeling like Riley had betrayed me back then only compounded my issues.

Riley pulled back from our embrace, and his lips found mine. His kiss pulled me into some kind of vortex. Maybe it was the darkness. Maybe it was the stress of everything that had gone on. Maybe it was just me getting the best of me.

But our kiss deepened. It was filled with heat and intensity that scared me. It scared me because it took me back to an old part of my life, a part I was desperately trying to move past. I put my hand firmly on his chest and pushed him back. It took every ounce of willpower in me to do so.

Riley stepped back, but my world was still spinning. My soul felt like it was reeling. What had just happened?

"What was that?" I whispered. I stepped back, ran into the bed, and immediately jumped back to my feet.

"I just wanted to let you know that I love you."

"I love you too, but . . . " I raked a hand through my hair, waiting for my brain to settle down, and every other part of me, for that matter. "We can't do that again."

He rubbed my arms. "I know, I know."

"Is this about Veronica?"

He shook his head, his features soft as my eyes adjusted to the darkness around me. "It has nothing to do with her. I just can't wait to marry you one day, Gabby."

I nearly reached up and kissed him again.

But I knew there was no way I could do that, not unless I wanted to get myself into some serious trouble.

I backed up, careful not to fall back on the bed this time. "You should go."

He nodded. "I'll meet you for breakfast in the morning, okay?"

"Yeah, for breakfast."

He clicked the door shut behind him. I left the lights off still as I listened for any telltale signs that

Veronica and Lane were still out there talking. I heard nothing.

I fell back in bed, trying to control my thoughts. In the very least, I needed to try and sleep.

But all I could do was toss and turn.

***

At 1 a.m., I realized sleep was futile and a waste of time. I was already dressed, thanks to not having any other clothes, so I grabbed my cell phone and my keycard and quietly opened my bedroom door.

No one was in the living area. Thank goodness. Because I couldn't take facing Veronica right now. Maybe she was a perfectly nice woman. That didn't mean I wanted to room with her.

God, are You trying to teach me something?

Probably. Because I still had a lot to learn. Like *a lot*, a lot.

But at least I knew that now. At least I wasn't filled with the same arrogance that I had been at one time. I knew I didn't know everything. Simply knowing that was definitely a step in the right direction.

I quietly tiptoed to the door, opened it, and snuck into the hallway. Five minutes later, I was down in the same wing where I'd been last night. I wondered if Deanna was down here again. I kept my ears open for the telltale sound of someone else stirring at this hour but heard nothing.

I started down farther than I went last time, past the area where I'd spotted Clint and his friends talking. I never did find out what that was about, and I had a sneaking suspicion that his friends were somehow involved in all of this. Tomorrow, I'd ask more questions and hopefully figure out some answers.

At the end of the hallway was an elevator. I paused in front of it and read the sign there. If I went downstairs, I'd find a breezeway and then the pools.

Why not explore some more?

I hit the down button, and a moment later the elevator dropped me off.

I paused at a glass-enclosed breezeway before me. It was long and narrow. In the sunlight, I bet the area was beautiful. But right now, the expanse looked exposed.

Most likely, my imagination was just working overtime. I was convinced there was nothing scary here except what my mind could conjure up.

Despite that, my throat felt tight as I started walking through the enclosure. Why was I doing this again? Looking for Deanna? Just being nosy? I wasn't sure, but I'd already started the journey, so I might as well finish my exploration.

Halfway down the breezeway, the already dim lights flickered. I paused, my heart pounding in my ears.

Then everything around me went black. Pitch black.

What in the world?

My eyes adjusted to the change, and I was able to make out a table and a plant.

I blinked down at the end of the hallway. A man stood there.

Or did he? Maybe that was an artificial tree or my eyes playing tricks on me.

I rubbed my eyes.

No, that was a man down there. He stood in the center of the breezeway staring at me but not moving.

Blood pulsed through my veins when I noticed the all black clothes he wore.

And the ski mask.

I tried to scream but couldn't. Instead, I ran the other way.

CHAPTER 15

My fingers fumbled with the elevator button. "Hurry!"

I pounded the buttons. On second thought, knowing my luck, the man would get in the elevator with me. I looked back. He slowly walked toward me, like one of those people from a horror movie. Only in those movies, the bad guy always ended up catching up with you when you least expected it, even though they were moving at a snail's pace.

I jerked the door beside me open and saw a staircase. I jetted up the steps, taking them by two.

Was the man following me? How close was he?

I couldn't afford to look back.

Finally, I reached the next floor. My hands trembled as I pushed the door open and practically fell into the hallway.

Behind me, I heard nothing.

Had I imagined the man? No, I knew that I hadn't. Someone had been there.

And he still could be coming.

I dragged myself back to my feet and began running again. The farther away I could get, the better.

Just then, a janitorial cart wheeled out in front of me. Before I could put on my brakes, my waist hit the edge. My speed propelled my upper body to keep going, even though the cart stopped my lower extremities. My head flipped downward, into a sea of old sheets and towels. All the breath left my lungs in a *whoosh*.

I kicked my legs as I tried to right myself, but I couldn't move. The narrow confines of the cart trapped me.

Something wet rubbed against my cheek.

Dirty towels, I realized.

Ew . . .

I fought against them, punching, flailing, clawing as I tried to get away. Panic nearly seized me. Was the man still chasing me? Had he almost caught me? What would he do when he did?

"Oh, my goodness. Are you okay? I didn't see you coming," a voice muttered above me.

"Help me! Please. Someone's chasing me." I swatted away a washcloth.

"Chasing you? Oh, my."

Suddenly, the cart jostled. We were moving, I realized. Kind of fast, for that matter.

One of my flip-flops slipped off as my legs dangled in the air.

This would only happen to me. Seriously.

Two hands gripped my ankles. "Let me get you out." The woman pulled, tugged, squeezed.

My legs throbbed, ached, pinched.

"This is hard. The cart is so high, and you're wedged in so well."

I braced my hands on the bottom. "Try once more. I'll help this time."

"Oh, I'm so sorry about this. I hope I don't get in

trouble."

I froze. "Deanna?"

"Do I know you?"

"It's Gabby."

"Gabby!" Her voice warmed. "How did you end up in my cart?"

"It's a long story. I'd love to tell you about it . . . after I'm out of here and my face isn't pressed into someone else's filth." Death by airborne pathogen. Was this how it would happen?

"Point taken. Here goes." She pulled again with enough force to pull my ankles out of socket. But I didn't move.

"Can you tilt the cart over, and I'll crawl out?"

"Oh, no. I can't do that. The base is too wide, designed that way so the cart *won't* tip over. Let me grab Shirley. She can help."

Awesome. Before I could argue, the door opened and shut. I was left doing my handstand and breathing in germs in my contamination chamber. I thought of the figure I'd seen at the end of the hallway, and my pulse quickened. I was in a room now. He couldn't find me here. He probably wasn't even looking anymore, for that matter.

My heart rate didn't slow, though.

The door slowly creaked open. I wanted to hear a familiar voice letting me know Shirley was here with her. Silence crawled by without another sound.

"Deanna?" I finally asked.

Silence.

My breath caught. "Deanna, is that you? Did you find someone?"

Nothing.

Alarms were sounding at a furious rate in my head. I wished I'd stayed quiet. I should have simply pulled my feet into the cart and pretended not to be here. Now I was a sitting duck—or maybe more like a cow waiting to be butchered. I was destined to disappear like Jackie . . . or worse.

How was I going to get out of this one?

I listened for the sound of footsteps or a gun cocking. I waited to feel the undeniable feeling of someone's eyes on me. I braced myself for the rip of a knife blade or the sting of a bullet.

Oh, Lord. Here I am again. A screw up. I don't even deserve to ask You for help. But I'm asking anyway.

I could hardly breathe, and my heart beat so fast that I felt like a locomotive rushed through me.

That's when I heard the first footfall. Someone *had* opened the door. They'd walked in the room. Coming toward me.

I was helpless to do anything about it.

CHAPTER 16

"Gabby, I'm coming!"

Deanna's voice sounded down the hallway.

I held my breath, unsure whether to tell her to run or to help. The footsteps in the room quickened. But they were going . . . the opposite way? Another door clicked, just as I heard Deanna again. "Shirley is here with me. We'll get you out of there. Strange, I don't remember leaving this door open."

"There's someone in the room, Deanna," I whispered. The laundry around me muted my voice.

"What?"

My muscles tightened. I didn't want to speak louder and trigger the intruder. "Deanna, can you hear me?"

"I hear you, Miss Gabby. What did you say?" Her voice sounded closer to my head now, like she'd bent down so she could hear better.

"Someone else is in the room," I muttered.

"That's right. Shirley's here."

"No, someone else. He's either in the closet or the bathroom. He's somewhere!" I said it in the loudest whisper possible.

"You mean—?" Her voice caught.

"I mean, get out of here!"

The cart jostled again before taking off at a breakneck speed out of the room. We turned with enough force that my neck ached in protest, and I nearly lost my other flip-flop. My stomach dropped as we went down a little hill—most likely the handicap ramp, I realized—and finally we stopped and another door slammed.

Two sets of hands grabbed my ankles. It wasn't pretty, but they managed to manhandle me until I sprawled on the floor.

I just laid there, in the middle of a fancy hotel room, trying to catch my breath while two maids stared at me like I was a lunatic.

"Are you okay?" Deanna finally asked.

"I've never been so glad to see you," I mumbled. I rolled over and laid like a dead fish for a moment before finally sitting up.

I felt like an idiot, but I was alive.

"What were you doing down there?" Deanna asked. "Was there a fire somewhere?"

I looked at the door to the room, which was closed, hopefully locked. There was no one else in this room. Just the three of us.

"I thought . . . " I realized the absurdity of my words and stopped. "Never mind. I just got spooked, I supposed."

Deanna patted my shoulder. "This place can get creepy at night, especially the areas where there are no guests. Some people say it's haunted."

"I don't know about that, but someone was in that room with me."

That had been no ghost. I was sure of that. What I wasn't sure of was exactly who it had been.

"Why would someone have snuck into the room?" Deanna sat down across from me with her legs crossed. Shirley, a larger woman with short red hair, leaned against the bed.

I shrugged. "I have no idea. Tell me, what's beyond that breezeway a couple floors down? I think it's under construction."

"They're updating that entire section down there and putting in a new indoor pool and a spa just for children. Like children need spa treatments." Deanna snorted.

"What about outside? Is there anything near that area?"

Deanna and Shirley glanced at each other a moment. Deanna finally shook her head. "Woods. Lots of woods. The maintenance shed used to be out on a service road back there, but it caught fire last year and it hasn't been used since. As soon as they finish renovating this wing, they're going to tear it down. So, in short, there's nothing back there. What's with all the questions?"

"Did you guys hear about the girl who's missing?"

"She's been the talk of the staff. You knew her?" Deanna asked.

I shook my head. "No, I didn't know her, but my fiancé does. They went to law school together."

Shirley shook her head. "That's terrible."

I nodded. "I know. I've been asking around, and I'm afraid the wrong person found out about her disappearance."

"Is that why you wanted to see the video feed?" Deanna asked.

I nodded before glancing back and forth from the two women. "You don't know anything about her disappearance, do you?"

They glanced at each other and shrugged. "I see so many people, I wouldn't remember," Deanna said.

I pulled out my phone, brought up a social media site using Wi-fi, and found her picture on Riley's friends list. "This is what she looked like. Her name is Jackie."

Shirley got up to look first. She shook her head.

I held the phone up in front of Deanna. She gasped. "I do remember her."

Finally! Maybe the answers were in my reach. "What do you remember?"

She shook her head and looked into the distance. "She was wandering down the hallway in my wing. It was late, like two a.m. or something. I don't see that many people at that time of the night. And I thought it was weird because she was walking with three guys, and none of them looked like they should be guests here."

Clint's friends! Except . . . there were only two of them that I'd seen. I pulled my phone back toward me and pulled up another picture. "Was this one of the men?"

Deanna stared at the picture a moment before nodding. "I'm pretty sure he was. I remember that beard and flannel shirt."

I closed my eyes. Was Clint involved in Jackie's disappearance? I didn't want to believe it, but I was starting to suspect he knew more than he was letting on.

I looked up at my new friends, an idea forming in my mind. "I have one more favor. I need to borrow something."

***

I walked back to my room an hour later wearing only one flip-flop and desperately needing to decontaminate my face.

124

I tried to sneak back inside, praying that Veronica was still asleep and that I could avoid her. I closed the door behind me, ready to tiptoe to my bedroom and pretend like I'd been there all night. The light in the room was still dim, and all was quiet.

Relief filled me. Veronica was still asleep. I kept my steps soft against the carpet as I tiptoed toward my room. I needed some time by myself to decompress and chew on everything I'd learned.

Plus, I was still thinking about the man in black. Who was he? Where was he now? Why did I have the feeling that I hadn't seen the last of him?

My hand gripped the doorknob when I heard someone behind me.

I readied myself to fight for my life . . . with only my fists as weapons.

This wouldn't turn out well.

CHAPTER 17

"You don't have to sneak off to be with your boyfriend, you know. We're all adults here."

I twirled around and saw Veronica there, a smirk on her face. Her bedroom door was right behind the main door to the room, I reminded myself. It wasn't as if she'd been hiding, waiting to scare the snot out of me just for humiliation purposes.

Or had she?

I straightened as her words sunk in. "It's not like that."

"Whatever," she muttered. She stood in her doorway, wearing some kind of fancy silk robe that reached to the floor. Her hair was pulled back in a sloppy ponytail that somehow still looked like a million bucks. Veronica was just that kind of woman.

I wasn't even going to bother explaining myself to the woman. In fact, I wasn't going to bother speaking with her at all. Her smirk told me that she wouldn't believe anything I had to say anyway. Instead, I went to my room, shut the door, and hopped in the shower.

It was only after that I remembered my clean clothes were in my old room.

No way was I asking Veronica if I could borrow hers. Not that I could fit into them. I might be skinny, but I wasn't *that* skinny.

I glanced at the clock beside my bed. I had an hour before I met Riley.

I went through the dance of putting dirty clothes on my clean body. Gross, but I had little choice. It was only then that I noticed I had some kind of mustard stain on the front of my shirt. Great.

I quickly dried my hair. I desperately wished I had some gel to keep it from frizzing. It would look okay for the first thirty minutes, but after that I'd look like Ronald McDonald after he stuck his hand in a light socket.

I used the little bit of makeup I kept in my purse to cover the circles under my eyes. I almost slipped on my one flip-flop, but I realized I'd be better off going barefoot.

I glanced in the mirror.

It wasn't a great look, but it would have to do for now.

Why here at Allendale, of all places, did I have to do without my suitcase?

I went downstairs. Thankfully, the shops opened at eight. I wandered around looking for something—anything—that I could wear and that was in my price range. Certainly the police would release the room soon, and I could get my clothes back.

In the meantime, I bought some navy blue shorts, a stripped blue and white top, and white loafers. This was so not my style. But it would have to do.

I changed and was ready just in time to meet Riley.

When I saw him, my face heated as I remembered his goodnight kiss. I still had no idea what exactly that was about, but I hoped he might open up about it soon.

"That's a new look," he said, after giving me a kiss

on the forehead. Sometimes it was the sweet, most innocent kisses that really warmed my heart the most. There was so much tenderness in kissing someone's forehead; it was such a small but thoughtful way to show you cared.

"I had to run down to the gift shop."

"That's right. I forgot about your clothes." We walked side by side. "What are you planning for today?"

"I think I might go hang out by the pool for a little while."

"They're heated by natural springs, you know."

"So I've heard." I glanced up at him. I couldn't tell him about last night. He'd ask me what I was doing out at that hour, or why in the world someone might want to chase me. I just couldn't answer those questions right now. Instead, I decided to keep the subject safe and non-controversial. "So, is this the kind of place you see us vacationing at after we're married? Are you an upscale resort kind of guy?"

He shrugged. "Honestly, I'd be happier in a little cabin nestled in the mountains with no one else around. Or maybe in a beach house, but not one in a resort city, maybe on the Outer Banks of North Carolina or something."

I nodded. "I like that idea. I can't say I'm much of a fancy resort girl, although this place is awesome."

"Fit for royalty."

We sat down at a table for breakfast. A moment later, Derek and Lillian joined us. Derek offered a smile as he glanced my way, but there was something in his gaze that I didn't like.

Derek whipped his napkin in the air before placing it on his lap. "I ran into Clint a few minutes ago. He didn't look very happy."

"What did he say?" Riley asked. He held up his coffee mug, and a waitress filled it with warm liquid.

Just hold it up, and they fill it. Nice. I raised mine, but the waitress scurried away before she saw it. I scowled and set it back on the saucer.

"He said that he wanted us to stay out of it. He made that abundantly clear, didn't he?" Derek glanced at Lillian, who nodded.

"Abundantly."

"The police are involved now. This is all out of his hands," I added.

Derek shrugged. "I'm just telling you what he told us. He looked ticked. Wouldn't surprise me if he still tried to take this all into his own hands."

It wouldn't surprise me either if he tried to take things into his own hands. Maybe I'd revise my swimming plans for the day. Maybe I'd tail Clint instead.

I put in my breakfast order. From across the room, I saw Ajay sitting by himself again. He looked regal and cultured, almost exotic. What was behind the hurt in his eyes? Why had he traveled here alone and stayed for a month? He had no entourage, no family, no friends. Every time I saw him, he was alone.

I knew he had a story. I just didn't know what it was.

The waitress came back to refill Riley's coffee. I raised my cup again, determined to get some also. I'd hardly gotten any sleep over the past two nights. I needed something to keep me awake.

She stepped away.

"Excuse me! Miss—" It was too late. She was gone.

I sighed and put my cup back down. Not even fancy new clothes could make me look at home here.

"Excuse me," I mumbled.

I stood, grabbed my cup, and walked over to the little station where the coffee was set up. I pushed past my waitress and grabbed the pot, poured myself a cup, and slammed the carafe back down.

"I like a woman who makes her own way," someone said behind me.

I turned and saw Ajay. He offered a slight bow. I found myself offering a slight bow in return.

"Nothing stands between me and my coffee," I mumbled.

"You have been a bright spot in my day here, Miss St. Claire. Thank you for your authenticity."

I really hoped he wasn't getting the wrong idea about me. I'd been showing interest in him for Deanna's sake, not my own. Sticky, sticky, sticky . . .

"I appreciate that, Ajay." I raised my coffee mug. "Good seeing you again."

As I sat down at my table again, Derek raised his eyebrows at me. I glanced over at Riley, hoping he hadn't seen. He was engrossed in a conversation with Lillian. I had the odd desire to kick Derek under the table . . . and then keep kicking him. He annoyed me to no end.

"I can't believe that Lane didn't know you were engaged to Veronica," Derek said just as our food came. "How lame is that?"

Riley quickly glanced at me. "Well, Lane and I never were that close in the group."

"Are you surprised that Veronica didn't tell him?" Lillian asked.

Riley sucked in a deep breath. "I don't know. I won't speak for her or assume anything."

Lillian snorted and looked at me. "You're a bigger woman than I am. No way would I room with my fiancé's ex."

"Keep your friends close and your enemies closer." I cast a sharp glance at Riley. "Not that she's an enemy." I erased the smile from my face. "Besides, I think we can learn something from every circumstance, no matter how dire it may seem at the time. I'm going to learn something from this, too."

Riley smiled at me, admiration in his gaze. A year ago, I wouldn't have been able to say that. No, back then I was living in the moment. Things had changed, though, and for the better. But I was still a work in progress, and I had so much to learn.

Starting with all the secrets I'd been keeping from Riley. I was waiting for just the right time to share, but the right time never seemed to come—or got interrupted halfway through. I had to clean up the mess I'd made somehow, though.

Secrets in relationships weren't good. Speaking of which, Riley had a few secrets of his own, it seemed. When did he plan on sharing those with me?

CHAPTER 18

When Riley went to his conference so he could learn about "Conservatorship When the Ad Litem Guardianship Is Absolved" and "Technicalities in the Breach of Real Estate Brokerage Law," I wandered up to my room. I looked around, trying to figure out if Veronica was here or down at the workshops with the rest of the gang.

"Hello? Anyone here?" I was playing it safe this time.

No one said anything, nor did I hear water running or any other telltale sign that someone was here. That meant I had some time to myself.

I plopped down on the couch. I wanted to slouch, but the place was so nice that I found myself sitting up straight, "like I had a string running through my spine all the way up through the top of my head." Yeah, my mom had done some beauty pageants in her younger days and loved to pass on tidbits of advice like that.

I pulled out my cell and called the police. After getting transferred several times, I finally talked to the right person, and they agreed I could get my suitcase. They were going to send an officer to escort me into the room and retrieve it. He'd be at Allendale within the hour, he said.

I sank into the couch, trying to clear my head and ignoring the painting of the prim and proper woman who stared at me from across the room, chiding me for bad posture. Delores Allen, the nameplate read. I wondered if that was Bentley's great-grandmother, the one who'd started Allendale Acres three generations ago.

There were still some details of my plan that I needed to work out. And I really hoped that the police officer didn't show up at the same time as Shirley, otherwise I might find myself in a sticky situation.

My cell phone rang. I saw the number was my best friend Sierra's. Sierra was just the person I needed to speak with. She understood me just as well as anyone. I made fun of her for being such an animal lover, and she made fun of me for cleaning crime scenes, so we got along just fine.

"Gabby! You answered! What's going on?"

"I'm just sitting here, wearing this fancy fur coat at this luxurious resort. They're giving furs out because, you know, everyone here is rich and all. Maybe you should come and stop them."

"Ha ha. Very funny." She paused. "But if anything of that sort happens, let me know. I'll be right there."

"I don't doubt it." I smiled. I loved how passionate my friend was about helping animals. And thanks to her influence, I still felt guilty to this day if I ever wore leather or ate a burger or even stepped on an ant. "How are you and Chad doing?"

Chad was my business partner. He and Sierra had started dating not long ago, and I couldn't be happier for them. They seemed smitten.

"I don't want to talk about it," she grumbled.

"That doesn't sound good."

She sighed so loud I had to pull the phone away from my ear. "We had this huge fight. I really don't want to get into it over the phone."

"I'm sorry." I wanted to say more, but she didn't want to talk about it.

"Quick question before I forget. What's the best way to get blood out of carpet?"

I went stiff. "Are you serious?"

"Yeah, unfortunately."

"Are you in trouble?"

"I'm fine. I'm just doing a little undercover work. Puppy mill stuff. But the blood is human, not dog, so don't get sad or anything. I'd ask Chad but I'm not speaking to him right now."

"Okay . . . " I drew out the word for as long as I could. "Is the blood dry or fresh?"

"Fresh."

I didn't like where this was going. "Use cold water. Mix some hand soap with some water and blot it."

"I tried that already."

"You can use some ammonia."

"Tried that, too."

"Why don't you just go up to my apartment and grab some of my cleaning solution?"

"I was hoping you'd say that. Thanks!"

I twisted my head, trying to comprehend this conversation. "Are you sure there's nothing you want to tell me? Chad's alive, right?"

"Very funny. He's fine. I'll fill you in when you get back. Anyway, how about you? How's it going at Allendale Acres? You and Riley been practicing that scene with the song 'Love Is Strange'?"

So I may have made a *Dirty Dancing* comparison

before I left—minus the dirty dancing part. You know, fancy resort; rich girl, poor boy (only reversed). In all fairness, I'd also made *My Fair Lady* comparisons, and I may have even mentioned *Stand By Me*.

"No 'Love Is Strange' reenactments." I filled her in, not leaving out any detail.

Sierra sighed. "Oh, Gabby. It's no mystery that these kind of capers find you."

Capers? I don't think I'd ever heard her use that word before. Nor had I heard anyone else remotely near my age say it. "Tell me about it. There's this small problem that Riley asked me not to get involved."

"Oh, no. Does he know that you can't help yourself?"

I twirled one of my curls absently. "No, not yet. He's been distracted with his conference."

"You've got to tell him. You know that, right? For that matter, I think you should tell him that it is highly insensitive of him to even ask you not to snoop."

"Insensitive?"

"It's like asking you not to be you."

"I thought you liked Riley."

"I love Riley. And you two together are like Sonny and Cher."

"They got divorced."

"Okay, how about Romeo and Juliet."

"They died."

"Fred and Wilma Flintstone?"

I didn't even know what to say to that.

"Anyway, I think you're perfect together. But you shouldn't have to try and be someone you're not."

"It's called compromise. And it's just for a week."

"You know what? It doesn't matter. I'm just in a rotten mood, and I've got to get the blood out of the carpet. I have to ask, though. Did you tell Riley about your job yet?"

I let out a soft sigh. Sierra was the only person I'd talked to about my job situation. But between my job secret and my investigation, I was feeling like slime. "No. I just can't bring myself to do it. Riley seems so proud of me."

"He'll be proud of you if you're a crime scene cleaner or a medical examiner. You know that."

I did know that, but there were so many other small details that clouded my judgment at the moment. I twirled my curl faster. "I know, but medical legal death investigator just sounds so much better, especially around his friends. How do I explain to him that my job was over practically before it even started?"

"He'll understand, Gabby. Believe me. He loves you."

I sighed. I hated it when I sighed. "Relationships are so complicated."

"But they're worth it, right? I think you told me that once."

I thought of all the good times Riley and I had shared. We'd laughed together, cried together, argued together, and even prayed together. If our relationship could survive what it already had survived, then our chances for making it were probably pretty good. "Yeah, they're worth it."

We chatted a few more minutes before I hung up. Talking to Sierra always made me feel better. Except not really today.

Blood on the carpet? Trouble with Chad? Trying to be someone else for Riley?

The hotel phone rang.

I knew what that meant.

The police were here.

***

"I don't understand. My suitcases were right here." I pointed to the closet off of my bedroom. My first bedroom. The one in the room adjacent to Jackie's.

"No one was allowed in here. I don't know what happened to them." The police officer shrugged and looked anything but apologetic. Maybe annoyed would be a better description.

Annoyed definitely fit how I felt at the moment. "Well, are you going to try and find out?"

He shrugged again. "I'll check the front desk to see if anyone used their keycard."

"I'll go with you." I crossed my arms, irritated beyond belief. Why would someone take all of my clothes and make up? Were they trying to drive me crazy? To implicate me? I had no idea.

The officer, a middle-aged man with a mustache and receding hairline, nodded toward the door. "Let's go."

We walked side by side down the hallway, quiet for a moment with only the sound of his pants swishing back and forth, back and forth.

It was time to break the silence. "Any leads on Jackie?"

He continued to look straight ahead. "I can't discuss that."

"Did you check out the security footage?"

"I can't discuss that."

"What's your next move?"

"I can't—"

I interrupted him. "I know. You can't discuss that. You can't blame a girl for trying."

"I assure you that we're exploring every possible avenue in an effort to find answers." He offered a small glance as he said the words. I never could quite understand people with stoic personalities. It was the opposite of me, since I had a tendency to err on the side of dramatic.

"That's always good. I guess you don't get many cases like this out here in the middle of nowhere." I imagined the police out here dealing with stuff like rowdy hunters, property disputes, or moonshine—not that I wanted to stereotype or anything.

"Lost hikers? We get lots of those." His voice held amusement, like I had no idea what I was talking about. I'd probably seen more homicides in my lifetime as a crime scene cleaner in Norfolk, than he'd seen as a police officer out here in the boonies.

"If you just thought she was a lost hiker then why did you cordon off her room like something illegal happened?"

The hint of a smile disappeared. "I can't discuss that."

I nodded, mentally mocking him. "Yeah, yeah. I know."

We were at the front counter now. The officer explained things to the lady behind the desk, who then went and got the manager. Bentley Allen appeared.

"How can I help you?" The man's head bobbed back and forth between the two of us, his expression screaming, "Customer service."

"We just need information on who's been coming and going from room 3412," Officer Sharples said.

"Is everything all right? Satisfaction is our top priority here for our guests."

"We're just looking into a matter involving the

young woman who's missing."

Bentley pushed his glasses up on his nose. "Of course. Anything we can do to help."

He tapped away at the computer before looking up. "It says that a Gabby St. Claire used her key card at 2 a.m. to get into the room."

My palm hit the counter top. "I'm Gabby St. Claire and that's impossible! I did not go into the room last night. Besides, I thought my keycard was deactivated once the room became a potential crime scene."

Bentley shrugged. "I'm just telling you what the computer says. Do you have your card with you?"

I reached into my purse. The spot where I'd kept my key was empty. I felt like beating my head against the counter or, in the very least, doing a face palm. I settled for shrugging. "It's gone."

"You sure you didn't go into that room, desperate to retrieve some of your clothes?" the officer asked.

"I'm sure." I ran my hand down my outfit like a game show hostess might. "I had to buy this hideous outfit this morning, and it cost more than I make in a day sometimes."

He nodded slowly as if he didn't believe me. Finally, he said, "I'll file a report. In the meantime, I'd buy some more clothes, sailor."

CHAPTER 19

I was trying not to fume as I went back into my own room. I did not want to wipe out my checking account just so I could buy clothes I didn't even like from some fancy gift shop in some fancy hotel. I'd probably have to drive an hour to find anywhere else to buy clothes, and that was a problem because Riley's car was in the shop.

Besides, why had someone stolen my clothes? It didn't make sense. There was no incriminating evidence in my suitcase, nothing that someone would want to get rid of or need to hide. No, whoever did it had probably either wanted to annoy me or to somehow make me look guilty.

Just then, someone knocked at my door. I pulled it open and saw Shirley standing there. She had a maid uniform in her hands, and she thrust it toward me as she pushed herself into the room. "Here you go."

I stared at the polyester uniform. "Thank you. I know this is risky."

She shrugged. "I like the job and all, but I like justice more. Besides, if I help to find the bad guy and save the hotel's reputation, maybe good things will happen for me. Otherwise, I'm perfectly content to wait for my reward in heaven."

I smiled. "You're a good woman."

She sucked in a deep breath, looked side to side, and then held up a key card. "You'll need this."

My eyes widened. "I was just trying to figure out how I was going to get into his room. I had no idea."

"This is a master key. It will get you in."

"Won't you get in trouble?"

She shook her head. "Jasmine downstairs said she'd erase it from the records. Ricky is watching the security cameras. We've got you covered."

"You guys really believe in me, don't you?"

"We believe that rich folks shouldn't get away with murder. I call that a win-win." She shoved the keycard into my hand. "I need this back. And don't lose it or my hide will be toast."

I gripped it and gave a quick, tight nod. "You know it."

"Seriously. One of the valets got in trouble for giving a guest some special privileges about a month ago. I trust you."

"I won't let you down."

"Most of all, be safe."

She bustled toward the door, pausing only a second before bursting into the hallway. She hummed the theme from *I Love Lucy* as she hurried down the hall.

Sneaking into Clint's room could get me in big trouble. I knew that. If he saw me, of course he'd recognize me. But this was a risk I had to take. I had to figure out if he was involved in all of this.

I cracked my door open. Clint's room was only five doors down from mine, and that fact would work to my advantage. I hadn't seen him leave yet today, but I could have missed him when the officer was here.

Quickly, I changed into the maid's uniform. I said a

mental prayer of thanks that I didn't have to wear this every day on my job. It wasn't cute and fitted like the ones you saw on the movies. No, it was baggy and the grey color washed out my complexion. I pulled my hair back into a bun and put a handkerchief—courtesy of Shirley—around my head.

Up close, someone would recognize me. From a distance . . . maybe not.

I pulled a robe on over my clothes, just in case Veronica walked back in while I was waiting. I couldn't help but notice how plush the white, belted robe was—microfiber and cozy and softer than the clouds. I ran my hands up and down the length of it. *Oh, la la.*

I had to stop getting distracted, though. I put my hands on the side, resisting the urge to cuddle with my robe anymore.

Instead, I took my place at the door. I'd watch and wait for Clint to leave. Then I'd make my move.

***

An hour later, the door to Clint's room finally opened. I watched through the peephole as he went past. I counted to ten—the approximate number of steps to the staircase, which he always used instead of the elevator—and then I opened my door again.

I surveyed the hallway. No one was there.

As the saying went, *here goes nothing.*

I threw off my robe and stepped into the hallway. I smoothed my apron with my hand, touched the handkerchief at my hairline, and took a deep breath. I could do this. I had to.

Calmly, I walked down the hallway. Shirley had taken an additional shift and was cleaning one of the rooms between mine and Clint's. Her cart was in the hallway. I managed my breathing, though my adrenaline made my whole body want to move in fast motion.

Just a few more steps and I'd be home free. This first leg of my undercover investigation had been surprisingly easy.

As I reached the cart, someone called out from behind me. "Excuse me! Ma'am! Miss Cleaning Lady. You in the gray outfit!"

I didn't have to turn. I knew whose voice that was. Lillian's.

I stopped. Didn't turn. Didn't move. Didn't dare speak.

"Ma'am?" Lillian repeated, only a few steps behind me. One glance at my face, and I'd be a goner.

My heart hammered away in my ears. How was I going to get out of this one? There was more at stake here than my reputation.

"Ma'am? Did you hear me? Do you speak English?"

She did *not* just say that, did she? I realized I couldn't pretend like I didn't hear her. I had to do *something* or I really would look suspicious.

"One minute!" I called, trying to disguise my voice. I ended up sounding Fran Drescher—a mix of nasal and New York. I hurried to the other side of the cart and ducked down before she could see my face. "How can I help you?"

"I need another towel."

I pressed myself closer to the cart, remembering my last up close and personal experience with one all too well. "A towel, you said?"

"That's right. A towel."

I stared at everything in front of me and spotted a stack of fresh linens. I grabbed a bath-sized version and held it up, feeling a bit like I was raising a white flag. "Here you go!"

After a moment, I felt her take the towel.

"Okay . . . thanks," she muttered.

"No problem."

I heard footsteps padding away. I peered around the cart and watched her until she disappeared around the corner. I rocked back on my heels and let out the breath I held.

That had been close. Too close for my comfort.

I hurried to Clint's door, swallowed hard, and knocked. As I waited, I slipped off the "Do Not Disturb" sign and stuck it in my pocket.

I wasn't sure what I'd do if someone answered. Clint's friends could be here, but since he hadn't exactly introduced them around, I had a feeling they weren't staying at Allendale. I couldn't imagine there were very many other places to stay around here. Maybe they were camping.

Come to think of it, everyone else here was sharing a room with someone. Why wasn't Clint, the one other person here who wasn't a lawyer or rich?

No sounds escaped from the other side of the door. Just to be safe, I knocked once more. "Housekeeping!"

Still nothing. Carefully, I slid the key into the lock. When the light turned green, I twisted the handle, and stepped inside, searching for a sign someone was here.

My heart pounded in my ears as adrenaline heightened my senses.

I didn't see anyone. I did see soda cans and potato chip wrappers all over the table and couch. Dirty socks stretched across the carpet. The shades were drawn and the entire room smelled musty and dirty.

Where did I even start?

This room only had one bedroom. I assumed that's where all of Clint's stuff would be. I slipped inside. I didn't chance turning on the light. Instead, I pulled out a flashlight and shone it across his suitcase. I peered inside. I saw all the normal stuff—clothes, socks, shoes.

I opened a side compartment and saw pictures of him and Jackie together. I stared at one for a moment. There was something in their gaze that couldn't be faked. These two had loved each other.

Then why did I suspect that Clint was somehow involved?

I went to his nightstand. A container of pain reliever stood there. A half-drunk bottle of water. A map of Allendale.

I picked the map up and stared at it a moment. There were a couple of odd markings on it, almost as if he'd plotted out some course. Interesting.

I opened the drawer and froze. What . . . ?

I picked up two plane tickets to . . . the Bahamas? The names on the tickets read "Clint Miller and Mona Tyler." There were also three inhalers in the drawer. I was certain that Clint told the police Jackie had only brought one and that she'd left it.

Just then, the door to the suite opened.

I flinched at the sound and, in the process, my hand hit the bottle of pain reliever. Pills spilled all over the nightstand.

My heart raced. Someone was back. And I'd just clued them in to the fact that I was in the room.

I quickly put the tickets back into the drawer, quietly closed it, and begin brushing pills back into the bottle. I didn't get them all, but I was out of time.

I looked around. The closet. I had to get there and

now.

I slipped inside just as I heard the bedroom door open.

I could hardly breath as I crept toward some clothes hanging in the back. I had to get there, and I had to do it without making a sound.

This coming from the girl who had found herself upside down in a custodian's cart.

A voice came from the other room. Clint's. "Everything is still set? I'm doing the drop at three. Don't mess it up this time."

What did that mean? I couldn't make sense of the conversation. Right now, I just had to concentrate on staying hidden.

If Clint found me here alone, I didn't know what he'd do to me.

"Why are my pills all over the floor? You been in my room?" Clint asked.

The air escaped from my lungs. He knew someone had been in his room. Despite the mess he'd left, he'd noticed the one thing that hadn't been out of place originally.

I held my breath and pressed myself into the wall, waiting for whatever would happen next.

Something sharp jabbed into my arm. What was that?

I shined my light and saw a pad of paper sticking out from behind the safe. I had to restrain myself from grabbing it. Instead, I waited.

"Let me grab my bag," Clint muttered.

My pulse raced. His bag? Hopefully, it wasn't the one I'd seen right by—

The closet door opened. The light flipped on.

Yep, the bag I'd seen right by the closet door.

I shoved myself deeper into the dark recesses in the back of the space, thrusting my face into a couple of flannel shirts. One of the shirts swayed back and forth at my movement. I grabbed it, trying to still the action.

From between the shirts, I could see Clint. He glanced my way and furrowed his eyebrows together. I didn't have to be a mind reader to know that he was sensing something wasn't right. Would he trust his gut and investigate? Or would he blow it off as stress and lack of sleep? I hoped it was the latter.

Don't come closer. Don't come closer. Don't come closer.

He took a step closer.

I should have brought a weapon. A knife. A rolling pin. A bottle of cleaning spray. Anything!

Right now, he could kill me, dispose of my body, and no one would ever know.

Clint paused and pressed the phone harder into his ear. "Yeah, I've got the bag. I'll see you soon."

He slid the phone into his pocket and threw one last glance my way before grabbing the book bag, flinging it on his shoulder, and stepping from the closet.

Finally, I heard a door close. My heart counted each second as it passed. *Thump-thump, thump-thump, thump-thump.*

I refused to move. What if this was all a set up? What if Clint was waiting for me on the other side of that door?

I was staying right here, for a few more minutes, at least.

I remembered the pad of paper I'd seen. Slowly, carefully, I pulled it out from behind the safe.

I clicked my flashlight on and stared at the paper there.

It was yellow legal paper with blue lines. I checked the torn piece at the top. It was jagged, especially on the left side.

Just like the ransom note had been.

CHAPTER 20

I had to talk to Jackie's mom. In order to do that, that meant I had to get out of this closet. I moved a few shirts aside and took a step toward the door. I'd take it nice and slow. If I was caught . . . well, I had no idea what I'd do.

I pushed the closet door open slowly. As the bedroom came into view, it appeared empty. Just to be sure, I checked behind the door. That's where I'd hide if I were Clint.

My blood pounded in my ears as I slowly turned. I released my breath when I saw the space was empty.

I wasn't clear yet, though. I still had to get out of this suite without being seen. I tiptoed toward the bedroom door, which was still open. I paused there and soaked in the living room area. I didn't see anyone. I wasn't going to wait around anymore to find out if I was correct or not.

I darted toward the front door, threw it open, and then transformed into Ms. Composed as I walked back toward my room. A man and woman walked down the hall toward me, chatting to themselves.

My throat went dry.

But, as they passed, they didn't even glance at me.

I slipped into my room. I didn't even have time to change. Instead, I grabbed the robe from my room, threw it over my outfit—I didn't want to get Shirley in trouble—and ran up one flight of stairs to Carol's room.

4561. Mrs. Harrington had told me the number yesterday on the elevator.

I pounded on the door with more force than necessary. A moment later, she pulled the door open. Her lips curled back in . . . repulsion?

"Gabby?"

"I need to talk to you." I tried to catch my breath, but it came out in ragged gasps.

She blanched. "Are you wearing a robe? And a handkerchief?"

I pulled the collar of my robe closer. "It's a long story."

"Is everything okay?" Clint appeared behind Jackie's mom. His gaze looked equally as perplexed when he saw me.

I took a step back and straightened. "I just had a question."

"Well, go ahead. Spit it out." Jackie's mom stared at me, along with Clint.

My original question wasn't going to work. I had to think of something else, and quick.

"What's Jackie's favorite meal?" I blurted.

They both stared at me another moment. Finally, Mrs. Harrington said, "Braised lamb chops with risotto."

I nodded. "Okay, I'm going to make sure Jackie has some to eat this evening when she's back with us. It just seems like something small I can do."

"This evening?" Clint asked.

"I know you don't want us to get involved, but I

figure the kidnappers probably told you to drop off the money again today. That is what they want, right? If they hold up to their end of the bargain, Jackie will be back tonight. We want to celebrate."

"I wish I could be as optimistic as you are," Carol muttered.

"I'm sorry. I know this is hard for you." I glanced up at Clint. "For both of you. Let me know if there's anything else I can do."

As I turned to walk away, I heard Jackie's mom mutter, "What a strange girl."

I glanced at the time. It was noon. That meant I had three hours until Clint dropped off the money and completed whatever scheme it was that he was planning.

I had to figure out exactly what I was going to do about this.

But first I had to change and meet Riley for lunch.

***

"You seem preoccupied."

I jerked my head toward Riley. "What?"

"You seem preoccupied. Everything okay?"

I considered pouring out everything to him right then and there. But I couldn't, and that was part of my problem. If I told him everything I knew, then I'd also be fessing up to all of my snooping. Instead, I shrugged. "Just thinking about the pool." About how there was no way I'd be making it there today after all.

"Anyone talked to Clint since this morning?" Lane asked.

Headshakes went around the table. Somehow, we'd managed to snag a larger round table so all of Riley's friends could sit together for this meal. I actually preferred the smaller seatings, but there was no way to gracefully get out of sitting with the rest of the gang.

"So, tell us about your job with the medical examiner, Gabby." Derek looked at me. "I bet that's really interesting, as long as dead people don't creep you out."

I forced a smile. Again, this just didn't seem like the time to correct the facts as they were. So I drew on my knowledge that I'd obtained from my one month of working there. "It's interesting what a dead person can tell you. Even in death, they can speak to you."

It was true. It had been so exciting to work with the police and investigators in finding clues that would identify the person's cause of death. There was nothing I found more satisfying than putting the bad guys behind bars.

Which was why I'd decided that after lunch I would call the police and share what I'd learned about Clint and the ransom note.

My throat felt dry as I thought about what I'd learned. With every passing moment, it seemed like time was slipping away. The police had to know what was going on, and now. How could I be eating at a time like this?

I stood and placed my napkin in my chair. "If you'll excuse me, I need to run to the restroom."

I slipped out of the dining hall and kept walking until I reached the library. I stepped inside. No one else was here.

Quickly, I dialed the number to the police station and asked to speak with the officer who'd been here earlier.

"Officer Sharples, this is Gabby St. Claire. We spoke at Allendale earlier. I have an anonymous tip for you."

"But you just told me who you were."

I narrowed my eyes, getting annoyed again. "I know that. I just don't want anyone besides you to know whom the tip is from. Is it a deal?"

"I suppose."

"I think Clint is behind the disappearance of his girlfriend. I think he wants the money. He has two plane tickets to the Bahamas for the end of this week. His other ticket is for another woman. I'm pretty sure you'll find the paper used to write the ransom note in the closet of his room."

"How do you know all of this?"

"I have my sources. Oh, and he plans to drop off the ransom money somewhere at three today. I don't know where, though. I suspect his friends are supposed to be the ones who grab it."

He paused. "Why should I trust you?"

"If you Google my name, you'll see I have some credentials. But please don't waste time doing that now. I'm afraid Jackie will be hurt."

He was silent for another moment. "I'll look into it."

"Thank you."

I hung up and joined Riley's friends again. Now I'd just wait. I'd done my duty. I turned it over to the police and relinquished myself of any more investigating.

My conscience could be clear.

***

I dropped the maid uniform and key back off with Shirley and was walking to my room when someone called my name from behind.

I pivoted and glanced behind me. Jackie's mom. She wrung her hands together and her eyebrows formed a V on her forehead. The poor lady. I couldn't even imagine.

I paused and nodded toward my door. "Let's go

inside."

She caught up with me as I slid my card into the slot. Tension stretched through her voice. "What was that about up there earlier?"

"I didn't know Clint was there. I didn't want him to hear," I whispered.

My door made that gentle buzzing sound to let me know my card had worked. I twisted the handle and pushed it open. Jackie's mom followed me inside.

With the door locked, and Jackie's mom staring at me like a lunatic, I began to pace. Just like any good lunatic would.

Mrs. Harrington's hands twisted together, ever so subtly. She didn't bother to sit or to even move for that matter. She just stood there by the door, staring at me, her only sign of anxiety those fingers that rubbed together. "Why didn't you want Clint to hear?"

"Can we sit down?" I walked toward the couch and hoped she'd follow. She did. I sat on one end, and she sat on the other. I wished I had something to offer her to drink, but I had nothing but a half empty bottle of Mountain Dew. "Tell me about Clint."

Jackie's mom shrugged, her face vacant in a way that only grief and stress could be responsible for. Even her voice lacked a lot of emotion. It simply sounded raw from too many hours crying. "What about him? I certainly don't think he's good enough for my daughter, nor do I feel he's equipped to handle the family's money. Jackie's our only daughter. The estate will go to her when I'm gone one day."

"Did you tell Clint that?"

"In so many words, I suppose."

"Do you think your daughter loves him?"

Her fuchsia-colored lips twisted into a frown. "Yes,

I do think she loves him. But I think there's more to love than feelings of infatuation. You have to take a multitude of things into consideration, and I don't think she realized that."

Riley and I had talked about that a lot, how we couldn't base our relationship just on our emotions or our attraction to each other. Truth be told, I would have probably never thought about it had Riley not brought it up. My past dating record proved it. "How about Clint? Do you think he loves your daughter?"

Mrs. Harrington's eyebrows twitched. "What are you getting at?"

"I'm still trying to put all of the pieces together. I know the questions may not make sense, but I have to ask them." I swallowed, softening my gaze when I saw a touch of moisture in the woman's eyes. "Do you think he loves her?"

She nodded curtly, quickly, but her neck muscles looked strained. "He certainly appears to."

I shifted in my seat, trying to put everything together in my mind, all the while attempting to figure out the best way to approach this whole situation without sending her grief over the edge. "Do you know where Clint is taking the money?"

"It's a different trail this time than last. I only hope this whole drop off doesn't get messed up on the second go around. If it does, they threatened to . . . " A tear rolled down her cheek. "They threatened to kill Jacqueline if we messed up again."

I sat up straighter. "So the kidnappers were in touch again?"

"That's right. They called my phone. I couldn't recognize any voices. They were all muffled. I thought maybe there would be a clue or something." She waved her head back and forth, her chin trembling. "I couldn't figure out anything."

"Did you tell the police that?"

"No, Clint insisted it was better this way. It's so hard to know what to do."

I tapped my finger against the couch. Of course Clint had insisted that they not tell the police. That would have gotten in the way with his plan. I wondered if Mrs. Harrington had been introduced to Clint's sidekicks. They could be playing an important role in all of this. "Have you met Clint's friends that came to town?"

She frowned, obviously not approving of his buddies. "Once."

"Where are they staying? Did Clint say?"

She raised a shoulder, flicking a piece of fuzz from her arm as she did. "They rented a cabin somewhere. Now, what's this all about?"

I sucked in a deep breath before unloading the words that would rock her world. "Mrs. Harrington, I think Clint may be after your money."

CHAPTER 21

After the Attorneys' Conference was over for the day, Riley met me back in my room. Thankfully, Veronica wasn't there. We had a few minutes to kill before we met the rest of the gang up in Derek's suite.

Riley tried to tell me a few things about the conference and all that he'd learned today. My mind was in another world, though. I was thinking about Clint and Jackie and money.

Had Clint arranged for his friends to kidnap Jackie just so he could get money out of her? Was that the primary reason he'd dated her in the first place? Perhaps their whole relationship was just an elaborate scheme to get rich.

I played it out in my mind. Clint meets Jackie. Realizes she's loaded. Figures out he could use a relationship with her to his advantage. Maybe his first plan was to marry her and get her money that way. Then he found out that Jackie wouldn't get any of her money if she married him. Then he'd come up with an alternative plan.

Kidnap her. Demand a ransom. Run away with someone else.

Riley rubbed my shoulders as I stared off into

space, letting everything sink in. "You want to talk?"

I glanced up at that hideous picture of Delores Allen. "I'm thinking about people's heritages, I suppose."

"What about it?"

I nodded toward that painting. "Think about it. The Allen family has a heritage of starting this world-class resort. In their day, they were practically celebrities as they mingled with the affluent here at Allendale. Then there's Jackie. Jackie has this heritage of wealth. Her family who could buy their way into whatever they wanted. She's never wanted for anything. Whenever people hear 'Harrington Enterprises,' they think of Jackie."

"Look where their heritages took them? The Allens were disgraced when they lost the resort. Jackie has had numerous struggles, mostly because of her money."

I glanced at him. "Then there's my heritage. My dad was a drunk. My mom was too exhausted to shave her legs half of the time. How would things have been different for me if I'd grown up without my struggles? What if I'd grown up in a middle class neighborhood with a mom and dad who loved each other, with a brother who hadn't been kidnapped? What if I hadn't had to drop out of college?"

"Our struggles help to make us who we are. We may have never met if you'd grown up in the way you just mentioned. It's best if we don't toy around with the 'what ifs' in life. We can't change our past."

His words were true. There was no changing things that happened yesterday. We just had to make the most of today.

Riley squeezed my hand. "Besides, you have a great heritage now. You have a spiritual heritage. Your spiritual heritage is one of faith, sacrifice, courage."

I nodded. I hadn't thought about that before, but it

was true. When I became a Christian, I became a new person. My slate was wiped clean. There weren't many occasions you could say that in life.

Riley tugged me to my feet. "Want to skip out on my friends tonight?"

I shook my head. The idea was tempting. Very tempting.

But Riley had come here to see his friends, and that's what we should do. I could tune out the conversation once we met them and mull over my theories for longer, if I had to.

"I think they need someone to keep them straight. I designate you."

Riley smiled, but there was something sad behind his grin. My curiosity pricked again. When was he going to tell me whatever it was that was on his mind?

Soon, I hoped. Because curiosity killed the cat.

And I was pretty sure that would be my cause of death one day, as well.

***

Everyone gathered in Derek's room. Derek's suite must have been the *crème de la crème* of the Allendale. He had a full kitchen, a massive living room with a pool table and a hot tub, a huge balcony, and three bedrooms.

Everyone else—including Riley—seemed perfectly content to unwind with a movie blaring on the TV. Derek had apparently had some food catered because there were trays of fancy cheeses and crackers and fruit placed strategically around the room. Jack the Dipper stood over the veggie tray.

I kept an eye on him. Sure enough, he was up to his old ways.

While Riley chatted near the balcony with Lillian, I paced around, turning thoughts over and over in my mind. But turn is all I could do. My thoughts wouldn't rest or be still or even attempt to settle down.

Nor could I. I couldn't stay still. I just kept wondering what was going on. I wanted to be in the action. But I was trying to respect Riley's wishes and not let a guilty conscience get the best of me.

The rest of the gang was talking about the workshops they'd attended that day when Derek came into the room.

"Did you guys hear?" Derek asked.

He had four beer bottles tucked into the spaces between his fingers, and his hands were on his hips. His shirt was untucked in a trendy sort of way and he wore expensive jeans. No, I didn't recognize the label. But I already knew what kind of person Derek was, and he was the type who liked the best of everything. His job as a malpractice attorney must pay really well.

"Hear what?" Veronica stepped closer, a glass of wine in one hand, and her other arm was slung fashionably over her waist.

"You guys are never going to believe this. The police arrested Clint." Derek's eyebrows were suspended in the air, and I could tell he was proud of himself that he'd been the one to break the news.

"What do you mean the police arrested Clint?" Riley joined me. I was standing the closest to Derek at a couch near the door.

Derek shook his head, his voice alive with excitement. He probably fed on stuff like this. "He set up the whole kidnapping. He left the ransom note. He got his cousins to help with the whole thing. It was all about the money. Apparently this guy already had a rap sheet. I can't

CHRISTY BARRITT

believe Jackie even gave him a second glance."

Lillian fell back into the couch, her face white, and her eyes fluttering. "Poor Jackie. She's always been worried about people using her just for her money and now this." She glanced back at Derek. "Is she okay?"

"Apparently the police are searching for her now," Derek said. "They're hoping that Clint will give up her location now that there's nothing to hide."

Derek was a malpractice attorney. He had to know there was *always* something to hide. Always.

"How did you find all of this out?" Lane asked. His hands were on his hips, his forehead wrinkled, his jaw tight. Out of everyone in the group, he looked the most worried. Could that be because he still had feelings for Jackie? Or was I reading too much into it?

Derek finally set some of the beer bottles down on an antique-looking table. He shoved a silk flower arrangement out of the way like it was a piece of trash. "One of the valets told me. Apparently the police got an anonymous tip that led them to the arrest."

I held my breath. I dared not look at Riley and risk giving away something. Instead, I nodded. "That's great news."

Derek froze for a moment before a huge grin stretched across his face and he jumped on one of the couches. "I'd say so. As soon as the police find Jackie, we can officially party without guilt. No more of this walking around subdued and respectful. We came here to have fun, and now we can finally do it!"

"Derek, you're a pig," Lillian muttered. She waved a hand in the air as if to brush him off.

Derek ignored her and addressed the rest of the group. "So, tomorrow I say we go four-wheeling and hang out in the hot tub. We get our party on."

"Oh, come on, man. We know you've been hanging out at the hot tub all week anyway," Lane muttered. Was that a glimmer of admiration in his eyes? "We've all noticed how you're skipping the workshops."

"There are advantages to being your own boss." Derek shrugged, looking full of himself with that grin across his face. The words "full of himself" and "Derek" seemed to go hand in hand. This guy was a piece of work. His Light Bright teeth glowed at anyone looking his way. "You know me well, friend. You know me well. After we go four-wheeling, we can go hiking or maybe rent one of those Segways, maybe hit a bar or two wherever we can find one."

Lane remained silent. I was sure he would object, that he'd have some class.

Instead, he raised his beer. "Sounds like a plan to me!"

Riley and I looked at each other but said nothing. How would we get out of those plans without looking holier-than-thou? I wasn't sure.

"But for tonight . . . " Derek ripped off his shirt. "We're having a toga party!"

I had to look away from the spectacle called Derek. Perhaps his first dream had been to be a Chippendales dancer? I could only imagine what the man's commercials were like.

As someone cranked up the music, Riley pulled me back toward the door. "I'm sorry."

I was amused, and I couldn't hide it. "Toga party?"

He shrugged, glancing back at his friends. "Reliving the glory days from college. You know, back before there were responsibilities."

I glanced back and saw that Lane had taken off his shirt as well. "I wish they wouldn't." Besides, I couldn't relate. I'd dropped out of college to care for my ailing mom, so college was all about responsibility for me. There were times I dreamed about what it would be like to feel carefree, to not have to worry about paying my bills or if my dad would become homeless. I'd never had that luxury.

Riley nodded toward the door. "Do you want to leave?"

I shook my head. "No, I want to be a light in the darkness. I mean think about it. If you hadn't decided to hang out with me, despite how messed up I was, then I wouldn't have ever seen that you were different . . . in a good way."

Riley grinned and kissed my forehead. "I love you, Gabby St. Claire."

"I love you, too." *I love you enough that I didn't go watch the drop or see Clint get arrested.* I hadn't totally stayed out of the investigation, but I hadn't jumped in feet first, either. That was a good step for me.

All around us, Riley's friends were stripping sheets from the beds and out of drawers. Veronica sashayed over to me and began wrapping some bedding around my midsection. I raised my hands in surprise, though the action afforded Veronica a better opportunity to toga-fy me. "What are you doing?"

"Trying to get you into the spirit." She looked at Riley and playfully raised an eyebrow. "You're next."

I didn't like the undertones of her statement. I'd like to say I wasn't the jealous type, but I was. I knew she'd taken it hard when Riley broke up with her. She wasn't still holding out for a chance with him, was she?

Veronica had already expertly draped a sheet over her lithe figure. Lillian grabbed some flowers from a vase and began wrapping them into wreaths to go around people's heads.

Alcohol, already abundant, suddenly appeared from every direction. These people had just been waiting for the "burden" of Jackie's kidnapping to be resolved, hadn't they? I couldn't judge. I'd been in bad places in my life before. I knew what it was like to seek temporary pleasures and relief from the demons in our lives.

But something about all of this seemed sad.

This scene around me was so foreign from how I'd pictured Riley. I couldn't see him ever enjoying any of this. Had he been the good boy while everyone else partied? Had he been the designated driver to ensure no one got into accidents after a night of binging? Something just didn't compute in my mind.

"Beer?" Derek held out a bottle to me.

I shook my head and yanked up the white sheet around me. "I don't drink."

He stared at me like I was the most un-American person he'd ever met.

"My father's an alcoholic," I explained. I hadn't drank, even before Riley came into my life and I started going to church. Nope, I'd seen firsthand the negative impacts liquor could have on a person, and I didn't want anything to do with it.

Derek shrugged. "Suit yourself. Riley?"

Riley shook his head and casually raised a hand. "I'm good."

Derek raised his hands in the air as his mouth dropped open. "Oh, come on. What happened to the King of Guzzling?"

Riley grimaced. "I'm not that person anymore, Derek."

Derek finally shrugged and took a step back. "Just means more for me, I guess!"

Riley and I really needed to talk. Like *really* needed to.

We settled on the couch to watch the spectacle around us. I couldn't help but laugh when his friends, now fully inebriated, started dancing Gangnam Style. I couldn't help but join them when they started into the Harlem Shake.

I was laughing so hard that my side hurt when I sat beside Riley again. "Maybe you guys can do a *Dead Poets Society* thing after this. Isn't that what every rich college boy does?"

Riley chuckled. "I'll let you think that."

I licked my lips, realizing how thirsty I was, and then nodded toward the kitchen. "I'm going to grab a water, Oh Captain, My Captain. Do you want one?"

Riley ducked as a beach ball flew by his face. "Where did that come from?"

He didn't look uncomfortable here. In fact, the way he lounged with his hand across the back of the couch and a smile on his face reminded me of all I loved about him. He had standards that he didn't back down from, but he wasn't afraid to be around people who weren't like him.

"Some water sounds great."

I walked into the kitchen and nearly stopped in my tracks when I saw Veronica there digging through the refrigerator. Her toga showed all of her curves and way too much of her legs. Suddenly, I wanted to grab one of those plush robes and throw it over her before Riley remembered what he was missing.

She looked up when I walked in. A coy smile tugged at her lips as she stood, a canister of whip cream in hand. "Gabby. Nice moves out there."

I shrugged, trying to picture what I'd probably looked like. It was better if I didn't know. "Just having some fun."

Using her foot, she shut the fridge door, a little too hard if you asked me. She leaned there, staring at me, her eyes assessing. "You know, Riley looks really happy. I wanted to say congratulations to you both."

I was impressed. Veronica was being very mature about this whole thing. I couldn't honestly say that I'd do the same thing in her shoes. "Thank you." I grabbed two bottles of water from the counter and started to take a step away.

Veronica kept talking, though. "I was worried about Riley after I broke up with him, you know. I feared he'd be devastated for a long time."

I shook my head, thoughts colliding inside. She'd said, *after I broke up with him.* That wasn't the story I heard. I tilted my head and chose my words carefully. I set the water back on the counter. "He broke up with you."

She raised her eyebrows. "Is that what he told you? That's so sweet. He probably just didn't want you to feel like his second choice."

Anger ripped through me, but I pushed it down. I had to stay in control, but I clearly could see where she was going with this. "I realize that you're mean and vindictive, Veronica, but why don't you give it a rest? After this week is over, I'll never see you again."

The way she raised her eyebrows and glided from the room made me wonder what exactly she had up her sleeve.

I wasn't smiling this time when I sat beside Riley. "Where's the water?"

I looked down at my hands, half expecting the bottles to be there. Whether I liked it or not, Veronica had rattled me. "I must have forgotten."

"Is everything okay?"

I was determined not to let Veronica get to me, but despite my best efforts, her proclamation that I was Riley's second choice still replayed in my head. "We really should talk sometime."

His eyes swam with emotions as he examined my face. Finally, he took my hand. "Let's talk now."

CHAPTER 22

He tugged me to my feet and led me from the room. As soon as the door closed, the loud music and raucous party noise instantly muted. We kept walking until Riley opened a door leading to a small porch overlooking the back of the resort. The pools glimmered under the moonlight, and the mountains seemed to guard the entire place.

No one else was on this porch, so I took one rocking chair and Riley took the other. He looked off into the distance, and I could tell something was weighing heavy on his mind. Finally, he leaned toward me.

"There are parts of my life that I've never told you about, Gabby." His voice sounded scratchy.

My heart began pounding in my ears. I'd gotten a few insights into how he was at college, but what if there was more? What if I didn't like something he told me? "Like what?"

"I'm not very proud of some of the things I've done." He rubbed his hands together. He stayed quiet, swallowed, and then swallowed again. Finally, he looked at me. "You know I grew up in a Christian home."

"Right. We've talked about that before." I'd heard

all about how his family had celebrated other people at Christmas by serving at homeless shelters. They'd done without so others could simply live. Apparently, every time the doors of the church were opened, Riley was there. His parents were still married and still happy, and his mom called him every week to make sure he was doing okay. They were basically a *Leave It to Beaver* family.

"Well, my junior year of college, I was roommates with this guy named Scoggins. He was a people magnet, if you know what I mean. Everyone just loved him. He had charisma. He was always riding me about my beliefs."

"That's hard."

"I found myself slowly being worn down. I saw how happy Scoggins was, and he wasn't a prude. I convinced myself that I could have it both ways. I could be a Christian and a partier. I could be a witness by infiltrating crowds of people who weren't like me. They were going to see something different in me."

"But . . . "

"Instead of me influencing them, they influenced me. I joined a fraternity and gave in to the party scene. I'd thought I was stronger than that, but when it came down to it my faith was actually pretty brittle. I found myself feeding on the popularity and the fast times and the rush I got when I did crazy things."

"That does not sound like the Riley I know, at all."

He nodded. "Tell me about it. The person I was disappeared before my eyes, yet, in truth, it was a slow process. One choice at a time. One decision at a time. One party. One beer. Before I knew it, I was this person I never thought I'd be. I thought I was happy, but I always had to feed myself more, you know?

"I think you're the one who told me that worldly pleasures won't fulfill you. I just had no idea you knew that firsthand."

"There's more." He looked up, and the pain in his eyes nearly sent me toppling out of my chair. I wanted to reach for him, but I sensed that he needed some space to get through this.

"Scoggins and I went to a party one night. It was close to graduation, and we were just ready to be done. I'd told myself that this was it for me. After I graduated and had my degree, I was turning my life around. No more partying or drinking. That night, Scoggins and I had probably both been drinking too much, truth be told. Actually, we *were* drinking too much; we just didn't think we were. He drove." Riley paused, swallowing again and closing his eyes. "Scoggins hit a car. Killed the driver. Scoggins died, too."

I sucked in a soft gasp. "And you?"

"I was unscathed." He shook his head. "That really woke me up, and I realized what an idiot I'd been."

"I had no idea." I half expected to blink and discovered I'd daydreamed this conversation. I'd never imagined Riley to be that kind of guy. In my mind, he was the opposite of me and, since I was a screw up, that meant that he was near perfect.

Riley continued. "I went through some really dark days, Gabby."

"Why didn't you tell me any of this before?"

He let out a long breath and stared out into the distance. "Honestly, I just try to put that part of my life behind me. I know God has forgiven me. Sometimes, I haven't forgiven myself. I should have known Scoggins was too drunk to drive. I should have stopped him. But I didn't. Two lives were taken from this earth as a result."

I put my hand on his arm. "Oh, Riley . . . "

"I'd hoped it would be a wake-up call and set me

back on the right path. I got in deeper, though, trying to numb my pain. At the end of my internship, Ed Laskin invited me to his home. That's where I met Veronica. We started dating. Then I went out to California to work as a prosecutor. Veronica came with me. I won a huge case and really let everything go to my head. I started drinking more, partying more."

Ah, he must be speaking of his days out in L.A. That was right before he moved to Norfolk.

"But, the good news," he looked up at me and a soft smile tugged at his features, "is that all of it eventually led me back to my faith. I realized how empty living for myself was."

"If not the death of Scoggins, what caused the change?"

"One of my friends at the district attorney's office actually. He was a Christian. He saw what a mess I'd become and really helped to point me in the right direction. He was patient and always there when I needed him. He gave me chances when I didn't deserve them. I vowed that was the kind of person I wanted to be, someone who simply showed people love and who reflected Christ."

I squeezed his arm again. "You have been."

He just stared ahead. "So, when I made all of these life changes, Veronica was kind of caught in the crossfire, so to speak. She'd gotten engaged to one man, but I'd turned my life around and become someone else."

I tried to picture all of that playing out. It couldn't have been pretty. "What happened?"

Riley shrugged. "We broke up. That's when I decided I had to get away from everything. I moved to Norfolk. I met you."

I shook my head. "But then Veronica showed up

again. I clearly remember, because I was there that night."

He nodded. "Right. Veronica said she wanted to give my new lifestyle a shot. She insisted that we could still be a couple, that we both just had to compromise some. It just wasn't going to work, Gabby. We were two totally different people. I wanted to run away from that materialistic lifestyle. She wanted to run toward it."

"So she broke up with you," I muttered. My heart thudded. What Veronica had told me was true.

Riley's eyebrows squeezed together. "No, I broke up with her. I'd known from the beginning that things weren't going to work out the second time around. I should have told her that from the start. She's very good at getting her way. She was not happy with me, though, and I can't blame her."

Relief filled me, feeling like a balm to my heart. I hadn't been his second choice. "You broke up with her? Really?"

He grabbed my hand and stroked his thumb over my knuckles. "Yeah, really. Why do you ask it like that? You don't believe me?"

"No, it's not that. It's not that at all. It's just because Veronica told me . . . " I stopped myself and shook my head. I didn't really want to go there. "Never mind. It's not important."

"Do you want me to talk to Veronica? I know it's gotta be awkward rooming together. She has a way of getting in people's heads and messing with them."

Did she ever. But, for some reason, moving rooms would seem too much like letting Veronica win. I wasn't about to let that happen. "No, I'm going to tough it out. It's only for a few more days, right?"

"I'm sorry I never told you any of that before, Gabby. I just . . . I don't like to think about it, really. I became everything that I didn't want to be. I was so self-focused that I couldn't see anyone's needs but mine."

I squeezed his arm. "That could be a great part of your testimony, you know."

"I know. And I know that I'll get there eventually. But really, Gabby, it's only been a couple of years since it all happened. My friends here this week haven't seen me since then. They know the old me."

"Who was one heck of a partier, apparently."

He turned toward me and caressed his fingers against my cheek. "Forgive me for not telling you sooner?"

I nodded. "Of course." That brick appeared on my chest again. He'd been so open. Now it was my turn. I had to share my secrets. "There's something I've been meaning to talk to you about also."

"Of course. You can tell me anything."

Just as I opened my mouth, I heard someone running down the hallway. As I looked back, I saw Derek and Lane. They stood at the French doors staring out at us. I jumped to my feet. "What in the world?"

"Sorry." Riley stood. "One minute."

He strode across the patio and opened the door. "What are you doing?"

"Get this," Derek said. His voice was alive and animated. "Jackie's missing. She's not where Clint said he left her."

I closed my eyes. I wouldn't be sharing my story tonight.

No, tonight, Jackie was taking center stage again.

CHAPTER 23

After Derek and Lane had left to join the rest of the crowd, I turned to Riley. I really wished I could explain this a little more. "I need to go talk to Carol."

Riley squinted. "Carol? Who's Carol?"

"Jackie's mom."

He squinted more. "You're on a first name basis with her?"

I tossed my head back and forth on my shoulders, trying to find something safe to say. "We've talked a few times. She confided a few things to me. I need to check on her."

He grabbed my hand. "Let's go."

I put a hand on his chest, hating the guilt that pressed in on me. I'd brought it on myself, though. I'd explain everything to Riley soon. I just prayed I wasn't too late. "I should go alone. She's very private."

He stared at me a split second before shrugging. "Sure. If you think that's best."

"I'll be right back. I promise." I squeezed his hand before taking off down the hallway. I jogged up the stairs until I reached the next floor. There, I started to pound on Carol's door when it opened. It hadn't been latched all the way.

Inside, I saw Carol in tears, and her male friend squeezing her shoulder, trying to offer some sympathy, while two police officers stood in front of her. She looked up as the door swung open and spotted me.

"Gabby, did you hear?"

I stepped inside, nodding to the rest of the crowd in the room. "I did. What's going on?"

She held a tissue under her nose and breathed fast—too fast. That woman was going to pass out if she wasn't careful. "You were right. Clint was behind this whole thing. Can you believe it? All along, he just wanted our money."

"So he kidnapped your daughter and demanded a ransom." I sat beside her and squeezed her hand. "What happened?"

"Clint said they—his friends are actually his cousins, apparently—were keeping Jackie at a cabin. After Clint admitted to faking the ransom, the police went to get Jackie, and she was gone." She shook her head. "I just don't know what to believe now."

"What else did Clint say?"

"He claims Jacqueline was in on the whole plan. Can you believe the nerve of the man, saying my daughter plotted her own kidnapping?"

I blinked at the new twist. "Clint is claiming this was an elaborate scheme on both of their parts?" I clarified.

She nodded and dabbed under her nose again. "Something about trying to get some money."

I sucked in a breath. "Carol, is Jackie your daughter's real name?"

"No, it's Mona. She's always hated that name, so she used her middle name instead. Why?"

Dread filled me. Maybe Clint was telling the truth. I needed to talk to him, look him in the eye, so I could find out.

***

I held on to the seat in front of me as the van rumbled down the road the next morning. Thankfully, the laundry service here was amazing. They'd cleaned my jeans, T-shirt and underclothes last night while I slept, so I actually had some clean clothes to wear this morning.

If only laundry was that easy to do at my apartment.

I'd discovered that the hotel offered a shuttle to various places. Most people used the service to go to one of the resort's many golf courses or to off-site locations for whitewater rafting in the summer or skiing in the winter.

Me? I was using it to go to the county jail. I had no other choice with Riley's car being in the shop.

Thankfully, I'd found out the jail was located in Healthy Springs.

Last night, after I'd talked to Carol, I'd found Riley and told him the gist of what had happened. It was late at that point, so Riley had walked me to my suite, kissed me goodnight, and I'd escaped to my room before seeing Veronica.

I'd slept hard, probably because I hadn't had a good night's rest since I got here. I had to admit that I missed my nightly chat with Deanna. Maybe I'd run into her today, though.

After breakfast this morning, Riley and I had gone our separate ways, promising to meet a little later so we could go four-wheeling with his friends. I guess his friends wanted to enjoy part of their stay here at Allendale, and a part of me couldn't blame them. The other part of me thought it seemed slightly disrespectful, but I was trying not to judge.

As if Riley had ESP, he'd reminded me about my promise not to snoop . . . again. That's how I ended up here in the shuttle with a bunch of people wearing their golf clothes and carrying tennis rackets.

I didn't miss the looks of curiosity that people gave me when I reminded the driver to stop at the police station.

"I'll be back on the hour, if you want a ride to Allendale," the driver mumbled as I climbed out.

I stepped onto the sunny sidewalk. I looked around the town surrounding me. It was quite quaint with cozy looking buildings, neat trees, and inviting benches. Too bad I wouldn't be enjoying any of that.

I walked one block, found the police station, stepped inside, and asked the lady at the front desk if I could speak with Clint. An officer was called to help me with the request, and it took several minutes for them to verify and approve me talking to him, but somehow it all worked out.

I was the kid who somehow always missed my bus in elementary school, didn't get into the classes I wanted at college, and who'd just lost her dream job, so any time that things worked out in my favor, I felt grateful.

I was escorted to a room with wood paneling on all sides, a clean vinyl floor, and a metal folding chair. Clint sat on one side of a glass partition, and I sat on the other. I looked at him for a minute, at how quickly he'd aged. I never noticed his wrinkles before or the lines under his eyes or how brittle his hair looked.

I picked up a telephone to speak with him.

"What are you doing here?" Clint stared at me as if

waiting for accusations to pour from my lips. "Did you come to crucify me also?"

"I just want to know where Jackie is."

"I wish I knew. She was supposed to be in the cabin. That was the plan. It was always the plan."

I pulled in a long breath. I was going to have to cut to the chase if I was going to get anywhere with him. "Look, Clint, I'm an investigator. It's what I do. I've cracked some pretty big cases before, and yours has me curious. I know you were planning to take off to the Bahamas at the end of this week."

His eyes widened. "How did you know that?"

"I have my ways. But let me tell you this also." I leaned closer to the glass, close enough that Clint could see the truth in my eyes. "I believe you when you say that Jackie was in on this with you."

"You're the only one."

"Can you tell me what happened?"

He shook his head. His eyes were bloodshot and red, his skin pale, his hair rumpled. "Jackie's mom wouldn't give her her inheritance if she married me. She had to marry someone in her own class." He said "class" as if it was a dirty word.

"Really? That's harsh." And it was. Discriminating against someone because of how much money they made was not cool. I could kind of understand the place he was in.

"Yeah, Carol wanted her daughter to marry someone with his own money. Definitely not a construction worker. So Jackie and I concocted this plan. Two hundred thousand wasn't a ton of money, but it would help us get on our feet. I was supposed to leave the money, my cousin was going to pick it up, and Jackie was going to be returned. We set it up so the police would never figure out who'd actually kidnapped her. In the meantime, I would look like a hero and hopefully Carol would soften toward me. We'd have the money. Take our little trip. Disappear if we had to."

"What went wrong?"

He buried his face in one of his hands. "I wish I knew. My cousin went to go get Jackie, and she was gone. No one knew we were there. No one. I just don't understand . . ."

I leaned back, processing what he told me. I had to find out more information in order to verify what he was saying. "Where was Jackie staying?"

"We kept her at this cabin in the mountains under a fake name. She was just hanging out, biding her time until the drop happened. Of course, she was already supposed to be free, but that woman at our first drop off attempt screwed everything up."

"Is there anyone who would want her dead?"

"Doug Matthews." He didn't hesitate. Apparently, he'd had a lot of time to think while he was behind bars.

"Who is Doug Matthews?" This visit just got interesting.

"He's a colleague of hers. They work together at the local D.A.'s office. Every time Jackie turned around, she was telling me how she couldn't stand him."

"Any reason in particular?" Wasn't he the same person Clint had mentioned earlier who Jackie never talked about? Apparently, jail time had brought Clint some clarity.

One of his shoulders pulled up in a half-shrug. "He was always trying to tell her how to do her job."

"I'll check him out. Anyone else?"

He nodded. "Derek Waters."

"Why Derek?" There was a name I wasn't expecting

to hear.

"I don't know. He just seems to have his sights set on Jackie. Always has, if you ask me. He even stopped by Atlanta a month or so ago for a surprise visit. I told him to get lost."

"What did Jackie think about that?"

"Nothing. I mean, she thought his visit was weird, but I don't think she lost any sleep over it."

"You have no idea where Jackie is now?" I needed the truth. I didn't let my eyes off of Clint, watching for a sign that he was lying. A gesture. A blink. A twitch.

"No idea. I wish I did. It was never supposed to happen like this." He stared at me, his eyes red and bloodshot. He didn't flinch or fidget, though. "You can talk to my cousins about it. They're locked up, too, and our stories match—because we're telling the truth."

"Where is the cabin where she stayed?" I was sure the police were there now, so knowing the location probably wouldn't do me much good.

"You'll never find it. It's on an unmarked service road. The area is called Willow's Reach."

"Did she go anywhere else?"

"There was this overlook she liked not too far from the cabin. I think there's a trail that leads there. But you have to be careful. The area is called Ominous Valley. She loved it, and it's so secluded she went there a lot to think."

Ominous Valley. That didn't have a good ring to it.

"Do you think you can help?"

I stayed silent a minute. I believed Clint's story. Maybe no one else did, but his grief and anguish seemed real.

The problem was—how did I help him? These mountains were vast and wild. It would take teams of rescuers days—if not weeks—to comb through each nook and cave there. Even if they did that, there was no guarantee that's where Jackie was.

Maybe she'd taken off. Maybe she'd staged the whole struggle, gotten cold feet, and decided to run. There were so many uncertainties, so many reasons why I wasn't sure I could help.

I stood. "I'll see what I can do. Is there anything else you can tell me that might be beneficial?"

Those bloodshot eyes met mine. "She left all of her inhalers in the cabin. Really, this time. Earlier we just said that because we knew her mom would think the situation was more urgent. We didn't want to give Carol too much time to think. Jackie would never, ever leave her inhalers, Gabby. She's out there without any medicine. If the people who grabbed her don't kill her, her asthma might."

CHAPTER 24

It seemed like such a mundane thing to do, especially considering all that was going on. But I still had twenty minutes before the shuttle came back, and I wanted to check on Riley's car. We were supposed to leave in three days, and I didn't want to be here any longer than I had to. Provided Jackie was found, of course.

I was ready to get back to my life in Norfolk. There was a part of me that even missed cleaning crime scenes, as weird as that might sound. That job had been a part of my life for so long now. Plus, I found crime scenes fascinating—not in a morbid way, but in the way the evidence told a story.

I blew a hair out of my eyes. Too bad I wouldn't be an official part of any investigations for a while.

Just as I walked into the repair shop, a tow truck pulled up with a Jaguar behind it. The driver I'd spoken with in the tow truck had been correct—that crazy mountain road did mess a lot of people up.

I stepped up to the counter. A new face was behind the desk, this one younger. He had a mullet, crooked teeth, and four gold chains around his neck. I thought the chains went really well with his flannel shirt, which happened to have the sleeves cut out and was unbuttoned halfway down his chest. "What can I do you fer?"

Where was Jeff Foxworthy when I needed him? "I need to check on my car."

"Your name?"

I gave him my information, and he disappeared into the back for a moment. He returned and said the parts had been back ordered. "The car should be ready by midweek."

I leaned against the counter to get a better look at his eyes. Surely he was jesting. "Midweek? Midweek is today."

He twirled the toothpick in his mouth. "Midweek next week."

My mouth dropped open. I had a feeling these people knew they were the only shop in town, and they were taking advantage of it. "That's not acceptable. I've got to get back home."

He shrugged, indicating he could care less. "You may want to look into renting."

"Even if I rented, I'm just going to have to drive all the way back out here to pick the car up when it's ready."

He leaned toward me, his elbows propped on the counters. "We do have a delivery program. It's kinda pricey."

I shook my head. "This is unbelievable."

"Happens all the time on these roads. People don't know how to drive on them."

"Apparently." I shrugged. "I'll be back in touch."

***

I wasn't sure what I was doing, but I found myself texting Riley and telling him I'd catch up with him on the trails.

Then I went and rented a four-wheeler myself. I got a map and found the approximate location of Ominous Valley. Just earlier I'd been thinking that no smart woman should go on one of these trails alone. Now, here I was, going on a trail alone. But I had a four-wheeler, which, to me, seemed to be an added safety measure. If I saw anyone crazy, I'd just hop on and roar away. In theory, at least.

The attendant gave me quick directions on how to operate the four-wheeler, warned me about the dangers of getting lost, insisted that cell phone service was nearly nonexistent, told me the path to Ominous Valley was both unsafe and not well traveled, and recommended that I four-wheel with someone else.

Then, just like that, I'd mounted my vehicle and headed toward a mountainous trail. Since I didn't have a car or anyone to travel with me, this would have to work.

A tinge of apprehension crept up my spine as I wondered what I was getting myself into, from the four-wheeler all the way to being out in these woods alone.

This was about justice. Finding answers. Helping people. I just couldn't get those things out of my blood.

I wondered if Riley would ever fully understand that? Certainly the rest of our relationship together wouldn't consist of me sticking my nose where I shouldn't and trying to hide what I was doing from him? Sierra wasn't right. Riley wasn't asking me to be someone I wasn't. That was just my insecurities doing what they did best—rearing their ugly heads at the worst of times. Half of the time I had to play a mental game of "Whack a Mole" with them.

My ATV climbed up the narrow path. I reached a fork, glanced at my map, and went right.

But my mind stayed on Riley. What if I had to choose between investigating and our relationship? No, he would never make me choose. But still . . . why did the choice seem like such a hard one? I should choose Riley. But my heart didn't feel convicted or like the choice was a no-brainer, and that fact bothered me as I bounced up the mountainside.

I paused at another split. According to my map, if I went right again, I'd get to the approximate area of Jackie's cabin, but if I went left, it would take me to the overlook that had been Jackie's favorite. I figured the police had already searched the cabin, so my chances were better at the overlook.

Across the way, on another ridge, I spotted three other people four-wheeling. I tried to imagine what it would be like to be out here, not to investigate but simply to have fun. Then I decided that without investigating, it wouldn't be any fun at all.

The tension in my chest pulled tighter. What was wrong with me? Why couldn't I just be normal and do normal things?

I knew the answer. It was because just like fingerprints—and tongue prints, for that matter—we were all created uniquely. I wasn't supposed to be like everyone else. But, at this moment, that didn't make me feel any better.

I saw a railing in the distance and eased off the accelerator. I puttered for a moment until I was close enough to cut the ignition. I pulled my helmet off and walked toward the overlook.

A soft breeze hit my face while an earthy scent rose up around me. Dried leaves, dusty pollen, fragrant dirt. I closed my eyes for a moment, enjoying nature.

Birds sang around me. Somewhere, a stream

trickled. The wind brushed the leaves together.

I opened my eyes. I wasn't sure what I was expecting to find here. In all honesty, I wasn't truly expecting anything. But if I did find something, I wouldn't complain.

I sucked in a breath when I saw the deep gulch below. The mountain steeply dropped and dropped and then dropped some more. The depth of the decline almost made my head spin for a moment. Thank goodness for the railing to hold me up.

"So this is where you liked to come, Jackie," I muttered, picturing her standing here. "Did you wonder about the wisdom of your scheme? Did you question your decision to go through with this, maybe even consider turning back?"

Of course no one answered me. Truth was, I doubted very many people knew about this trail at all. If I hadn't asked the guy at the four-wheel excursion adventure place about it, I wouldn't be here right now.

I cast one last glance over the mountain before stepping back. It was time to try and meet up with Riley and his friends. I needed to text them and see where exactly they were. I only hoped I could get a signal.

I pulled out my phone, saw that I had an ever-so-slight signal, and sent the text. As I glanced at my phone, something on the ground caught my eye. A spot of red.

Blood?

I squatted beside it. No, it was a . . . jelly bean.

I tried to recall what Riley had told me about his friends before we came. I was nearly certain he'd mentioned that Jackie had an addiction to jelly beans.

My heart rate sped.

Jackie had been here, just like Clint said. I had no idea when or if it tied in with her disappearance, but she'd been here.

Before I stood, I spotted another piece of candy a couple of feet away, a yellow one this time. A little farther toward the edge, there was an orange one, then a blue one, and a green one.

I paused at the edge. It wasn't a straight drop down. The ground was probably slanted for twenty feet or so before a total drop off occurred. I could probably slide and hang on to some trees to lower myself farther. That's the direction these jelly beans were leading.

Had Jackie fallen?

A quick glance at the foliage made it appear nothing had been disturbed on the mountainside lately. There were no marks in the dirt. I looked for a line in the leaves or a section where the underbrush was broken. Nothing showed any signs of a struggle. The whole "take only pictures, and leave only footprints" thing had apparently worked here.

I needed something to go on, and all I had at the moment were jelly beans leading down a mountain.

Of course, in Hansel and Gretel, following a candy trail had led them to a witch who nearly ended up eating them. The thought wasn't comforting. In the least.

Lord, watch over me.

I prayed that prayer a lot.

I grabbed a twig-like tree and lowered myself the first step of my journey into the gulch. Slow and steady wins the race, I reminded myself. I had to keep my footing. I'd just go down a few feet.

I spotted another red jelly bean.

As I took another step down, my foot hit a patch of leaves and slid. Gravity pulled me downward. I reached for something—anything—and grabbed a pine tree. The rough bark dug into my hands, but I didn't care. I jerked to a halt, the action so swift and harsh that my arm ached in its socket.

My breath caught. My heart pounded in my ears. In an instant, I'd envisioned myself passed out at the bottom of the gulch with no one to find me. Was that what had happened to Jackie?

I shook my head. Again, there was no evidence of that. Certainly, there would be broken tree limbs and marks in the dirt and disrupted leaf patterns on the ground.

Then why was there a trail of jelly beans? How had they gotten here?

I looked down. I could see three or four more pieces of the candy below me.

I paused. Above me and to the left, a rock jutted out from the mountainside. Above that was the overlook where I'd stood earlier. The craggy boulder had dark recesses below it that made me think of bears and wildcats and other wild animals that needed shelter.

Maybe coming down here wasn't a good idea. I should have gotten Riley. Or the police. Even Deanna would have worked. Someone, for goodness sakes!

There were so many things that could go wrong. Like me hanging from a tree with nowhere to go but down.

I tried to find my footing, but the leaves kept slipping out from underneath me, making it impossible for me to pull myself back up. My hands burned against the sappy bark of the pine tree. My arm ached, and I was losing my strength quickly.

That's when I heard a piece of bark crack. Then crack again. And again.

The bark was coming off the tree.

No. No. No. This could *not* be happening.

At once, my hold on the tree disappeared. I slipped

down the mountainside, right toward the cliff. Right toward my death.

I reached for something—anything—but only grabbed leaves and a loose rock that tumbled back toward me and knocked me in the forehead. Finally, my hand caught a root.

But not before my feet dangled over the edge. I looked down.

The gulch was even deeper than I'd thought. It was a long way down. Like, a *long*, long way down. A river—so far away it looked more like an oversized snake—cut through the landscape below.

And all I had to hang onto was a root.

This had been such a bad idea. A bad, bad idea. Even though I jogged and my job kept me physically active, I didn't have the upper body strength I needed to pull myself up.

I pushed on my elbows, hoping that would give me leverage. Instead, my arms felt like Jello—wobbly, mushy, and easily torn apart.

How was I going to get myself out of this one?

I glanced back up and saw the railing of the overlook. Was this how Jackie had died?

My palms sweated under the pressure, under the heat of the afternoon, and I felt my grip slipping. If I lost hold of this root, there was no way I'd make it. There was nothing—nothing—between this root and the edge of the cliff except me.

If I could take one hand off my lifeline, I could reach into my pocket, grab my phone, and call for help.

If I had reception.

I had reception up by the overlook. But it was spotty at best. It was a big risk to take for something so uncertain. Besides, holding on with only one hand could lead to my death.

What was I going to do?

"Hello? Are you okay down there?"

My heart stuttered for a moment. Someone else was here. Since I was hanging on to a root for dear life, I only hoped the person out here was a good guy and not a bad one.

A face peered down at me. I blinked in surprise. "Ajay?"

"Miss St. Claire? What are you doing?"

I tried to shrug, but it was a little hard since I could barely move my shoulders. "I've gotten myself into a little predicament, I suppose."

"Do you need a hand?"

"I'd love one." I glanced down. "But first I have to finish checking something out."

"Can I help?"

"If I fall and hit my head, just call the police. That would be awesome."

In a graceful motion, he practically repelled down the mountainside without any ropes until he was at my side. "Let us hope that is not needed."

He grabbed my hands and pulled me up until my feet landed on the ground. He didn't let go until I was practically hugging a tree. I made a mental note to never describe myself as "sure-footed."

"Thank you," I gasped, realizing just how close that had been. Just glancing down once more made me feel lightheaded. That could have been really ugly.

I stared at Ajay, realizing I was seeing him in jeans and a golf shirt for the first time. He didn't seem like Ajay without the suit and the sash. He did wear a gold chain necklace with the symbol of a sun on the end. In the center of the emblem was a large diamond.

I drew in another ragged breath. "How'd you climb down like that?"

He shrugged, not looking the least bit shaken by the massive drop only a few feet away. "I grew up in the mountains, exploring nature. It is second nature. Now, what can I help you with?"

"I'm following a candy trail."

"I could have bought you some candy, you know. There are far simpler ways to get these things."

I stared at him a moment until I realized he was joking. Then I chuckled. "You're funny."

"I try." He glanced to the side. "The candy leads that way, it appears."

I followed the direction he pointed, and my throat went dry. The candy led to the boulder under the overlook. The dark, scary place where animals of prey should live. Lovely.

"What are you doing out here anyway?" I asked as I tried to find my footing and follow the clues.

"Enjoying nature. Thinking. Pondering life."

I sensed something burdening his soul, and I wanted to ask what. But this whole being engaged thing was messing with my head. Asking this man to share what was on his heart just seemed a little too personal, especially since we were out here in the woods alone.

I had to think about how I'd feel if Riley were out on a mountainside with another woman, alone and talking about the things that grieved their hearts.

What if he was out here with someone like . . . Veronica?

At that moment, my foot slipped from the root I'd stepped on. I felt myself falling backwards. A scream escaped.

Air loomed beneath me. My arms flailed. My

stomach dropped.

Ajay reached behind me and pulled me back up. I found my balance and laughed so hard I cried. How had that just happened . . . again?

I put a hand over my heart and drank in deep gulps of air. "Oh my goodness. My life flashed before my eyes."

Ajay only grinned, apparently having the agility of a monkey as he gracefully held on to the tree with one hand without even the slightest hint of strain on his features. "Never be afraid of falling. When you get back up, you will be stronger."

"Interesting take on it. I'll chew on that thought." I chuckled, feeling silly for my overreaction. "My goodness. What a day. I can't wait to tell my fiancé about all of this." I felt better mentioning Riley, just in case Ajay was getting the wrong idea.

"Your fiancé is a very lucky man."

My cheeks heated. "Thank you. I think I'm the lucky one."

"Then it sounds like the two of you will be good together."

I sighed. "Maybe. It's hit me with some clarity today that I'm keeping too many secrets from him." So much for not getting personal.

"Secrets can ruin a relationship. You should tell him. Trust him."

"You're right. I should." I nodded. "I'm going to. I'm not going to let anyone interrupt this time."

"Good for you, Miss St. Claire."

I glanced over at the rock again, knowing I needed to focus here—which wasn't something I was very good at sometimes. I soaked in the leaves, a tangle of roots, and several smaller rocks.

My heart froze. Something was out of place. I

squinted, trying to get a better look. Was that? Could it be . . . ?

I gasped, shaking my head, sure my eyes were deceiving me. "Hand . . . "

"You need a hand?"

I shook my head. "No, there's a hand over there. I think I know who it belongs to."

CHAPTER 25

Ajay helped me over to the rock. Suddenly, I forgot about my fear of mountainous heights. I sank into the dirt and brushed some specks off the fleshy appendage there.

"Oh, dear God," I prayed, closing my eyes a moment.

"It is a woman," Ajay muttered.

Using my fingers, I swept away some more dirt. That's when a face emerged. Jackie's dead, lifeless face. I quickly soaked in the bruises on her neck, the cut on her forehead, the bluish tinge of her face.

She hadn't fallen to her death. She'd been murdered, and her body had been stashed here.

I lowered my head, mourning this woman and whatever had happened to her.

Ajay's hands covered mine. "I am sorry. Did you know her?"

I shook my head. "Not really. My friends did, though."

I heard the squeal of four-wheelers in the distance. Was that the killer coming back to make sure no one discovered his stash?

"We might want to hide," I muttered. I made the

internationally known sign for "Murder." Okay, maybe not. But I put my hands at my throat as if I were being choked. Close enough, right?

Ajay's eyes widened, and he stepped deeper into the recess of the boulder. I stepped back, too, wishing I hadn't. Dead body. Possible spiders or wild animals. The cliff of death one good slide down the mountain away.

Creepy crawlies—either imaginary or real—danced across my skin. The cool, damp boulder crept through my shirt. The smell of dank earth filled my senses.

My ATV! I realized. It was still on the trail. Visible. An obvious sign that someone was here.

Ai yi yi.

The sound of the four-wheelers got louder and louder until finally, I knew they were right above us. I waited to hear rough voices. To see a gun. To look into the eyes of a killer.

Voices drifted downward. "This is . . . remote. Nature at its best."

Was that . . . Derek?

"I know she said to meet us here," someone else said, someone else who sounded an awful lot like Riley.

Riley! Of course!

I took a step away from the cavern where Jackie had been buried. I grabbed a tree to steady myself, noting all of the dirt caked onto my fingers. I could only imagine what the rest of me looked like.

"Riley?"

He stopped and squinted, his gaze searching his surroundings. "Gabby?"

I waved a hand in the air. "Riley, I'm down here!"

A moment later, I saw my fiancé looking down at me, along with Derek, Lillian, Jack, Lane, and Veronica.

Riley's eyebrows came together. "What are you

doing? And who's that with you?"

I looked back, knowing how strange this must look. Me out in the woods with a strange man, and both of us covered in dirt and under a rock. But I didn't have time to explain Ajay now. My lips pulled down as the grimness of the situation hit me. "Riley, I found Jackie. We need to call the police."

"What do you mean you found Jackie?" Riley slid down the mountain until he reached me. I didn't miss the scowl he gave Ajay. Could Riley actually be a little jealous? It wasn't an emotion I'd ever seen on him before.

"She's . . . she's dead." I pointed to her body.

Riley closed his eyes and turned his head away. "Oh, Jackie."

"I'm sorry," I mumbled. "I wished it were good news."

Riley turned back to his friends. His hands were on his hips, and he looked all lawyer-like and in charge. "Why don't you guys go call the police? We'll wait here until they arrive."

His friends all looked pale and slightly shocked, but they nodded and climbed back on their ATVs. Even Derek. A moment later, they roared away.

Riley eyed Ajay for a moment, and that's when I realized I hadn't introduced them. "Riley, this is Ajay. Ajay, Riley."

They shook hands, but I could feel tension stretch between them. I wasn't sure if I felt flattered or annoyed by it. Maybe a little of both.

Ajay seemed to sense it also because he nodded toward the path. "I should stay up there to direct the police on where to go when they arrive."

I nodded. "That sounds great. Thank you."

He disappeared down the path, leaving just Riley

and I standing there. Riley and I and a dead body, at least. I wanted to use what I'd learned as a medical examiner to look her over, but I knew I'd be disturbing the scene. I didn't have gloves or evidence bags or a camera even. I'd touched too much already.

Riley's thumb rubbed against my cheek. "You're filthy, you know."

I looked down and saw the dirt stains on my knees, leaves in my hair, a small gash on the side of my arm. I could only imagine what my face looked like. Probably like I'd just been mud wrestling.

"It's all in a day's work." I offered a weak smile.

"How . . . ?" He looked behind him at Jackie and shook his head.

"It's a long story."

He pointed back at Ajay. "And him?"

I shrugged. "It's another long story. Right now, I guess we should think about Jackie."

***

"I can't believe she's dead," Lillian mumbled.

We'd gathered in Derek's suite. That was, after the police had come, I'd been questioned and finally been told I could leave, but to stick close by in case they had any questions.

Been there, done that before.

Too many times.

I still couldn't believe Jackie was dead, either. If Clint was telling the truth, then what had happened?

Derek shook his head. His normal smugness was gone, replaced with what I guessed was shock. "Who killed her?"

Silence stretched a moment. That was the question

of the hour. I had absolutely no idea. I didn't think Clint was guilty, though.

Lane's finger suddenly jutted out, and it was pointed toward . . . me?

"Gabby was the one who found her body." Accusation stained his voice.

Riley's hand slipped around my waist. "That doesn't mean she had anything to do with the murder," Riley said. "She's a professional investigator."

Veronica stepped forward. "Or is she?"

"Of course she is. What are you talking about?" A touch of anger hinted in Riley's voice. I appreciated the fact that he was standing by me in what was turning out to be an ugly game of Clue.

Veronica's eyes lit with what I could only call vengeance. "I overheard her conversation. She was fired from her job with the medical examiner."

Tension stretched every part of my insides until I thought I might break over and over again. Veronica must have been in the other room when I talked to Sierra. She'd purposely been quiet so she could overhear our conversation.

Fire lit through my veins. "It's not like that. I wasn't fired."

Riley turned to me, confusion in his eyes. "What is she talking about, Gabby?"

Panic galloped through me, destroying every sane emotion in its path. "I've been trying to tell you," I started. "They had budget cuts. I was let go."

His eyes widened. "Why didn't you tell me?"

I nodded toward the group around us. "It's complicated. I tried to, but . . . " I shook my head. "It just didn't work out."

Certainly he had to acknowledge that I'd started

the conversation several times, but we'd been interrupted.

"She's been sneaking around with that Indian man also," Derek added.

I jerked my head toward Derek. "I have not. You don't understand."

I felt dizzy, like the whole room was spinning. Or maybe I was the only one spinning and the rest of the room was just fine.

"Gabby?" Riley asked.

I sighed. "It's not like it sounds."

"I saw her leaving his room in the middle of the night," Derek said.

"I can confirm that she snuck back into the room a couple of nights ago. I thought she'd crept out to see you." Veronica shrugged. "I guess not."

I pinched the skin between my eyes, nausea growing in my gut. "None of you know what you're talking about."

"Maybe she wasn't discovering Jackie's body. Maybe she was *burying* Jackie's body," Lane said.

Everyone in the room went silent and stared at me. I wanted to crawl into a hole and not come out. That wasn't a possibility, though.

"I think I saw her in a maid's uniform. I thought it was strange, but with all of this that's been mentioned, maybe she was plotting her getaway," Lillian said.

I threw my hands in the air. "I was hired to investigate. That's why I was creeping around. I was looking for answers, trying to help!"

"You promised not to investigate," Riley muttered. "I thought we both agreed."

"Jackie's mom asked me." I shook my head, feeling like the whole world was collapsing around me. "I just wanted to help."

I tried to keep explaining, but no one seemed to hear me.

"She would know how to cover up a murder since she did work for the state medical examiner for a couple of weeks," Veronica said. "Plus, who better to clean up a dead body than a crime scene cleaner?"

"I can explain all of this."

"Gabby's not a killer," Riley said. His eyes held disappointment that broke my heart. I wanted everyone else to disappear so we could talk. No one made any move to leave, though. At least Riley had defended me.

"Do you ever really know someone?" Derek asked.

Riley sighed. "I know Gabby well enough to know she wouldn't do that."

"If she lied about one thing, there's no guarantee she wouldn't lie about another," Veronica continued.

I wanted to throttle the woman. I really did. But that would be no way to prove my case that I was innocent. "I don't have to explain anything to any of you," I said. I looked up at Riley. "But I do need to talk to you."

The look in his eyes—part suspicion, part disenchantment—caused my gut to clench. Finally, he nodded toward the door. "Let's go."

We walked silently down the hallway. I just kept going, knowing he'd stop when he was ready. We went downstairs, out the front door, and kept walking until we reached a gazebo overlooking a pond.

With each step, dread built. It bit into my muscles, squeezed my lungs. My mind raced. How was I going to explain all of this? Where did I start?

I carefully sat on the wooden bench there, wishing we were here to enjoy the water and the stars and the crickets. The breeze hinted at a coming storm, and lightning cracked just over the mountains.

I never wanted to feel like this again. I knew that. "Riley—"

"Why did you lie to me, Gabby?" His voice held a tone I hadn't heard before. Disappointment? Resentment? I wasn't sure.

A million excuses rushed through my mind. But none of them seemed right to share right now, because it didn't matter how I tried to paint the picture—I'd been wrong. And now I may have ruined the best relationship in my life.

"I wanted to tell you the truth. I did." Words escaped me, leaving me shaking my head. "I don't know."

He leaned with his elbows on his knees, like he had the weight of the mountains on his shoulders. "I thought you respected me more than that."

"I respect you more than anyone, Riley." I did. He had to believe that.

He shook his head. "I find that hard to believe."

"I do, Riley. I messed up. I really did. Just for the record, I never cheated on you, though. Never. The Indian dignitary . . . he was . . . " Where did I start? I had no idea. Instead, I ran a hand through my hair, unable to face the mess I'd made. "It's hard to explain."

His eyes—wide and hurt—met mine. "You could have told me about your job, you know. That wouldn't have changed anything."

"I know." And I did know that now. I knew it with absolute clarity. At the time, it had seemed so hazy, though. Looking back, maybe I'd purposely avoided the subject. Maybe I'd wanted to wait until after this trip so I could hold on to my new title for just a little while longer.

He suddenly straightened and pointed to my hand. "Where's your ring?"

I gasped when I saw my bare finger. "It was here

earlier." When had I seen it last? I'd had it when I left for my ATV excursion. "It must have come off when I almost fell down the mountainside." I wanted to throw up. Seriously. "I'm so sorry, Riley. I'll find it. I promise."

He let out a little grunt and stood. He remained silent a moment, and I couldn't stand not knowing what he was thinking. I wanted him to take my hand and tell me he forgave me. Instead, he shook his head. "I just need some time."

My heart dropped. "Some time?"

"Yeah, some time."

He half-waved and walked away. The burden on his shoulders seemed to grow from Appalachian proportions to the size of the Rockies.

And I'd caused that heaviness to press down upon him.

Maybe I had been right. Maybe I was no good at relationships. I'd prayed that I would change, that I would turn over a new leaf. But maybe turning over new leaves was just some kind of fantasy. Maybe relationship failure was just in my blood, passed down from generation to generation.

I felt like I'd just failed some major test of my faith. I'd prayed that God would wash me clean. He had, but I'd gone out and wallowed in the mud.

Was there any hope for me?

I pulled my knees to my chest and leaned against the gazebo. Alone.

Just like I'd always known I was destined to be.

I couldn't stand the thought of going back to my room and possibly running into Riley's friends along the way, not to mention seeing Veronica in our suite. Instead, I collapsed into one of the rocking chairs along the front of the resort. The night sparkled around me, but instead of being filled with wonder, the blackness seemed ominous, a foreshadowing of what was to come with my so-called reformed life.

I'd always been a bit of a screw up. Why did I think things would change?

I sucked on my lip for a moment, trying to keep my tears from spilling over.

I shouldn't have put off the inevitable. I'd known Riley would want to know about my job and my inability to keep my nose out of other people's business. I'd avoided the subject, rationalized that we'd had no time to talk, insisted to myself that it was better if his friends didn't know the truth. Was I ever wrong . . . again.

I closed my eyes, the exhaustion of not getting much sleep over the past couple of nights catching up with me. Not to mention that my head ached, throbbing right behind my eyes as I tried to hold off any moisture that wanted to push out.

How was I going to make things right?

Or the even bigger question . . . what if I couldn't?

CHAPTER 26

"Ma'am?"

I jerked upright and searched for the source of the voice. My eyes darted around me. Darkness. A chilly breeze. An eerie calmness. Rocking chairs.

I blinked again until a man in a suit came into view. A gray suit, double-breasted, lined in burgundy.

A valet.

My gaze traveled to his nametag. Bill.

I ran a hand over my face and pushed myself up even farther. "I fell asleep."

"I noticed. I was going to let you sleep, but you almost tumbled head first out of the chair two different times. I didn't want you to get hurt. Plus, the storm's getting closer."

I nodded, raking a hand through my curls just as a big fat raindrop hit my cheek. "What time is it anyway?"

"Almost two a.m."

I stood and wobbled as I tried to find my balance. A heavy haze from my sleep still hung over me, making me unsteady. My eyes felt swollen, almost like I'd been crying, even though I hadn't been—unless I'd done so in my sleep.

"Rough night?"

"You could say that." Everything hit me, each remembrance coming at me like a bullet from a machine gun. I closed my eyes, wishing I could shut out the thoughts. I couldn't.

"Where you from?"

I opened my eyes just as another drop of rain splattered on my arm. "Norfolk."

Bill nodded. "Nice area with all the military around—patriotic and all, you know? Not to mention the beach and the ports."

I cast a sharp glance his way. "Most people don't necessarily drool over the area because of the ports, but to each his own, I suppose."

He chuckled. "My cousin works out there, so I always think of the ports when I think of Norfolk. One of the largest ports on the East Coast. That's what he always tells me, with a lot of pride at that."

"I've never really thought about it, but you're probably right." I got a better look at the man. He was on the shorter side, heavy set, and had blond hair that was shaved close. His round face made him look heavier than he actually was, and maybe even older. I guessed him to be somewhere in his late thirties to early forties. "You from this area?"

He shrugged. "From Roanoke, not too far away."

I shivered from the chilly breeze, but immediately thought of Jackie. My shakes intensified as I remembered looking at her lifeless body. My job as a crime scene cleaner meant I worked with the aftermath after the body had been taken away already. Seeing dead bodies . . . that could shake anyone up.

The snoop inside just wouldn't die. I supposed being nosy was just like breathing to me. I just *had to* fish for more information. Besides, if Riley and I broke up—the thought caused something hard and sharp to lodge in my chest—snooping would be all I had left.

That's why I found myself saying, "This area seems so peaceful and safe, but I heard about that girl they found dead on the trail."

He shrugged. "It's still safe. I'm sure she just fell. That's why you should never hike alone. There's no one to get help for you if you need it."

"Are you sure it was an accident?"

He cocked his head. "Did you hear otherwise?" Of course the hotel wouldn't want people to know the truth. It would make them look bad.

"I heard she was murdered."

One of his shoulders popped up. "Don't believe all the tales you hear. This area is truly one of the safest around. I don't even lock my doors at night. That's how safe I feel."

I nodded. "That's good to know."

I said goodbye and wandered back inside. Who had Clint said I should investigate? Doug Matthews, an associate of Jackie's who was here this week, as well as Derek "Playboy" Waters. Both had known Jackie was going on a hike, both were here, and both had some type of disagreement with Jackie in the past.

I had no idea what Doug looked like, so I decided to leave him a message at the front desk. I asked him to meet me before breakfast down here in the lobby and that I was a friend of Jackie's.

I suddenly got a second wind, so I decided to wander down to the wing where Deanna usually worked. I needed a friend. Deanna was the closest thing I had right now.

I remembered the masked man I'd seen last time I was down this way and shivered.

Just because things looked perfect on the outside didn't mean they were. This hotel was a case in point. Something was going on here, something secret and sinister. Riley's friends were Exhibit B on my list. By the world's standards, they had everything. In reality, they each seemed to be hiding something.

As I walked down the hallway, I saw no sign of Deanna. No carts. No piney scents. No one mumbling, "I could get in so much trouble for this."

My throat went dry when I spotted the elevator leading down to the breezeway where I'd seen the masked man last time. Did I dare?

I knew one thing: If I traveled down to the lower level, I wasn't taking the elevator. I'd take the stairs.

With this whole area being under construction, I doubted very many people came down this way. Why would they? What had Deanna told me? That beyond this wing, there was only an old maintenance shed that wasn't used anymore and miles and miles of woods?

Why had that masked man been down here, then?

I took each step slowly, carefully, trying not to make a sound. My throat felt dry and tight. I tried to ignore the tremble in my hand as it found the railing so I could steady myself.

This was not a good idea. When had that ever stopped me before, though?

I reached the landing and stared at the door that would lead to the breezeway. Maybe I'd just take a peek. I wouldn't do anything foolish or to put myself in danger. I could do this.

Slowly, I pushed the door open, praying it wouldn't creak. It didn't. I stuck my head out, just enough to peer both ways.

Nothing.

I held my breath as I stepped out. I stood there a moment, listening for something, a sign that someone else was down here. All I heard was silence.

As I glanced at the plastic covering a couple of windows and the caution tape over a nearby doorway, I reminded myself that this was a construction site. Clint worked in construction. Was that just a coincidence? Perhaps he'd told one of his friends about how rich Jackie was, and they'd betrayed him. Come here to Allendale. Pretended to be working down here, all the while plotting on how to get Jackie's money.

I shook my head. I didn't think so. I had to keep my mind open to all possibilities, though.

I crept forward, and the breezeway came into view. My skin crawled just looking at it. I stayed close to the wall and crept toward a nearby window. I snuck a glimpse out of it.

Outside, I mostly saw the darkness. Beyond the well-manicured lawn surrounding Allendale stood the forest, mighty and strong. Just beyond that, I caught a glimpse of the old maintenance shed. I wondered why it was no longer used. What had Deanna said? Something about a fire several years ago and that as soon as they finished renovating this wing, they'd tear that old one down.

I watched for movement, for a sign of something outside. But I saw nothing. Only the wind swaying the tree branches. Thunder suddenly rattled the building, including the eerie breezeway. The glass panes seemed to clatter together at the booming sound.

As lightning lit the sky, I expected to see a figure appear down the hallway. There was nothing, no one.

I turned to walk away, and my foot hit a piece of the plastic. The rumpling sound made my blood freeze.

I stopped, as still as a statue, and listened. Still nothing.

Or was that a thump?

My heart pounded in my ears. Maybe I was just hearing my own heartbeat.

My lungs tightened. That was it. It was my heart thumping. Nothing else.

Another sound hit my ears. That wasn't my heart this time. Someone was on the other end of the breezeway.

As lightning lit the sky again, something beneath the plastic caught my eye. I scooped down and picked up a small metal plate with some numbers engraved on it. The top of the piece was broken off.

What could this be? I didn't know if it was a clue or not, but I stuck it in my pocket, opened the door to the stairway, and slipped inside.

As soon as the door closed, I ran for my life back to the main floor, not stopping until I reached my room.

CHAPTER 27

I'd snuck into my room last night and fallen into bed. I'd gotten maybe four hours of sleep before my alarm went off. The loud, echoing thunder outside hadn't helped, but the smattering of rain against my window did.

I didn't know how Deanna did this every day. My body was crying out for rest. Maybe I'd come back after everyone else was at the conference and take a nap. It could only help me to think more clearly.

I quickly took a shower and threw on the nautical outfit. I was going to have to go shopping again. I couldn't ask housekeeping to keep washing these two outfits over and over each day. The thought of buying any more clothes here pained me, however. What I wouldn't do for a mall to be nearby. I'd even take a thrift store to the shops they had here.

Thoughts of Riley and Jackie slammed into my mind. Anxiety began to ricochet through my gut. Would Riley seek me out today? Would he want to talk? Or did he need space?

Would he avoid me if I ran into him? I couldn't stand the thought of that. But I'd told him I would give him some room, no matter how painful that might be.

I was sure Veronica had to feel really proud of herself. I took full responsibility for my actions, but Veronica had been looking for something—anything—to be the damning piece of evidence that sealed my fate. Certainly she didn't want Riley back. I mean, she had Lane. So what was up with that? Was the woman simply vindictive? She'd even gone as far as to lie about her and Riley's break up.

I ran a finger under my eyes. Maybe I should splurge and go down to the spa. Maybe they could help freshen me up a bit.

I sighed and grabbed my purse. I had to run and see if Doug was going to meet with me this morning. Before I stepped into the hallway, my phone rang. I paused and glanced at the number. I didn't recognize the area code.

Hesitantly—and against my better judgment, most likely—I put the phone to my ear. "This is Gabby."

"Ms. St. Claire? Gabby St. Claire?"

My spine muscles pinched. If I weren't in so much trouble all the time, maybe I wouldn't be gripped with worry every time I got a call like this. "Speaking."

"This is Sue Smith. I work for the Medical Examiner here in Kansas City."

My spine went from pinched to ramrod straight. "Yes, Ms. Smith. What can I do for you?"

"We got your application, and I wanted to let you know that we'd like to do a job interview with you. We've narrowed down our selection to just two people. You're one of them."

I blinked, dumbfounded. I'd applied for the job on a whim, not thinking I'd ever hear anything about it. It had happened on that first day when I'd found out I was being let go from my previously held position.

"Are you still there?"

I rattled my head back and forth. "Yes, I'm here. Thank you for calling."

"We were very impressed by your credentials and by your endorsements. We'd like to set up a time for a Skype interview. Maybe next week? Wednesday is the exact date we're looking at."

"Wednesday sounds wonderful."

She offered a few more details, and we hung up.

I stood there, still dumbfounded. Kansas City? Could I really move across the country? Did I even want to? Where would that leave Riley and me?

I shook my head. I couldn't think about it now. I had to go meet Doug. Just as I stepped into the hallway, I heard Veronica's bedroom door open. Thank goodness I was gone before she emerged. I really didn't want to talk with that woman. In fact, if I had a car, I might toy with the idea of packing up and leaving. But I didn't have a car, and Jackie's murder still hung over my head. I hated leaving things unfinished.

I hurried downstairs and to the library.

Please be here.

To my surprise, someone was in the room. A tall man with broad shoulders and a round stomach paced there, jingling some change in his pockets as he walked. He stopped when he saw me walk in.

"Gabby?"

I nodded and extended my hand. "That's me."

"I'm Doug. What's this meeting about?"

His directness made me pause for a moment. I had to make sure I handled our talk correctly, or my gut told me this no-nonsense lawyer was going to walk away. "I was the one who found Jackie yesterday."

He nodded. "Okay. What does that have to do with

me?"

"I've been asked to look into her death."

"What are your credentials?"

I wanted to say *Is that any of your business?* Instead, I said, "I worked for the medical examiner, but I'm on my own now."

He stared at me, as if uncertain of my level of trustworthiness. Finally, he nodded slowly. "What can I do for you?"

"Jackie was your colleague, correct?"

He nodded. "That's correct. We worked together at the D.A.'s office down in Atlanta. As soon as her death is ruled a homicide, I'm sure the feds will get involved. The death of an assistant D.A. is never taken lightly, even if the boyfriend has already been arrested."

"Had any threats been made against her?"

"I'm not at liberty to discuss that."

"How about you then? Did you have any reason to be upset with her?"

He let out a quick burst of air and then did a half-chuckle, half-coughing thing. "Me? What exactly are you implying?"

"I'm not directly implying anything. I'm just saying that I heard the two of you didn't always see eye to eye."

"How in tarnation did you hear that?"

I shrugged. "Look, it's like this. There are only a limited number of people who could have known who she was and that she was here at Allendale this week. You just happened to be here, know that she was going on a hike, and you could possibly even have motive."

He shook his head, his finger waving across the air. "I don't know who you're talking to, but that is just plain ludicrous. Besides, all the evidence points to the boyfriend. He even admitted to writing that ransom note, last I heard."

"Did Jackie reject you for a construction worker? Is that why you had a problem with her?"

"Jackie? Me?" His voice climbed a few notches. "You're off your rocker. No, I'm happily married. I was never interested in Jackie."

"Then what did you have against her?"

He stopped and blew out a breath through his nose. Finally, he looked at me again. "You want to know the truth? Because I have a feeling you're not going to stop asking questions until you get it, are you?"

"You know me well, especially when considering you don't really know me at all."

"It's like this. Jackie was blowing it. Big time. She wasn't cut out to be a D.A."

"How'd she get a job doing it then?"

He pulled back his lips and shook his head. "Easy. Her mom. Her mom has a lot of money. There's power in money. She has friends in high places and pulled strings for her in order for her daughter to get a job. I don't know exactly. I just know Jackie wasn't hired on merit."

"How exactly was she so bad?"

"She just made stupid choices. She didn't think things through. We were in the middle of this huge investigation that involved an auto theft ring. Customs and Border Patrol, the FBI, and other agencies were involved and had been gathering evidence for almost two years. She almost blew it for us by letting some information leak that would have ruined everything."

"That's what your disagreement was about?"

"Absolutely. I was the one who walked in on her trying to cut a deal with someone who was in no way trustworthy. He would have gone back and told all of his friends the low down. Jackie didn't take very kindly to my reprimand."

"Did she ruin everything?"

Doug shook his head. "No, thank goodness I got to her in time. She still hadn't forgiven me, though. She thought I purposely embarrassed her because I wanted to get her fired."

"Didn't you?"

He sighed again. "Not really. I just didn't think she was competent. I was hoping she might leave on her own. She only ended up making more work for the rest of us. I can't be sure, but I don't think she ever really wanted to be a lawyer anyway. I honestly think she would have been happy just as a stay-at-home mom."

I nodded. I couldn't say that I thought this man was a killer. He may have been a terrible co-worker and an arrogant attorney, but nothing gave an indication that he had murder in his eyes. "Is there anything else you might be able to add that would help?"

He shifted and crossed his arms. "Why are you convinced that her boyfriend isn't behind this?"

"Nothing concrete, just a gut feeling."

He stared at me another moment before bobbing his head up and down. "I wish I could help. I really do. The last thing I wanted to hear was that she was dead. But I don't know what else to tell you. I'd find it hard to believe that anyone from Georgia would have followed her here and concocted this scheme."

He had a point.

He nodded toward the door. "I've got to grab some breakfast before the conference starts. Sorry I can't be of more help."

He wasn't the only one who was sorry about that, I thought.

***

After Doug left the library, I sank back into the couch. Well, I sank about as much as someone can sink into something that felt like it was made of upholstered concrete. Where did this leave me now?

My thoughts wandered to Riley. Was he eating breakfast now? I glanced at my watch. No, he should be on his way to his conference. My heart pounded harder at the thought. This trip was supposed to bring us closer together, not pull us apart.

I sighed and reached into my pocket. I pulled out the metal plate I'd found last night. Upon closer inspection, it looked like part of it had been broken off. But seventeen numbers remained.

What could they be? It was too long to be a phone number or a social security number. It almost seemed like some type of serial number.

It had probably just fallen off some of the supplies they used during the construction downstairs, I realized. Despite that, I wasn't ready to give this up. I wanted to think on it a while longer, just in case.

I stood and stretched. I'd grab some breakfast and figure out what to do for the rest of the day.

As soon as I stepped into the lobby, I spotted Carol Harrington. My heart thudded in my chest. What that woman must be going through.

I'd intended on stopping by to check on her last night, but then all the chaos with Riley had broken out.

When she saw me, she stepped forward. I hurried to meet her and gave her a quick hug. She sniffled in my arms.

"I heard you found her."

I nodded. "I'm so sorry. This wasn't the outcome I

wanted."

"None of us wanted this. This just goes to prove why you shouldn't get mixed up with the wrong people. If Jacqueline had never met Clint . . . " Mrs. Harrington shook her head. "If only I could turn back time and try to convince her to stay away from that man."

"It might have only driven her further into his arms. Love sometimes works like that."

She nodded. "I suppose you're right."

Just then, I noticed the suitcase at her feet. "You're leaving?"

"I'd rather grieve in the comfort of my own home. This place . . . it's now shrouded with bad memories." She shook her head and a little gasp escaped. "My life will never be the same, you know."

"I'm so sorry." I wished there was something else I could tell her, but I had nothing.

"Keep searching for answers, Gabby."

I shifted my weight from one foot to the other. "Really?"

She nodded. "You're the one who found her body, not the police. You're the one who's going to be able to get to the bottom of this. I'll have no peace until I know Jacqueline has justice. I want evidence that will put the final nail into Clint's coffin."

"And if it's not Clint?"

"Justice, Gabby. I want justice."

Her shoes clicked against the floor as she went out to her car.

CHAPTER 28

A plate with a steaming ham and cheese omelet, freshly diced hash browns, and a piece of watermelon sat in front of me. Any other day, this breakfast would have my mouth watering. But not today. Today, I had no appetite.

Troubled relationships could do that to a person.

Normally, when a relationship went south, I just let it go. I wasn't used to fighting for people in my life. I could fight for issues and fight for justice and fight to solve other people's problems. But there was this part of me that still hung on to the idea that I was damaged goods. There was still a part of me that was convinced that I was destined to mess up every relationship, even my relationship with God, for that matter.

I sighed and lifted my coffee mug. The server had somehow skipped over filling my upturned cup again, so I'd gotten my own, something I was getting quite good at. Of course, I'd always been good at doing things for myself. I'd learned early on not to sit around and wait for things to happen; if I wanted something in my life then I was the one who'd have to make the effort to obtain it.

"May I join you?"

I looked up and saw Ajay standing there, looking

like a true dignitary with his sash around his waist and white suit on. I pushed myself up straighter in my chair and nodded. "Please do."

"I generally eat alone, but I thought it might be nice to have some company after our ordeal yesterday." He settled across from me, raised his cup, and a server instantly appeared.

I scowled at the attentive waitress as she poured the coffee. You could put a girl in a fancy resort, but that definitely didn't make the girl fancy. I was okay with that, though. I just wanted to be me, warts and all. Apparently, I had a lot of warts.

"You look downcast this morning." Ajay stirred his coffee. "Our discovery yesterday has you shaken?"

I shrugged. "Maybe a little. Truthfully, I got into a fight with my fiancé."

"I am sorry to hear that."

"Thanks. Me, too. But I wasn't upfront with him about a couple of things, so it's my fault. I just don't know how to make it right."

"Miss St. Claire, true love always conquers all. If he does not see how wonderful you are, then he is not for you, nor is he your true love."

Love always forgives, always protects, always trusts, always hopes. Love never fails. The Bible verse floated through my mind. Was I even capable of finding that kind of love? I had my doubts.

"I appreciate the advice, Ajay. I do."

"My wife was my one true love. There will never be anyone else like her. I would do anything to have one more day with her."

My throat tightened with emotion. "What happened?"

"A tragic car accident." He shook his head. "I was

supposed to be here for her. But I just had to work a little more and then I would join her." His eyes met mine. "If I had been here, she might still be alive." He pulled out his necklace, the one with the sun on the end. "She gave this to me.

"I'm sorry, Ajay. You said here. Was her accident in the States?"

"Right here at Allendale. I do not know why she did not hire a driver or take the shuttle, in the very least. Both were at her disposal. But she decided to drive at night down that mountain road. A truck ran her car off the mountain."

"That's awful. How long has it been?"

He grimaced. "Three years. I kept trying to get over my loss back in my home country, but I could not. I thought maybe if I came here, I could finally get some closure."

"Is it working?"

His lips pulled back in a line. "I wish I could say yes, but I cannot. Losing a loved one leaves a hole in your heart. I am not sure I want to fill it."

"I pray that you'll find peace."

A hint of a smile tugged at his lips. "I pray the same for you as well."

I set my coffee cup back down and stabbed one of my potatoes, not wanting to waste this meal that cost more than I wanted to think about. "What's on your agenda for today?"

The waitress set a plate of fruit in front of him. I didn't recall him ordering and wondered if he got the same thing every morning. As she stepped back, I saw a familiar face in the distance. Deanna. She gestured wildly to get my attention. Her face clearly showed she was elated that I was talking with Ajay.

He looked over his shoulder, following my gaze. As soon as he turned, Deanna stopped motioning and leaned against the wall, looking off into the distance. "Everything okay?"

"Just fine. Sorry. I thought I saw someone." I tried to keep my eyes off of Deanna, but she began gesturing again. "Let's see. You asked about my agenda? I was actually thinking about going back to that overlook today. I'm desperate to find my ring."

"Going out in the woods alone like that is not a good idea. Not to be a joy kill."

"A kill joy." I corrected with a smile. "And I know it's not smart, but I've got to find it, and the one person who might go with me apparently isn't speaking to me at the moment."

"How would you feel if I joined you?"

I blinked. "Really? You want to go out on an ATV?"

He shrugged. "Having some company would be refreshing, even if I understand that you are taken."

Relief filled me. Good. He didn't think this friendship was anything more. Now, if only I could convince Riley of that. What a Catch 22. To prove that I was taking our relationship seriously, I had to find my ring. To find my ring, however, I had to go into the woods with a handsome, single man who wasn't my fiancé.

I mentally shrugged. If Riley spoke to me again, I'd explain everything to him. No keeping secrets. But until he had his "space" then I had no choice but to explain later.

"That sounds great, Ajay."

Deanna motioned in the background, jumping up and down now. I put my napkin on the table. "Could you excuse me for a moment?"

"Of course."

I slipped across the room toward Deanna, promptly

giving her a scowl. "What are you doing?"

"You're eating. With him. The man of my dreams."

"We're just chatting."

Her eyes widened. "About what?"

I wasn't sure if she was hoping I would say "about her" or what she was thinking. I went with the truth. "We're going for an ATV ride."

She squealed. "I want to go! Please, let me go!"

"Really?"

She nodded. "It would be like a dream come true."

"One condition." I remembered her whole, *I'll scratch your back if you scratch mine.* Maybe this would be a good time to employ that method of reasoning.

"Anything."

"I need to meet with a few of your colleagues."

Her head jerked back. "My colleagues? You mean the other maids?"

I nodded. So much for trying to sound refined. "Yes, the other maids."

"About what."

I leaned closer. "It's a long story . . . I'll explain later."

***

Nobody puts Gabby in the corner. That's what I kept telling myself, at least.

Thirty minutes later, I had finished picking at my breakfast, changed into my tennis shoes, and taken the shuttle from the resort into the town that cozied up beside the place.

I paused in front of the shop where I had rented the ATV. Down the road, I spotted Buck's Garage. A familiar figure stepped out the front door. Who was that man? Where had I seen him before?

I snapped my fingers. The valet. Bill. The one who'd spoken with me last night. He looked different without his uniform on. What was he doing in the shop?

I shrugged it off. There was nothing illegal about him being there. Even valets had to have their cars worked on, for goodness sakes. Now that I thought about it, he was the same person I'd seen leaving the shop when I was here before. Maybe he had a friend who worked there.

I pushed open the door to the rental shop and spotted Ajay there. He'd traded his "dignitary wear" for jeans and golf shirt again. "Nice look. I meant to tell you that yesterday, but I got distracted by my near death experience."

He looked down and smiled. "Thank you. I feel underdressed."

"Look, I was wondering if it would be okay if my friend joined us. She's been wanting to explore the mountains, and then she heard I was going today."

He offered a slight bow again. "Of course. That is fine. What is the saying? The more, the merrier."

I grinned. "Perfect. She should be here any time now."

We were filling out the paperwork when the door opened again, and Deanna stepped inside. I had to blink twice. Her makeup looked perfect. Her hair had been straightened. Her clothes practically looked new. How had she transformed herself like that in thirty minutes? The woman was a miracle worker.

"Ajay, this is Deanna," I introduced them.

Deanna reached her hand forward. "It's a pleasure."

He did his little bowing thing. "No, the pleasure is mine." He tilted his head and squinted at Deanna. "Do I know you?"

She shook her head, a bit of a sparkle in her eyes. "I don't think so. I think I just have one of those faces. I get that a lot."

He nodded, satisfied with her answer. A few minutes later, everything was complete. I'd rented a metal detector and strapped it to the back of the four-wheeler. I'd also purchased an overpriced book bag down in one of the shops at Allendale and had found some cheap rope at a General Store that I put inside, along with some water, peanuts, and my cell phone.

I cranked my engine. I was pretty sure I remembered the route back to the overlook.

I was going to find my engagement ring, one way or another.

I zoomed to the front of the pack. There was no chatting over the roar of these ATVs, so I didn't bother to try and be polite. Instead, I climbed and climbed and climbed the mountain. The moisture from last night's storm made the path a little more slippery than it had been yesterday. A couple of times my wheels slid before finding traction again, making my heart speed with adrenaline.

Finally, the overlook came into view. I motioned toward it, and Ajay nodded behind me. We pulled the ATVs up to a clear patch of land and tugged off our helmets. I glanced back at Deanna as she pulled hers off and couldn't help but grin when she shook her hair out like one might see on a movie.

I was going to miss that lady when I left the resort in a couple of days. If Riley's car was ready in time.

And if Riley would still let me ride with him.

There were too many variables in there for my comfort.

I was going to make this right—starting by finding my engagement ring. I walked to the edge of the boulder and looked down. Just as had happened last time, my stomach clenched as the drop soared downward. It would be a long, steep fall to the bottom. "That's where I lost it. It has to be."

Ajay peered down behind me. "I must say, after that rain last night, I am not certain you will find it. What is that saying? It will be like a needle in a haystack?"

I couldn't argue with that. "I agree. But what other choice do I have?"

I glanced at the railing and the gigantic boulder. Shivers raced through me as I remembered Jackie's lifeless body. Police tape still marked off the area. I was going to have to go out to the left to avoid the crime scene area. My guess was that they'd collected all the evidence they could yesterday before the rains came.

I pulled the metal detector from the back of my vehicle and tossed Ajay the rope from my backpack. He looped it around a tree and tied it securely.

"Just in case," he explained.

I shoved the metal detector through my book bag. "Just in case," I explained.

I caught Deanna putting on some lipstick. "Just in case," she mouthed.

I hid my smile.

Ajay pointed to a path a few feet away. "It is not as steep there. It might be a good location to go down. We will have this rope to help us back up if we need it."

"Sounds great." Sounded like Ajay was a person who liked to think things through. As much as I hated to admit it, I needed people around me who helped me to think before jumping. I'd gotten myself into more than one pickle before by being rash. I thought Riley was the one who'd be the *ying* to my *yang*, the one who'd help balance me out.

My heart thudded in my chest.

Relationships never seemed to be easy for me. The happily ever after where someone swept me off my feet and I never looked back wasn't destined to be written as a part of my life story. But I also realized that I wasn't the type of person who wanted someone who'd kiss my feet and drool over my every word. I liked someone who challenged me, who got my blood boiling at times, who wasn't afraid to speak his mind around me. Those things made a relationship seem real.

Ajay started down first, insisting that I follow his footsteps. I gripped a tree branch and lowered myself onto a rock. It wasn't as unsteady as I'd feared it might be. I let out the breath I held.

Deanna brought up the rear, already slightly out of breath with sweat sprinkling across her forehead. That didn't stop a broad grin from stretching across her face every time she looked at Ajay.

Deanna and Ajay talked back and forth about India and Tandoori chicken and the number of factory jobs the U.S. had outsourced to his country. My mind went to Riley.

Our relationship had definitely had its ups and downs. I'd been attracted to him when he'd first moved into our apartment building, but then Veronica had shown up. Then I started dating a detective named Parker. We'd broken up, and Riley and I continued to build our friendship.

Finally, Riley and I had both been ready to take things to the next level. I'd almost blown it again when my past had pounded at my psyche so badly that I felt destined to fail at every relationship. I thought I'd moved past that issue, but maybe I hadn't. Maybe there were things that no amount of prayer would change. Maybe they were the thorns in our flesh, so to speak.

I shook my head. I wasn't sure I believed that, but I wasn't sure I didn't believe it either. I just knew that prayer wasn't some magical potion that made everything right in your life, nor was God a genie who granted your every wish. No, a relationship with God and prayer was more about changing you than it was about changing the circumstances around you.

I reached the bottom and tuned back into the conversation around me just in time to hear Deanna say something about how much she hated calling customer service numbers and speaking to people in India. I glanced back at Ajay and saw him squirm. He'd reached the bottom of the incline and found an area where the ground leveled off for a moment. He squatted and began moving some leaves out of the way.

I needed to do the same, but first I took in a deep breath. I glanced up at the mountains around me. I felt so small here, surrounded by the massive creation of God.

Faith could move mountains, the Bible said. I needed to have more faith in my life to believe that God's hand was in everything. He knew what the future held. I had to learn to trust Him more . . . I had to learn to trust Riley more, too, for that matter.

"Are you sure you lost it here?" Ajay stood and squinted against sunlight that snuck in between two trees.

I looked around at the vast wilderness around me and sighed. "It's the only place I can think of where it might have slipped off."

We continued to search. Deanna chattered, this time about white water rafting and mountain biking. I pulled out the metal detector and found some coins, some bottle tops, a couple of screws, but no engagement ring.

I kicked some more leaves to the side, feeling like this whole trip was hopeless. My ring was gone. Was this some kind of symbolism of my entire relationship with Riley? I had been crazy to think I could ever find it.

Something unusual caught my eye. I bent down and picked up a . . . business card?

"What did you find?" Ajay asked.

I read the words there. Derek Waters, Malpractice Attorney. A Glamour Shots version of his smiling mug stared at me.

What was his business card doing down here?

I closed my eyes as the worst-case scenarios began playing out in my mind.

This wasn't good. It wasn't good at all.

The only reason Derek's business card would be here was if . . . Derek had also been here. If Derek had been here, that meant he had some kind of secret of his own, one that possibly had to do with Jackie's death.

CHAPTER 29

Two hours later, we'd given up on our search, returned our ATVs, and headed back to the hotel. Ajay had thanked us for our company and then scurried off.

Derek's business card burned in my pocket. I had to figure out how to best approach this subject and what exactly to do with the evidence. I was walking a tight rope here, and I had to handle this situation carefully, lest I fall to my death in front of a crowd of cheering onlookers.

That's why I was glad I'd had Deanna do a little favor for me earlier. I was even gladder that it was time for my meeting to begin. Deanna led me upstairs and into one of the closets where the maids kept their supplies. It was bigger than I thought, which was good considering there were already four other women in there.

"Everyone, this is the woman I've been telling you about. Gabby St. Claire," Deanna introduced me. "Because of her, I was able to go hiking today with Mr. Super Hot, which I found out today there's an Indian word for 'good morning' that's 'suprahaat.' Kind of sounds like 'super hot,' huh?"

I waved hello, feeling for a moment like I was in a closet AA meeting.

I glanced at the circle of ladies around me. I recognized Shirley, and I was pretty sure the woman who cleaned my room was here too, but there were also three others I didn't know.

"Thanks for meeting with me. I know you all have jobs to do, so I appreciate your time," I started. I tried to take a step back, but the space was too tight. I hit the wall instead.

Two carts had been pushed out into the hallway, and the place smelled like lemon and pine . . . and a little bit of B.O.

I remained focused. "I'm investigating the death of Jackie Harrington."

Shirley's hand went to her heart. "That woman who was found dead?"

I nodded. "That's right."

"I heard her boyfriend did it," another woman said.

"There's evidence that he may have been set up," I said. "He did do some unscrupulous things, but I don't believe he killed her."

"Who did then?" Deanna asked.

"That's where I need your help. You're all the eyes and the ears of this hotel. Did any of you see anything strange going on here recently? It may seem minor, but that's okay. Anything could help."

Everyone took turns glancing at each other. Finally, a skinny woman with dirty blonde hair spoke up. "The management has been coming down hard on us lately."

"About what?"

"We have to maintain the image of a luxurious, safe hotel." The woman shrugged. "I guess there have been too many mistakes lately. The manager's not happy."

"You mean Bentley Allen?" I could picture him clearly in my mind from my brief encounters with him.

"What kind of mistakes?"

The maids looked at each other again. Finally, the dirty blonde spoke again. "It varies, really. I mean, we've had a couple of cars stolen from the parking lot. That never looks good. Then Maurice—the bellhop—died in that kayaking accident. A couple of the valets quit."

"Those are all unrelated, right?" I asked, not putting anything together.

"Most likely. I mean, I don't see how they're connected, other than making us look bad," Deanna said. "Image is everything here, if you haven't noticed. It was a big snafu when the valets quit because it left us shorthanded. It's not that easy to fill positions out here in the middle of nowhere."

I nodded, trying to absorb the information and what it might mean for my investigation. Finally, I reached into my pocket and pulled out Derek's business card. I held it up and showed the group Derek's picture. "Have any of you seen him?"

The dirty blonde snorted. "He makes himself known."

I tilted my head. "What do you mean?"

"He hits on everyone with an X chromosome," Deanna said, shaking her head. "He's the talk of the hotel."

Interesting. "Did any of you see him talking to the woman who died?"

Shirley raised her hand. "I did. It's funny that you asked because I haven't thought about it since then." She stopped talking and stared at me with her hand raised, as if waiting for permission to continue.

"You definitely don't have to raise your hand. Please, share."

She leaned closer. "I accidentally walked in on them arguing. They didn't put the 'Do Not Disturb' sign on their door, so I went into his room to clean. Whatever they were talking about, it was heated. I started to leave, but they both got quiet and told me to go ahead."

"Did you hear anything they were talking about?" I asked.

Shirley shook her head. "Not really. But I did see something while I was cleaning."

I leaned closer this time, waiting with bated breath. "Okay . . . ?"

She looked from side to side. "It was a contract with Jackie Harrington's name on it. It had the name of a law firm at the top."

"What kind of contract?"

Shirley shrugged. "It had a whole bunch of numbers on it. And it wasn't signed. It was from Waters and Associates? Does that ring a bell?"

I leaned back and let the information sink in. Did that have anything to do with Jackie's death? There were so many pieces floating out there. Certainly one or two of them had to connect.

"If any of you find out any more information and remember anything, please let me know. This woman deserves justice. Everyone does."

The group around me nodded.

I took a step back. "Thanks again, everyone. This really means a lot."

I opened the door and stepped out, nearly colliding with someone. I jerked my head up, an apology on my lips, until I spotted Derek . . . and Lane, Veronica, and Lillian. They all stared at me, occasionally glancing back at the maids who filed out behind me. The looks on their faces were a mix of curiosity, disgust, and amusement. I got that. We were like clowns fleeing a tiny car at the circus.

Only I wasn't supposed to be part of the act. But

the truth was, I fit in more with these ladies than I'd ever fit in with them.

I heaved in a deep breath. "Hi, guys."

Derek raised his chin in the air. "Gabby. If we'd realized you were so down on your luck that you'd been forced to stay in the maid's closet, I'm sure we could have all pitched in to get you another room."

I let out a mocking laugh. "Save it, Derek. Have any of you seen Riley?"

Lane shrugged. "Last time I saw him, he was in his room."

I pushed past the group, not afraid of their looks of pity. "Thanks."

Derek mumbled something, and everyone in the group laughed. I was sure his comment was about me. That's when I pulled out my wild card. I stopped and turned toward them. "And Derek?"

He glanced over his shoulder. "Yes?" He drew out the word a little too long with that smug little voice of his.

I held up his business card. "Did you lose something?"

His face went pale. "Where'd you get that?"

"I found it not far from where Jackie died."

He stepped closer and held out his hand. "Strange. I'll take it."

I pulled it back and shook my head. "Not so fast. I'm taking this to the police first."

His lips parted ever so slightly. "Why would you do that?"

"It's evidence. Why don't you tell all of us where you were on the night Jackie died?"

His eyes narrowed. "Why don't you mind your own business?"

"This isn't about minding my own business. This is

about justice for Jackie."

"I'm going to report you," he growled.

"Go ahead." I smiled and turned.

Just as I took a step away, I heard him mumble, "You little . . . " Thankfully, I didn't hear the end of his sentence.

As soon as I rounded the corner, and I was sure that group couldn't see me anymore, I took off in a jog. I found the emergency stairway and raced up a flight. I reached Riley's room and pounded on the door. "Answer. Please!"

I waited, tapping my foot impatiently. I'd given the man almost twenty-four hours to think things through. Wasn't that enough?

I heard no movement inside, so I knocked again. Still nothing.

I sighed. Okay, I had to think things through. And right now that meant that I needed to call the police, just in case Derek made good on his threat to report me. I slipped into an area filled with vending machines and pulled out my cell phone. I dialed the number for the officer whom I talked to earlier. Officer Sharples.

He answered on the first ring, and I explained what I'd found. He promised to come out right away and told me I should meet him in the lobby.

My pulse was still racing as I hurried down the stairs. So many things could go wrong. So many things *had* gone wrong.

I had to turn this all around. The answers were getting closer. I could feel it.

I paced across the marble floor, the business card still burning in my back pocket. I had to believe that things would turn out for the best. I had to. Otherwise, I'd lose my mind with anxiety.

I glanced across the room, feeling someone watching me. Finally, I found the source.

Lane.

He was at the courtesy phone.

As soon as we made eye contact, he hung up and hurried away. I started to go after him, when someone called my name.

"Miss St. Claire?"

I stopped pacing as I saw Bentley Allen staring at me. "Yes?"

He pulled his lips in a tight line before saying, "May I have a word with you?" Each of his words was crisp and sharp.

They left a bad feeling in my gut. I shoved my hands down into my pockets. "About?"

His nostrils flared as he leered at me. "I'd rather discuss this in private."

Oh, no. I really hoped I hadn't gotten any of the staff in trouble. That was the last thing I wanted. "This is a bad time."

"It's urgent." He nodded behind him. I followed his gaze and saw a security officer standing there.

My eyes widened as the entirety of the situation began to sink in. What in the world was going on? I shook my head. "I'm waiting for the police. Can't you just tell me here?"

His scowl deepened. "We've had some complaints about you."

"About me?" I jabbed my finger into my chest as my voice rose at least an octave.

"That's correct. Apparently, you've been disturbing some of our guests."

At the word "guests," I narrowed my eyes. I could only guess that those "guests" were Derek, Lillian, Jack,

Lane, and Veronica. "If they have a problem with me, they can take it up with me. That's what real people do. They don't have other people do all of their dirty work . . . or wait on them hand and foot for that matter."

"Ma'am, can you please keep your voice down?"

My index finger shot out. It came out at the worse times and seemed to take on a mind of its own. Right now, my digit pointed at the hotel manager accusingly, wagging back and forth with more sass than a scorned Southern Belle. "You're the one who started this conversation."

He raised his chin, obviously taken back by the finger. "And I asked if we could do it in private for a reason."

My finger began wagging again. "Whatever someone has said against me, it's bogus."

His chin rose even higher. "Disorderly conduct. Running through the halls. Taking their things. Sneaking into rooms." His voice contained the lilt of someone who thought they were better than everyone else. I really hated that lilt.

My eyes widened as I moved beyond his snotty ways and focused on his words. Taking their things? What had I taken exactly? "That's ridiculous."

He cupped my elbow. "Miss St. Claire, we're going to have to ask you to leave Allendale Acres."

CHAPTER 30

My mouth gaped open, and I dug my heels into the floor. "Are you serious?"

He nodded. "Very serious. We can't have our guests unhappy."

I swatted his hand away from my arm. "I'm a guest here! Don't you care about my happiness?" People were starting to stare, but I didn't care.

"Please, lower your voice." If steam could come out of ears, the vapor would be pouring from Bentley Allen now. The man was seething, his face turning red, until finally he motioned the security guard. The man appeared on my other side. He was probably only twenty and built like a twig. I could take him if I had to.

As the security guard took my other arm, I shook my head. "I'm going to talk to my lawyer. This is discrimination." My lawyer? I knew about five of them here, but I doubted any of them would jump at the chance to be legal counsel for me. Not even Riley.

They began leading me to the stretch of front doors. "Ma'am, I can file formal charges against you for theft," Bentley said.

"I did not steal that business card. I found it, and

now I'm turning it in to the police. Besides, it's just a business card." Had the man lost his mind?

Bentley stopped. "What business card?" He blinked, as if the conversation had just taken an unexpected U-turn.

"Derek—" I stopped before I incriminated myself. I shook my head and ran a hand over my face as I bought time and gained my composure. "What are you talking about?"

Bentley actually sighed. I made people do that a lot. Like, *a lot* a lot. "A necklace that's worth half a million dollars was stolen from someone. He doesn't want to press charges, but he doesn't want anyone else to be deceived by your charms."

I glanced over at the man's office in the distance. I knew from all the time I spent wandering the facilities where it was located—right behind the check-in area.

Ajay stepped out and stared at me. Gone was his earlier friendliness.

Heaviness pressed on my chest as I tried to comprehend what was happening. "Ajay?" Dread filled me when I remembered his necklace. I'd just been asking him about it—totally innocently—and now it was gone. This was *not* looking good for me.

He stepped forward, a new solemnness about him. "I am sorry. I fell for your act. Now I realize that you are just a con artist."

Fire shot through my veins. "I'm not a con artist. I didn't steal anything."

He stared at me, suddenly looking less like Prince Charming and a lot more like a royal pain in the buttocks. "Are you saying you did not slip my keycard while we were out today and then use it to sneak into my room?"

"Of course I didn't do that." I didn't even have to

think about my words. They came out fast and adamant and passionate.

The manager shifted, that hungry gleam in his eyes again as he looked at me. "Then why did we find the necklace in your room?"

My mouth gaped wider. "I was set up, that's why! That's the only possible explanation."

Ajay shook his head. "I am sorry. I truly am. I do not want retribution. I only hope that others do not suffer from their choices as I have."

"You've got to believe me. I would never do something like that!"

Ajay only continued to stare at me.

Great. The screw up has struck again. The problem was that this time I didn't do anything.

Bentley spread his hand toward the door. "If you don't mind. I've already had your key card de-activated. We're going to have to ask you to leave."

I sighed and shrugged out of both the manager's and the security guard's grasp. I could do this gracefully. Now that I knew what the charges were that had been leveled against me, I had to accept the fact that I was being kicked out. "I don't have a car even."

The manager's eyebrows flickered upward. "I'm sure you'll figure out something." He gave me one last little shove.

I shook my head and stepped outside just as a police cruiser pulled up. I might as well throw myself inside and tell Officer Sharples to lock me up.

"Jailhouse Rock" wasn't my song of choice, however.

Besides, if I did that, someone would get his way, and I wasn't about to let that happen.

***

Two hours later, from the front seat of the police cruiser parked in front of the hotel, I'd turned in the business card and explained how I found it. I got a lecture about why I wasn't supposed to be at the scene, and then I explained how when I'd discovered Jackie's body, I'd lost my ring and how when I went back to look for it, I'd stayed away from the area that was taped off, etc., etc., etc.

I'd seen curtains fluttering from the hotel as guests had peered out, wondering exactly what was going on. I'm sure they were all more than glad that a troublemaker from the wrong side of the tracks was leaving their fine facility.

Only, at the end, I stepped out of the cruiser. I waved goodbye to Officer Sharples. He waved goodbye to Valet Bill behind me, and pulled away.

I ignored the curious look from Bill and grinned up at the hotel, just in case anyone was watching. I realized how absolutely psycho that seemed and stuffed my hands down into my pockets instead.

I glanced at the nighttime around me. What now? I'd been kicked out of the hotel. How was I going to break *that* one to Riley? What would he think when he found out about this mess I'd gotten myself into?

I pinched the skin between my eyes and pushed my head back. Every time I thought that things couldn't get worse, they did just that.

Now I was homeless, in the middle of nowhere, with almost no money left, no clothes, no fiancé, and no car.

"You okay?" Bill asked.

I shrugged. "Just peachy."

He stepped forward. "Listen, you don't want Mr.

Allen to catch you loitering around here."

I pointed toward the distance. "I think I'll just walk into town then."

That seemed to satisfy him because he nodded. I started walking, not necessarily to the town, though. I wouldn't go in the woods or anywhere too secluded. But maybe I'd just walk around the resort for a moment and clear my head. Maybe I could finally figure out a plan.

As a last option, maybe I'd call Sierra or Chad to see if they could pick me up. I could even call my brother, Tim, or my dad, if worst came to worst.

I walked past the pond where Riley and I had our talk last night. Crickets and frogs sang their evening song and some bugs buzzed by in the not-so-far distance. Humidity hadn't set in around here, and I was grateful for that, at least.

Guilt continued to pound at me as I remembered the disappointment in Riley's eyes. I had someone really great in my life, and I'd let him slip away.

I shook my head. I didn't want to feel sorry for myself, but it felt like all of my other emotions were drying up. Guilt and self-loathing . . . they were abundant. I just wished Riley understood me better. I wished he'd never asked me to make that promise.

I rounded the West Wing of the building. Inside, windows were lit with a warm glow. I could see silhouettes of people happily moving about, enjoying their lives and all the fine things that came with it. I shoved my hands deeper into my pockets.

In the distance, the pool area came into view. It wasn't just any pool area. There were five pools, some with slides, others with jet sprays, some with sprinklers. Everything you could imagine. Right now, the area was dark and the lifeguards had gone home.

I walked between some lounge chairs. I wondered if I'd be caught if I slept here tonight? I wasn't tired right now, so it didn't matter. I just kept wandering.

My phone buzzed in my pocket. I pulled it out and saw a text message.

From Riley! My pulse quickened.

Where are you? I've been looking for you all day.

My heart soared and then immediately crashed. Looking for me with good news or bad? I couldn't be sure.

I texted him back that I was down by the pool.

My throat tightened again. I prayed that our meeting would be good. I prayed that this mountain of a misunderstanding between us could be moved.

All things worked together for good in Christ, right? That's what I believed. So I had to believe that all of this would turn out the way it was supposed to. Sometimes, when things turned out the way they were supposed to, that didn't mean they turned out my way. The thought made my heart ache, though I believed in the truth of the words.

I paused as I spotted that breezeway in the distance and the area under construction beyond that. I wasn't going any closer. No way.

I heard a footfall behind me and turned, fully expecting to see Riley.

Instead, a gloved hand covered my mouth.

CHAPTER 31

"You couldn't leave well enough alone, could you?" someone growled in my ear.

I struggled against my captor, desperate to get away.

He tried to move me forward, but I dug my heels into the concrete. I was not going with this man. I was certain I wouldn't come back alive, if I did.

My captor was broad and solid. He easily lifted me off my feet and carried me away from the safety of the hotel and toward the endless woods surrounding it.

I thrashed back and forth. I kicked. I tried to scream. Nothing worked.

"Put her down!" someone yelled behind us.

I'd know that voice anywhere. Riley.

The man paused. That's when I saw Riley's fist collide with my captor's nose. The man groaned, and his grip loosened enough for me to squirm away. But then he turned toward Riley, all bulk and beefy mass.

He charged toward Riley and tackled him. I screamed. I couldn't bear the thought of Riley being hurt at my expense. I ran toward the masked man and hopped on his back, desperate to stop him.

The masked man reared, trying to throw me off, but I held on tight. My distraction gave Riley enough time to stand and grab a beach umbrella from its stand nearby. The pole was made of iron, thick and heavy. Riley pulled it back and crashed it into the man's knees.

The man threw his arms behind him. I fell back, landing with a thud on the concrete. My head cracked and immediately pulsated with pain at the impact.

The thug grabbed the umbrella and charged at Riley again. Riley ducked, but the man turned at the last minute. The pole clocked Riley in the arm. He moaned.

Someone yelled in the distance. Security was coming.

The man spotted them and started to run. I grabbed the first thing I could find—a chair—and threw it in his path. The man fell headfirst onto the concrete. But, before security could reach him, he'd pulled himself back up and darted into the distance.

I turned over to check on Riley when my gaze skimmed the pool beside me. I let out a scream.

There was a man floating there, face up.

That man was Doug Matthews.

***

After the police, EMTs, and hotel staff disappeared, it was just Riley and I. We'd both been through the ringer with questions from everyone who'd arrived at the scene. Doug was dead. He'd only been dead for less than an hour, so I guess that cleared me from being a suspect.

The EMTs had treated Riley's cut, checked out my head, and given us all the warning signs that we might need further medical help.

Bentley had glared at me from across the crowd

the whole time. I'd successfully avoided him, and the police had kept him busy with lots of questions before finally leading him inside to check out the security footage. I guess the murder overshadowed his need to humiliate me publicly, at least for the moment.

Now that everyone else was gone, Riley looked at me, a depth of unreadable emotions in his eyes. My heart squeezed again. Those unreadable emotions seemed an awful lot like the ones he might have if he was breaking up with me.

Instead of saying anything, he took my elbow and led me inside.

"I can't go in here." I pointed toward the hotel.

He didn't slow down or miss a step. "What are you talking about?"

"They kicked me out." Scenes from that ugly confrontation flashed through my mind. Not one of my better moments.

Riley's voice rose in pitch. "Who kicked you out?"

"The manager. It's a long story."

One shoulder shrugged up. "I'll sneak you in the back way then."

Sneaking me into a place where I was forbidden just might be one of the most romantic things Riley had ever done for me. Too bad he was doing it right before he dropped the bombshell that we were breaking up.

He kept his hand on my elbow. Using his card, he opened a back door and took the emergency stairs all the way to his room. I stepped inside, trembling and nauseous and feeling washed up. What a night. What a trip, for that matter.

Riley locked the doors and stepped back. His gaze was heavy, burdened. I wished I could come up with a cleaning solution to wash away people's pain. I'd be a millionaire if I could.

My gaze perused the room and came to a stop on . . . Veronica?

She sat on the couch, a look of alarm in her eyes as she sat up straighter. Why had she been sitting alone in the dark?

My eyes zeroed in on the low cut blouse she wore, as well as the bright pink lipstick. Her hair cascaded down her shoulders, and she had a goblet of wine in hand.

"Where's Lane?" Riley asked. He looked equally as confused by her presence.

She pulled a hair behind her ear. "He's . . . um . . . he's asleep."

Riley shook his head methodically. "I guess you couldn't sleep?"

She grabbed her purse. "I should be going."

She swooped past me and was out the door. Out of curiosity, I walked across the room and pushed Lane's door open. There was no one in there.

My mouth dropped open. "She was here for you," I mumbled.

"I had no idea she was going to be here, Gabby. Please believe me." He locked gazes with me.

I did believe him. But I also believed that Veronica still would do anything to be with Riley.

Riley moaned, grabbed his arm, and stripped off the sweatshirt he was wearing, revealing a torn T-shirt underneath. He glanced at his arm and grimaced.

I sucked in a breath when I saw the blood there. "You're hurt."

The EMTs had treated one cut. They must have missed this smaller one on his other arm.

He examined the deep gash on his bicep. "I'll be okay."

I stepped closer, starting to reach for it but thinking better of it. "No, you need to get that cleaned up." I grabbed a washcloth from the bathroom and held it under the sink until warm water soaked it. I took it back to Riley and gently pressed the cloth into his cut.

My throat ached when I thought about how he could have been hurt.

Those thoughts were immediately followed by the realization of how defined his muscles were. He must be sneaking in some workouts on his lunch break. It wasn't that I hadn't ever noticed before. It was simply that my emotions were going haywire at the moment.

I focused and stared at his cut. "That's deep. You might need stitches."

He shook his head, his jaw locked in place. "I'll be fine. Some butterfly bandages will work."

"I'd get some for you, but no one can see me here." I offered an apologetic smile.

His hand covered mine, which covered the washcloth over his wound. "I'm going to be fine, Gabby. Stop worrying."

I swallowed and left him to hold the washcloth. My head still pounded from my fall. I caught a glimpse of myself in the mirror and saw my lip was busted, my hair was a tousled mess, and dirt smudged my cheek. I was a mess, in more ways than one.

How appropriate that someone who cleaned up messes was such a disaster herself at times.

I turned around, ready to get this conversation over with. Riley and I both started at the same time. We stared at each other a moment, tension crackling between us, until finally Riley said, "You first."

I nodded and leaned against the table behind me. How did I even begin to explain everything to Riley? My emotions didn't even make sense to myself half of the time.

"I've been thinking a lot lately, Riley," I started. "Aside from God, you're the best thing to ever happen to me, and I'm so sorry that I wasn't open and honest about everything." I sucked in a deep breath. "But I also know that I'm doing what I was created to do, Riley. I'm good at solving crimes. My passion is to find justice for people who desperately need it in their lives."

"You are good at what you do, Gabby. I've never argued with you there."

"Every time I try to investigate, you ask me not to."

"Because I worry about you."

"Is that really the reason?"

"Of course it is. Why would you ask that?"

"Because sometimes I think you want me to be someone I'm not. I can't stand feeling like that." I blinked as my words escaped my lips, etching a moment in my life that I could never take back.

Riley stared at me, a wrinkle between his eyebrows. "What are you saying, Gabby?"

I shook my head, fighting back tears. What *was* I saying? I pulled in another breath. "I guess what I'm saying is that I can't choose between you and doing what I love." A tear spilled down my cheek.

Riley stood, his eyebrows forced together, his shoulders tight. "Are you breaking up with me?" His voice sounded low, laced with surprise, regret.

I wasn't sure. Was that what I was doing? My gaze flickered back up to his. "I just want someone who loves me for me. For all of me."

"Gabby—" He reached for me, but I held up a finger to stop him. I had to get through these thoughts that suddenly hit me with clarity.

I sliced my hand through the air above my head as high as I could reach. "I've had you up on this pedestal for so long. The problem is that I keep trying to climb up this huge base at the bottom so I can reach you, and I just don't think it's ever going to happen."

"Gabby." He reached forward and brushed a tear from my cheek. "Please stop. Don't do this."

I shook my head, my chin trembling. "It's true."

"We can leave this silly resort. I don't need it. I don't need to be around my old friends. None of this was supposed to make you feel bad. I wanted you to enjoy yourself. I wanted time with you, away from the craziness of our usual life."

"Maybe my problem is that I haven't had time to discover who I am now that I'm a Christian. You've helped me change in so many ways, for the better, but now what?"

"Now we get ready to start a life together. You and me. Forever."

I shook my head. "I don't want to feel like this forever."

"Feel like what?"

My throat burned as the words stopped up my throat a moment. When they emerged, they sounded raw, exposed. "Like I'm not good enough."

"Gabby, I'm not the one who's making you feel like that. I love you as you are. I just want you to be honest with me. I want you to trust me enough to be yourself."

I wiped my hand across my forehead, and when my fingers reached my temple, I rubbed vigorously, as if trying to wipe out a stain. "I don't know. I don't know anything right now."

Silence stretched between us for a moment as we stared at each other. Finally, Riley fidgeted. "Maybe you should get some rest. Your thoughts will be clearer after you get some sleep."

I nodded and stepped toward the door, my head feeling like it weighed a hundred pounds. "Yeah, I should."

"Where are you going? Why don't you stay here? I'll go to Derek's room for the evening."

"Derek's probably not going to be speaking to you anymore," I admitted feebly.

"What?" His confusion disappeared as he shook his head. "Never mind. I don't want to know. I can just stay on the couch, and if people ask questions, I'll explain myself to them. I'd rather do that than be worried about you all night. Besides, Lane will probably be back and be sleeping in the other room."

I thought of my options. There weren't many. Finally, I nodded, too exhausted to argue. "If you wouldn't mind, then that would be great."

He put his hand on my back and led me to a door on the other side of the room. "Let me just grab a few things."

Bile rose in my throat as I watched him collect his bag and some clothing from the closet. My dream getaway with Riley was not supposed to work out like this.

CHAPTER 32

I woke up the next morning and felt like I'd been run over by one of those antique carriages downstairs. My head pounded. My chest ached. My eyes were swollen, and I couldn't even remember crying.

I sat up and everything from last night came crashing back. Derek's business card. Being accused of taking Ajay's necklace. Doug's dead body. A possible break up with Riley.

I glanced at the clock. It was twenty minutes past noon. I rubbed my eyes. I had been tired.

I jumped in the shower, trying to wash some of the grime off myself. After I dried off, I realized I had no clean clothes, so I pulled on some of Riley's shorts and a T-shirt.

I glanced in the mirror. This was not a good look. Not in the least.

Stepping outside the room, I fully expected Riley to be gone. I expected him to run for his life, truth be told. That's what any normal person would do.

Instead, I saw him sitting on the couch, his elbows propped on his knees, and staring off into space.

He looked up when I stepped out. That same tortured look remained in his eyes. "Morning," he mumbled.

"You're still here. I figured you'd be off with your friends."

"There's only one person I want to spend time with." His gaze was intense on me. "You."

"Where's Lane?"

"He never came in last night. Probably stayed with Veronica, if I had to guess."

I plopped down beside him and pointed to my Georgetown T-shirt. "I don't have any clothes. Again."

That got a small smile out of him. "How about if I go get you some downstairs?"

Something in his hands caught my eye. "What's that?"

"I found it on the floor."

I looked more closely. It was the metal plate with the numbers on it. "That's mine. It must have dropped out of my pocket. Do you know what it is?"

He flipped it over and over again. "I'm not sure. If I had to guess, this is a VIN for a car."

"VIN for a car?" I closed my eyes, knowing I knew what that was, but I couldn't for the life of me remember at the moment.

"The serial number that's assigned to each car by the manufacturer. Every car has one. It's how they're identified."

I hooked a hair behind my ear, trying to think this through. "Why would that have been downstairs in the construction area?"

Riley flipped it over in his fingers. "You found this inside the building?"

I nodded. "That's right."

He set it on the table. "Your guess is as good as mine then. I have no idea."

I leaned back into the couch and nibbled on my thumbnail a moment. The bigger picture was starting to come into focus. I just needed to hammer out a few details, including the *who*.

Riley stood. "How about if I go grab you some clothes and some food? As cute as you look in my workout clothes, you probably want something a little more . . . fitting. You're going to stick out like a sore thumb wearing that around here today."

The strain in his eyes was enough to make my soul ache. Riley was hurting just as much through this situation as I was. Were relationships supposed to be this hard?

I nodded. "I appreciate that."

As soon as he opened the door, I heard Deanna's voice sound from the hallway. "Have you seen Gabby? Rumor has it that she came in here last night. You didn't hurt her, did you?"

"What? Me? No, of course not."

"Where is she then?"

Riley turned back to me, confusion clearly written on his face. "Gabby . . . ?"

I nodded, and Riley stepped back. Deanna flung herself inside the room and rushed toward me. "I'm so glad you're okay. I heard what happened last night. All of it. You'll never believe what I saw last night."

I had no idea. "What?"

"I saw Ajay walking down my wing in the middle of the night. I hid, of course, because I didn't want him to realize I was a maid. But then I got curious and started to follow him."

"Is that the guy from India you've been hanging out with?" Riley asked.

"The gorgeous, handsome one who's destined to be my husband one day?" Deanna nodded enthusiastically. "That's the one." She turned back to me. "He went down to the breezeway."

My blood felt ice cold at the moment. "Really?"

She nodded. Deanna continued, going sixty miles an hour and waving her hands in the air. "I couldn't stop myself. I kept following him. He walked through the construction area and out the back door."

Tension squeezed my spine. "What then?" I didn't think this was the time to mention how unsafe what she'd done might be. Of course, I would have done the same thing.

"He pulled a ski mask over his face and kept walking." She swallowed, visibly shaken. "He went outside to that old maintenance shed located in the woods back there. I got close enough to peer inside the door."

Her dramatic pauses were really starting to get to me. I shifted and tried to keep my voice even, despite the anticipation that coursed through me. "And?"

"There are cars inside. Lots and lots of cars. Nice ones, too. I'm talking high-end Mercedes and BMWs."

I shook my head and began to pace. "What sense does that make? Do the valets use that for some kind of overflow parking?"

Deanna shook her head. "The building is condemned. I hope not."

I reviewed what I knew about Ajay so far. This new information didn't fit. "He said his wife died here a few years ago. That she was killed after being run off the road by a truck while driving up a mountain road."

Deanna shook her head. "That never happened."

"How do you know?"

"This is a small community. We remember things like that. The whole staff would have been alerted. It never happened."

Was Ajay the one behind all of this? Was he the masked man who'd followed me in the hallway? The man who'd attacked Riley and me last night?

"I need to talk to Clint."

Deanna shook her head. "You're practically a fugitive."

My shoulders pulled up in confusion. "What does that mean?"

"It means that the manager showed your picture to everyone on staff and told them to keep a lookout for you. We're supposed to immediately report you if we see you on the premises."

I glanced back at Riley and sighed. "Well, I need to get out of here somehow."

Deanna tapped her finger against her mouth. "I can help. Just give me fifteen minutes."

"Deanna, I don't want you to lose your job."

"Are you kidding? This is the most excitement I've had around here in years. Besides, I know there's no way you took that necklace."

I pulled my arms across my chest. "I was set up."

She nodded and stepped toward the door. "I know. I'll be right back."

As the door clicked shut, I pulled my eyes up toward Riley. "I didn't do it."

"I know." His words sounded soft, believable, soothing. "How about if I go get you something to eat and I'll pick up a few other items for you down at the market. Okay?"

I nodded, feeling at his mercy. At everyone's mercy, for that matter. "I appreciate that."

"Don't open the door for anyone, not even my friends, okay?"

His words chilled me. He thought one of them

could be involved also. "Got it."

He closed the door, and I turned both locks and pulled the chain across it. Then I sank onto the couch and tried to sort out my thoughts.

CHAPTER 33

Thirty minutes later, I glanced in the mirror and frowned. "This is your best idea?"

Deanna nodded, a little too much excitement in her eyes. "It's perfect. No one will ever know it's you."

She'd brought me what I could only consider a muumuu—a large, billowing dress with no shape or form to it whatsoever. She'd also brought me a large straw hat and oversized sunglasses. I'd pulled my trademark red hair into a bun and stuffed it under the hat. I kept the shorts on underneath also.

Riley pulled on a ball cap and kept it low over his eyes. I couldn't see his gaze, but I was sure he was amused by this costume.

"I figured you could just be pretending to escort your grandma or something," Deanna told him. She extended her hand. "By the way, I'm Deanna."

His fingers connected with hers. "I'm Riley."

"You're Riley? I've heard a lot about you. You two are both so fortunate to have each other. I would love to be in your shoes."

My throat tightened as I remembered everything that had transpired between me and Riley over the past two days. If she knew the whole truth, Deanna wouldn't be so quick to want to be in our shoes.

I straightened my oversized potato sack. "What happens when we get out of this hotel? I can't exactly hop on the shuttle, and Riley's car is in the shop."

"I can fix that." Deanna pulled out her phone and dialed. She took a few steps away, mumbled something, and then came back. "All settled. Let's go."

I had to swallow a lot of pride to leave the room wearing the get up Deanna had provided. At best, the outfit looked like something Maria from *The Sound of Music* had made out of leftover curtains. At worst, I looked like a pincushion, all the way from the shapeless, puffy dress to the straw hat on top. I only hoped that wouldn't give the killer any ideas to poke me with something sharp.

Deanna's phone rang again, and she held out a hand to stop us. She talked into the mouthpiece, her words clipped and tight. Finally, she hung up and turned to us. "Mr. Allen is in his office, so the path should be cleared. But we should move fast. He will call the police on you and have you arrested if you're caught."

That probably wouldn't look great for future job opportunities. I nodded, grabbed Riley's arm so he could escort me, and we took off toward the opposite end of the building. We moved quickly unless we saw someone, then we slowed to a normal pace.

Deanna's phone rang again. After she hung up, she informed us, "Mr. Allen is on the move. I repeat, he's on the move, headed toward the back of the hotel. We've got to pick up our pace."

I pulled my hat lower. More than getting caught myself and getting in trouble, I feared what might happen to Riley or Deanna. Riley, he'd probably be okay. I mean, I didn't think there was any law against harboring a hotel fugitive. He'd probably be asked to leave, at the most. Deanna, on the other hand, she could lose her job.

Our exit came into sight at the end of the hallway. Just as we reached it, a deep voice called behind us. "Deanna?"

Deanna paused and whispered for us to keep going. I didn't argue; I knew whose voice that was.

Bentley's.

Deanna hurried toward him. Meanwhile, Riley and I kept our pace steady so we wouldn't aggravate Bentley's suspicions. We reached the door, and Riley casually opened it for me. I took my steps slowly, trying to look like I belonged in this outfit and that I was supposed to be here.

As soon as we stepped outside and the door closed behind us, I breathed a sigh of relief. I only hoped that Deanna was okay inside. I wanted to turn around and check on her, but I knew I couldn't. We kept walking until we reached the street behind the resort.

When I stepped on the sidewalk, I heard the door open and someone come running out. I held my breath. Bentley? Security? The police?

"You guys, wait up."

My shoulders sagged with relief. Deanna.

"What was that about?" I asked her as she joined us.

"Mr. Allen was just reminding me to be on the lookout for you. I don't think he suspected a thing. He asked me why I was here since my shift was over, and I told him I left something in my locker. He seemed to buy it."

"He seems awfully uptight," Riley said.

"Uptight is an understatement," Deanna told us. "He's impossible to please sometimes. Of course, my theory is that if he didn't live in such a big house or drive such a nice car, maybe he would have money to buy this place back. But he's all about image. I heard he lives from paycheck to paycheck, but he would never admit that to anyone."

"It's the American way," I mumbled. Of the many vices in my life, image wasn't one of them. At least, it hadn't been until this trip. I was pretty content with my apartment, which was nothing fancy. I liked wearing jeans and T-shirts. Fun for me didn't involve spending lots of money. It meant being around good friends and occasionally maybe helping out someone who was down on their luck.

Deanna stopped in the middle of the sidewalk. "Well, this is it."

I glanced around and saw nothing. Not a car, not a van, not a truck. I looked back at her. "This is what?"

She pointed at a mailbox in the distance. "Your ride."

"Huh?" What was I supposed to do? Put a first-class stamp on myself and pray that I got to the police station by morning?

Riley moved me over until a red moped came into view. It was so tiny that I couldn't even see it behind the mailbox.

"Shirley said you could use it. I'd let you use my car, but I don't have one." Deanna held out a key. A little yellow troll dangled from the keychain. "It's all yours."

I glanced at Riley quickly. Just as I thought. Amusement danced in his eyes. Finally, I grabbed the troll and started toward the moped. "Thanks for your help. I'll return this just like I found it. Promise."

Deanna nodded. "I know. I'm waiting for you to prove that Ajay is innocent."

"What if he's not?" I stared at her, watching carefully for her reaction. This whole plan could backfire majorly if I wasn't careful because Ajay *could* be guilty. Then what would Deanna do? Turn on me? Report me to Bentley?

She shook her head, not even a hint of doubt in her eyes. "He will be. You'll see."

I didn't argue. Instead, I handed her my straw hat and gave Riley the keys. "Let's go find some answers."

We climbed on the moped, and Riley cranked the engine. Trickles of our conversation crept into my mind, and my heart twisted with each remembrance. I squeezed Riley's arm, trying to push away the guilt pounding at me. "You sure you want to do this? It's not too late to back out."

"Why would I want to do that?" He took off, and my arms slipped around his waist.

This was Riley. My Riley. We were meant to be together . . . weren't we? I mean, how much did the man care about appearances if he was willing to be seen with me in this outfit? Maybe I'd been too hard on him. Maybe my emotions were getting the best of me. It wouldn't be the first or the last time.

I leaned into him and inhaled the scent of leathery cologne. I felt the ripple of his muscles beneath his shirt. I remembered our conversation about how the little things in life were the most important.

Images filled my mind. Images of Riley chasing me through the apartment with icing on his face. Images of Riley spontaneously doing a dance move when I talked about *High School Musical*. Pictures of how safe I felt when I was in his arms. Pictures of how my life had changed for the better since he came onto the scene.

I pointed in the distance, directing him to the

police headquarters. We pulled to a stop, and I climbed off and straightened my caftan. The wind whipped up and filled the outfit with air, making me gain about a hundred pounds. I was a sight to behold.

I looked up and saw Riley staring at me. There was no embarrassment in his eyes, just . . . love? I tucked a hair behind my ear, observing a once a year practice I employed known as "being speechless."

Finally, I cleared my throat. "What are you thinking?"

He shrugged, his lips in a line. "I'm thinking that I want to grow old with you."

"Even if it means I'll wear stuff like this?"

Part of his lip tugged up. "Absolutely. You'd still be gorgeous to me."

Tears stung my eyes. "Oh, Riley . . . "

"Talk later?"

I nodded. Now wasn't the time. But we definitely needed to talk.

We walked into the jail, hand in hand. A few minutes later, we were seated across from Clint. He looked worse than before. Dark circles hung under his eyes. His skin was pale. His gaze is what shook me the most, though. The life looked gone from him.

"How's it going?" My question almost sounded mocking, I realized. It was obvious the man wasn't doing well.

"She was strangled," he mumbled. "Strangling is a sign of passion. Everything is stacked against me. Even I have to admit that I look guilty."

I got straight to the point. "Doug is dead."

His eyes widened. "Doug? The guy who works with Jackie?"

I nodded. "They found him last night in the pool. I

haven't heard the official cause of death."

Clint ran a hand through his hair, leaving most of it standing on end. "Wow. At least they can't frame me for that one. I was locked up."

"Listen, Clint, I have a question, and I'm really hoping you can help. Doug told me that he and Jackie had a disagreement about a case they were working on. It was some kind of big investigation that spanned more than one state and involved multiple agencies. Did she ever talk to you about that?"

He shook his head, quickly and barely. The action almost made him look like his spine was vibrating and taking his head with it. "Maybe. I dunno. Why?"

I tapped my finger on the table. "I just wonder if it's all connected somehow. That's the only reason I can think of that both Jackie and Doug would be murdered."

"It sounds like a theory, but I don't have any idea what that case might be."

"Did Jackie act strange after she got here? Did she say she recognized anyone or that someone looked familiar?"

"No, I have no idea. Believe me, I wish I could think of something. All I have to do all day is think, and I come up short."

I pressed my lips together. "What about Derek? Did she have any disagreements with him?"

"Not that I know of. She never talked about him."

"She never mentioned a contract he may have drawn up for her?"

Clint jerked his lips back in surprise. "Contract? I have no idea. She wouldn't have Derek draw it up. She didn't trust him as far as she could throw him."

I told Clint goodbye and promised him that I would keep looking into this. I filled Riley in as we walked over to Buck's.

CHAPTER 34

As Riley haggled with the guy behind the front desk about his car repairs, I thought about the VIN plate I'd found. Jackie had worked on a case involving an auto theft ring. Deanna had mentioned that there'd been a couple of stolen vehicles here at Allendale and that she'd seen some high-end cars in that maintenance shed.

Could Derek and Jackie have gotten involved in some kind of auto theft scheme somehow? There was probably a lot of money involved in a crime like that. Maybe Jackie was trying to get her hands on more money so she could marry Clint and still maintain a rich lifestyle.

Or maybe the mysterious contract Shirley had seen was something Jackie was going to slap on Clint. Maybe she was afraid he was just after her money, and she wanted to safeguard herself.

Or how about Ajay? Maybe he was here from India to oversee the entire operation. That would explain his long stretch of time here and his made-up story about his wife dying.

Then there was Derek. I'd overheard him telling Lillian something about getting some guy who owned a chop shop off on his charges because he'd been injured on the way to the jail. Maybe Derek took a piece of the cut when he agreed to be the man's lawyer.

For all I knew Lane or Veronica or Lillian could be involved. After all, Lane had dated Jackie. Maybe he wanted her back. Maybe they'd had a little quarrel on the mountaintop and one thing had led to another.

Then there was that look that Officer Sharples had given the valet. What was that about? Nothing? Maybe. Everything? Possibly.

Riley was still arguing with the guy at the front desk about his bill when an idea hit me. "Excuse me, where's your bathroom?"

The man cocked half of his lip dubiously. "You sure you want to use it, lady? It's not the cleanest place."

"A girl's gotta do what a girl's gotta do."

"Your choice." He nodded toward the hallway. "It's back there."

I sneaked a glance at Riley as I slipped away. The look in his eyes told me that he knew exactly what I was up to. As soon as I was out of sight, I turned toward the garage. It was going to be really hard to hide in this floral monstrosity—maybe impossible—but I had to figure out a way.

The garage was actually bigger than I expected. There were two men working back there, one of them the man who'd driven the tow truck. They chatted in short, choppy sentences that I couldn't make out. I had to get closer.

When one man called the other over to look at the undercarriage of a car on the far side of the garage, I seized my opportunity. I snuck through the open doorway and crouched behind a car in the corner. The Honda hadn't been looked at yet, apparently, because it wasn't up on a hydraulic lift.

"Tonight the shipment's going out," one of the mechanics said. "The boss told you about it, right? He needs us all there. It's hush hush. There's been too much going on around town lately, and he's afraid people might get suspicious."

"Oh, I'll be there. I want my cut," the tow driver said. "Now, we need to get our story straight on this car . . ."

Before he came back to the other side, I slipped out. My heart pounded in my ears as I stood in the hallway. That had been close. But now I had information that might lead to some answers as to who this "boss" was.

I started back toward Riley.

"You sure your friend's okay? She's been back there a long time," I heard the guy at the front desk say.

"She has stomach issues," Riley said. I could only imagine his expression.

Nice.

I stepped into view and rubbed my belly. "Sorry about that. I've got issues." Did I ever.

Riley nodded toward the door. "Let's get out of here. If I stay another minute, I'm going to blow a fuse."

"What's going on?" I asked as we stepped outside. I had a feeling I already knew the answer.

"They're telling me I'd be better off to junk the car, that the amount it's going to take to fix it is more than what the car is worth anymore. They offered to give me a couple thousand bucks for the parts."

I shook my head. "I think they're running a chop shop, and I think they're using people who get involved in the accidents on that mountain road as their victims."

"You think this is all about selling car parts?"

I shook my head. "No, I think it's bigger than that. I

think it may have started as simply selling car parts, though. There's something going down tonight, and I need to figure out what." I looked down at my dress. "And I've got to get more clothes if I'm going to do that."

***

I looked in the mirror at the jeans and "Virginia is for Lovers" T-shirt. Much better.

Riley and I had ridden the moped a little farther up the road and discovered a consignment store. The clothes were nice, but they cost more used than most of my clothes cost new. I was so happy to have decent clothes that I didn't care. Besides, I was doing a stakeout. Muumuus never worked for stakeouts.

Riley's cell phone rang. "It's Lillian," he mumbled before answering. A moment later, he hung up and turned toward me. "Derek's missing."

"What?"

"Lillian said all of his stuff is gone and that it's like he just grabbed his things and jetted."

"Why would he do that?" My mind was already racing through the possibilities. Guilt? Or maybe he had to get ready for this big transaction that was going on tonight.

"Your guess is as good as mine. Wasn't it just last night that you confronted him about his business card being found at the crime scene?"

"I've got to call Parker." Parker was my former boyfriend. He was now with the FBI and about to have a baby with his new girlfriend. I was so glad we weren't together anymore. So. So. Glad.

"Hey Nancy Drew. What's going on?" Nancy Drew was Parker's favorite nickname for me.

"What do you know about auto theft rings?" I didn't waste any time with being polite, not when there was so much on the line.

"Okay . . . " I could imagine his expression. Eyes wide with incredulity, lips smirking, and shoulders tight. "What do you want to know?"

"How do they operate? What do they do? Anything."

"I've never worked one of those cases, but I know there's big money to be found in some of those crimes. The thieves usually steal high end cars and, depending on whether or not it's local or international, they have dealers set up to buy the cars and get rid of them."

"Where are they sold internationally?"

"West Africa is big right now. But other places too."

"India?"

"Yeah, India. What's going on?"

I gave him a brief overview of what had happened. He let out a sigh. "These people can be dangerous, Gabby. I'd stay out of this one. Where are you anyway?"

"Wealthy—I mean Healthy—Springs."

"Oh, getting fancy with your new job now, huh?"

"Uh, well, not really. That's a long story." I didn't want to explain all of my failures to my ex.

"I'd let the local authorities know and then stay out of it. You don't want to get in the middle of something like this. People will kill not to be discovered."

I nodded and hung up. I was totally getting in the middle of this.

CHAPTER 35

"You see anything?" Deanna asked.

I pulled down my binoculars. "Not yet."

Riley was being quiet beside us. He was probably thinking about all of the legal trouble we could get into. It was better if I *didn't* think about these things.

We sat behind a boulder in the woods. To one side of us was a hardly-used service road that led to the abandoned maintenance shed; on the other side was the shed itself.

After my phone call with Parker, Riley and I had split up to collect supplies. I'd gone to get some snacks and lots of Mountain Dew. Riley had gotten the binoculars and flashlights. We'd returned the moped, Deanna had found us, and we'd given her the update.

She'd shown up here at our stakeout and told us she'd taken the night off in order to help. Then she'd muttered the, "I could get in so much trouble for this" mantra.

Hopefully, the trouble these car thieves got into would overshadow any potential trouble we could get into.

"Someone's coming," Riley mumbled. "Listen."

We quieted. Sure enough, something rumbled in the distance. We waited and watched as the sound got louder and louder. Finally, an eighteen-wheeler came into view. A big container was on the back of the truck.

I could picture it clearly in my mind. Fill up the container with stolen cars with switched VINs. Take the container to a port, ship the cars overseas, and make a ton of profit. Meanwhile, the cars are gone, along with evidence of the theft. Brilliant plan.

The truck went past and turned by the maintenance building. It then backed up to a set of garage doors. Because of the angle of the building, I couldn't see what they were taking on or off.

"Who do you see?" Deanna asked.

I focused the binoculars. Ah ha! Bill the valet stepped out of the building. He was in on this. Of course he would know which cars to steal. As a valet, he could probably even have copies of the keys made. I just didn't see him as the ringleader of this whole operation, though.

I kept watching. I fully expected Ajay to step outside. Maybe even Derek. For all I knew, they were each in on this. Both exerted a certain amount of power. Power mixed with devious plans could quickly turn violent.

"By the way, if we're caught, I want you both to run," I announced, still looking through the binoculars.

"And leave you?" Riley's voice held disbelief.

"Yes, and leave me. I don't want the two of you to get killed."

"I'm not leaving you, Gabby." He stared at me like I was crazy.

"I seriously don't want you two getting hurt on my account."

"But we should all go separate ways if we're caught," Deanna chirped. "Maybe they won't catch all of us. Why should all three of us die?"

Riley's eyes widened.

Deanna shrugged. "What? It's true. I've watched *Criminal Minds* before. I know how these things work."

I didn't know what to say to that, so instead I watched as the garage door opened and nice cars were driven onto the truck. I counted at least eight. I had no idea how they were fitting all of them in, but apparently they had a way.

This was a huge scheme. The person behind this was set to make major bucks. They had to have connections with the hotel, influence at the garage, knowledge of the ports, and an idea of how to get overseas sales. They also had to be a genius at covering things up, otherwise, how had they managed to get away with all of this? It would almost need to be someone like—

A branch broke behind me. Before I could turn, I heard, "I thought I told you that you were no longer welcome here."

I flung myself around. "Bentley?"

He held a gun, pointed at me, with a smirk on his face. "I think you lost your shoe." He held up my flip-flop, the one I'd lost that night as I ran from the masked man in the breezeway.

This wasn't exactly how I saw my Cinderella story turning out.

I licked my lips. "You're the one behind all of this?"

He stepped closer and scowled. His forehead glistened with beads of sweat. "You couldn't just leave it alone, could you? You had to keep pushing and pushing."

Riley nudged me behind him. "We can talk this out."

I barely heard him as facts clicked together in my mind. "You're stealing these cars because you want to buy

272

your family's business back."

"You're smarter than I thought," he mumbled.

Why did my brilliance always hit me about five minutes too late?

"You recognized Jackie from the investigation, which stemmed as far south as Georgia, and were afraid she'd figure out who you were. So you followed her. You knew the whole time that she hadn't really been kidnapped. As soon as you saw your opportunity, you killed her and made it look like Clint was guilty."

"It's too bad your nosiness is going to get you killed tonight." Bentley still had that gun pointed at me.

"You planted that necklace in my hotel room so I would get kicked out. Only, Ajay didn't take the bait. He didn't press charges like you'd hoped." Bentley had probably had my suitcase stolen also, for that matter, and then erased the security footage.

He sneered and stepped closer. "And you somehow found a way to stick around and continue to cause trouble. Now things are really going to have to get ugly. I want all three of you to get on that container." He pointed with his gun toward the maintenance building.

I glanced at the truck. I pictured the three of us in that big metal box . . . for weeks and weeks on end as we traveled across the ocean with no food, no water, no air.

We'd die.

Of course, that was probably part of Bentley's plan. When someone was already in this deep, what were three more murders?

"No way." I shook my head.

He cocked his gun and aimed it at Deanna. "Then your friend dies."

I glanced at Deanna. Her eyes were as wide as saucers. *We should all run in different directions. He can't get all three of us that way.*

Did she remember her own advice? I was the one Bentley wanted—not Deanna or Riley.

I gave her a slight nod.

Then I came up with my diversion. I pointed at Bentley's feet and screamed. "Snake!" I remembered Deanna mentioning off-handedly that he hated the creatures. My knowledge of useless facts sometimes came in handy.

Bentley looked down, and that gave us just enough time to split. Only Riley didn't split from me. He stayed by my side.

We darted through the woods. The nighttime was dark around us. I could only imagine one of those gulches appearing out of nowhere, and Riley and I nose diving to our deaths.

A bullet screeched by. Riley reached for my hand and pulled me along faster.

Wilderness surrounded us. Trees stalked us. Blackness closed in.

My legs burned. My lungs screamed for air. My life flashed before my eyes.

Riley's grip on my hand was the only thing that kept me sane. I felt hunted, like a deer in open season. No matter how fast we went, Bentley was always just a few steps behind.

Thankfully, he was a horrible aim. He fired bullets like some people hurled insults. The ammunition hit trees, hit the ground, hit the air.

Finally, Riley pulled me behind a thick patch of trees. My heart thudded in my chest as I gulped in deep breaths of air. Bentley would find us. It was only a matter of time.

I just needed to catch my breath, gather my

surroundings, tell Riley how much I really did love him.

"Come out, come out, wherever you are," Bentley chanted, not terribly far away and sounding more and more diabolical by the moment.

Where was Deanna? Safe, I hoped.

A noise floated toward me. The waterfall. That meant the gulch was close. One wrong step and . . .

Riley squeezed my hand. We were going to have to run again. Soon. We had no choice.

But before we could, a stick crunched beside us. Bentley stood there. Winded. Sweaty. But as devious as ever.

"Perfect. I can make this look like an accident. Just like I did with Maurice," Bentley muttered.

"Let me guess—he was the bellhop who died in the kayaking accident," I said, buying time.

Bentley smirked again. "I didn't give you enough credit."

I took a step back. Could we dart away? Or would his bullet find us if we did?

Bentley made a *tsk* sound. "I know these woods. I grew up wandering around exploring them. If you run again, I'll find you. Either that, or the wilderness will do my job for me, and you'll fall to your death."

"Not so fast." Ajay stepped out of the darkness. He aimed the gun in his hands at Bentley. "You're not going to get away with this."

"An Indian dignitary is going to stop me?" Bentley snorted. "Really? Is this the best you all can do?"

Ajay scowled. "You killed my wife."

Bentley stared at him unflinching. "The only woman I killed so far was Jackie. You weren't married to her, were you?"

Ajay didn't back down. "Your actions have had far

reaching consequences that had led me here to investigate."

I stared at the men in the stand off. How was Ajay involved exactly?

Riley tugged me back as the tension between the men deepened.

Suddenly, Bentley's gun fired. Right at Ajay.

A figure appeared from the shadows and plowed into Ajay, knocking him out of harm's way. I held my breath, waiting, watching everything play out.

My stomach sank. Deanna. Deanna had just saved Ajay's life. Like any good woman with a crush, she'd never given up on her belief in his innocence.

I prayed she'd be okay. That they'd both be okay.

Riley pulled at me again, and I stepped back. We took off in a run through the woods.

With every step, the blackness felt deeper, darker, like a death sentence.

Then there was that gulch. It was close. Too close. I prayed for our steps. I prayed for help, for wisdom, for anything God might be willing to offer us at the moment.

That's when Riley disappeared. I screamed. I didn't mean to. Didn't want to draw attention to us. But . . .

"Riley?"

"I'm . . . here."

I glanced down. Riley. Only his upper body remained above the cliff. He held on to a crevice in the rocks to keep from falling to his death. I dropped to my knees and grabbed his wrists. I locked my legs against a tree.

Even in the dark, I could see Riley's eyes boring into mine. "Gabby, run before Bentley finds you."

"No." I didn't even have to think about my response. No way was I leaving Riley.

"Gabby, please. He's going to shoot both of us."

I squeezed his wrists tighter and pressed myself harder into the tree. "I'm not letting you go."

Tears rushed to my eyes as the words slipped from my mouth. Not tears of regret or fear. Tears that symbolized my love for Riley. He'd stepped in front of a bullet to save me before. No way was I walking away now. Love like his didn't come around more than once in a lifetime.

"You're willing to die for him then?" someone said beside me.

I looked up and saw Bentley standing above me, his gun only inches from my head. I pulled myself together for long enough to nod, despite the cold fear that rushed through me. "Yes, I would. You see, I've learned something lately."

Bentley sneered. "Humor me. What is it?"

My muscles ached. The tree cut into my skin. My fingers felt cramped and slippery at the same time.

It didn't matter. I wouldn't let go of Riley. I'd hold on for as long as possible. I was still praying for a miracle.

"I've learned that the happiest people in life aren't the ones who are always looking out for themselves. They're the ones who put others before themselves. Take you, for example. You may be richer than ever, but you're more miserable than most of the population."

Bentley's sneer turned into a scowl. "I don't have time for this little lesson in morality."

Riley slipped farther down. I was losing my grip on him. If a bullet didn't kill him, this mountain would. I felt powerless to do anything.

As I glanced down, two eyes caught my gaze. Not Riley's.

No, it was a critter.

A snake, I realized, drawing in a quick breath. A real one this time.

"What are you doing?"

I nodded toward the creature. "Sn . . . snake."

"I'm not falling for that one again."

I stared at the slimy little menace. "No, really, it's a snake."

Bentley shook his head and scoffed. "Sure, it is. You must really think I'm an idiot."

Just then, the snake slithered. The motion was just enough to distract Bentley and cause him to yelp.

I swung one leg around until they collided with his knees. He fell to the ground, only inches from the snake. He stuttered and gasped as he stared face to face at the creature.

I swung my head toward Riley. "Riley—"

"I've got this," he said, his voice smooth, even, solid.

I glanced at him, looking for the truth in his gaze. He nodded.

Hesitantly, I let go of his wrists for long enough to grab Bentley's gun. The man was frozen with paralysis as he stared at the snake. I figured the little Lucifer could handle Bentley for a moment.

I forgot my fear of heights and grabbed Riley's arms. I'm not sure how it all happened, but I pulled and he pushed and somehow his entire body ended up on the mountainside. Safe.

Before I had the chance to say anything to him, the snake coiled and rose up at Bentley. He jumped . . . and slid toward the cliff.

Not again.

"Help me! Please," Bentley said.

Riley and I glanced at each other. Was this just

another scheme? I couldn't be certain.

But I couldn't let the man die, either.

Riley took one of his arms and I took the other, just as the police surrounded us. They stepped in to help Bentley, and I didn't object. My arms felt like they might fall off.

But I still had enough strength to throw them around Riley. "I'm so glad you're okay."

His arms wrapped around me, and he squeezed tight. His breathing still came out in quick puffs, and I could feel his heart racing against mine. "I'm glad you're okay. That was awfully brave, what you did back there."

"Not brave. I was just following my heart."

"You always follow your heart. That's what I love about you."

I pulled back, and we shared a smile. "We'll talk later?"

He nodded.

As the police took Bentley away, I glanced around and spotted Deanna. I rushed toward her. The darkness made it impossible to see if she was hurt or not.

"Are you okay?"

She held up her hand. I thought I saw blood there. "Just a flesh wound."

"Oh, Deanna. You could have been hurt."

She wagged her eyebrows mischievously. "I'm going to have some great stories to tell the girls tomorrow."

I smiled. She was probably already trying to think of how she could work this to her advantage. One of the officers examined her arm.

My gaze focused on another figure putting his gun back into its holster a few feet away.

"Ajay?" I asked.

He stepped closer. "I am working with Interpol on these car thefts. I had permission from Interpol Washington to be in the country, on the contingency that I share any information with law enforcement officials here."

"So you were here investigating the whole time. That whole story about your wife was just made up."

"Not completely. She did die in a car accident, only it happened in India. The man who hit her was driving a stolen car. It came from America, just as I suspected."

"I'm sorry."

"You are a brave woman, Miss St. Claire." He looked back at Riley. "You are lucky to have someone so strong and beautiful. She reminds me a bit of my wife. I have confidence that you two will have a relationship like we did—only without the tragic ending."

I caught Riley's eye, and we shared a smile.

"I didn't steal your necklace," I told Ajay.

"I know. Bentley Allen set you up. He was desperate to get you out of here before you ruined all of his hard work." Ajay extended his hand. "And, since we were talking about being lucky earlier, I must mention that I am so lucky that I had this woman," he showcased Deanna, "save my life. Would you do me the honor of taking a carriage ride together?"

Deanna squealed before composing herself. "I'd love to."

"Tomorrow evening, then. We have lots to wrap up tonight."

"I'll be ready," Deanna whispered. "I'll be ready."

I smiled. I didn't see the two of them having a forever relationship. But what did I know? I could see the two of them having a nice, cozy little date here at Allendale. It would probably be all Deanna talked about for months, and she'd smile dreamily every time she told the story. And that would be worth it.

They walked away, and Riley squeezed my hand. "You were wrong about your inheritance, you know."

"What do you mean?"

"Most of the guests here wouldn't stand a chance at getting in good with the staff here. You reached out to the employees and related to them, and that made them want to help you. If you hadn't made that connection with them, this case may have never been solved."

His words sunk in. He was right. My heritage, for once in my life, had worked to my advantage.

All things did work together for the good of those in Christ. When would I ever fully learn that lesson?

CHAPTER 36

I looked in the mirror and adjusted the little black dress I was wearing. I'd gotten my suitcase back, but I'd decided to pay a visit to that little consignment shop to look for something new.

This was especially appealing now considering that the resort had decided to make my stay complimentary and to refund the money I'd already paid for my hotel room. They'd also offered to take us in the shuttle to the next town over so we could rent a car and get home.

Riley and I had talked about leaving but had decided to stay for the final gala that ended the Attorneys' Conference. Maybe we'd finally get some time together—without a gun being pointed at us.

Someone knocked at my door. I yelled for them to come in. Riley stepped inside and let out a wolf whistle. "Beautiful!"

I soaked in his tux. "You're not so bad yourself."

We'd basically secluded ourselves from the rest of his friends today. It wasn't entirely on purpose. The police had questioned us for hours. Other agencies had been called in as well, but there were so many different agencies that they all ran together in my head. Let's just say that this bust was big.

By the time we'd gotten back to the hotel, we'd been exhausted—and dirty. The assistant manager had offered me a room of my own. I'd happily taken a long, hot shower and then passed out from exhaustion.

And now it was time for the gala. Riley extended his arm. "Ready?"

I grasped his arm. "As I'll ever be."

As we headed down the hallway, I reviewed everything that had happened. From what I'd gathered, Valet Bill was involved in this whole scheme, as well as a couple of the mechanics from the shop. It had all started because Buck's Garage liked to make a killing off people who had accidents on that mountain road. They started as a chop shop, but then realized how much more they could make by stealing high-end cars and selling them overseas. Bentley had come to them with the idea and had been the mastermind behind it.

He'd recognized Jackie and Doug as the prosecutors from the case down in Georgia. Apparently, Jackie had recognized him also, and he was afraid that she would blow the whole case open.

Bentley was going away for a long time.

See? I didn't have to work for the Medical Examiner to put the bad guys behind bars.

As soon as we walked into the Grand Ballroom, Riley's friends surrounded us.

"Are you guys okay?" Lillian asked. "We heard what happened. I'm sure we can help you sue this establishment for all the mental anguish they've caused you."

Riley shook his head. "No suing will be necessary. We'll handle things just fine."

I glanced around the room. "Where's Derek? Does

anyone know where he went?"

He stepped out from behind the rest of the gang, raising his hands in surrender. "I went into hiding. I admit it."

"You were trying to get Jackie to come work for you," I said. "That's what that contract was for. But why?"

He shrugged. "I like Jackie. She was a fun girl, easy to work with. She wasn't the most motivated person—not the most motivated to work, at least. But I thought she'd look great in my commercials."

"So you went down to Georgia to try and convince her," I said.

He nodded. "Yeah, I tried, but she said she wanted to be near Clint. She said things were going to turn around in her favor. I couldn't convince her. Believe me, I planned on trying after we all got here as well."

"Why did I find your business card at the scene where her body was?" I continued.

He let out a long sigh. "I gave it to Jackie when we got here. I was poised to convince her to reconsider my offer. The card must have been in her pocket and fallen out."

I glanced at Lane. "And you. You kept calling Jackie from that courtesy phone. Why?"

He tensed. "I didn't call Jackie from the courtesy phone."

"I saw you using it in the hallway that day, and you clearly have a cell phone."

"I forgot to charge it, and I had to call Veronica about lunch."

Derek raised his hands. "That was me, too. I was trying to get with her to talk. I didn't want Clint to see my number on her phone and think something was going on."

I glanced back at Jack the Dipper. He shrugged and

raised his plate of food in the air. "I just came here for the food and for the peace and quiet."

I guess that cleared up most of my questions. I turned toward Riley. We still had a lot to talk about. I hoped to steal a few minutes while we were here tonight. He took my hand and began leading me to our table.

Just as we stepped away, Veronica called to me. "Could I have a moment with you, Gabby?"

I glanced at Riley quickly before nodding. We stepped away from the rest of the crowd. I could tell by the way Veronica frowned that something was on her mind.

"I was wrong about you," she started. "And I wanted to say that I'm sorry."

I wasn't ready to let her off the hook that easily. I didn't trust this woman as far as I could throw her, as the saying went. Now that I thought about it, that saying sounded awfully violent. "Sorry about what?"

She frowned. "About trying to ruin things between you and Riley. I actually think you two are really good together."

"Why would you want to ruin things between us? You have Lane."

"Lane bores me to tears. I'll probably marry him anyway. I mean, he's got a good job and my family likes him. But he's not Riley."

"Why were you waiting for him in the hotel room that night?"

She grimaced. "Because I still have quite a bit of growing up to do. I'm sorry. I know I've acted horribly. I was trying to collect dirt against you so that Riley would break things off. It was really brave what you did here, though."

"Thanks."

She reached out her hand. "Here."

I glanced at her palm and gasped. "My ring!" I snatched it away before it disappeared again. "How . . . ?"

"You left it on the sink when you were cleaning up after your tumble in the woods when you found Jackie." She glanced at the ground before pulling her gaze back up. "I'm sorry."

I slid the ring back on my finger. I'd missed wearing it and everything it stood for.

After Veronica walked away, I found Riley. His fingers laced with mine, and he pulled me onto the dance floor. I held up my hand.

His eyes widened. "You found it? How?"

I made a split second decision not to rat out his ex. "It's a long story. The important thing is that I have it back now."

"Let's talk," he started.

"Let's."

"I'd really like to start this week over. What do you say?"

"Absolutely." I was tempted to put my head on his chest as we swayed back and forth, but I really needed to look him in the eye. "I'm sorry I wasn't open with you, Riley. It was selfish and immature."

"And I'm sorry that I gave you the impression that I wanted you to be someone you're not. That's definitely not what I want for you. I love you because you're your own person. Maybe subconsciously I did want to put my best foot forward this weekend and not rock the boat too much."

"I'm a boat rocker."

He smiled. "Yes, you are. Through and through. And that's okay."

I bit down on the inside of my lip as reality washed

over me. "I'm continually afraid that I'm not long-term relationship material. I can't shake it. Riley, I'm constantly waiting for the day I mess up and you won't forgive me."

His thumb brushed over my cheek. "First of all, I think you are long-term relationship material. Every couple has arguments and doesn't see eye to eye sometimes. You and I are no different."

I nodded, knowing his words were true.

"Second, you have to embrace forgiveness if you love someone. Everyone's going to mess up. Everyone's going to need grace. It works both ways."

I paused for a moment as the song switched to "How Can I Be Sure." Was God a heavenly deejay who constantly ordained the music in the soundtrack of my life? "There's one more thing I need to tell you, Riley."

His gaze was intense on me. "Okay."

"I got a job offer this week." The rest of the people on the dance floor seemed to disappear. I felt like it was just Riley and I.

"A job offer? That's great."

I sucked on my bottom lip for a moment. "It's in Kansas."

His grip around me loosened. "Kansas? Really?"

I nodded. "Yeah, really."

"What are you going to do?"

I shrugged. "I have no idea."

"Oh." He squeezed my hand again. "If that's what you want to do, Gabby, then you should. You've worked hard. Those budget cuts at the state level really messed with your career."

"It would be kind of hard to get married if I lived in Kansas and you lived in Norfolk."

"We could figure out something." I heard the doubt in his voice.

I nodded anyway. "Of course we will."

My cell phone buzzed in my little black purse. I was tempted to ignore it until I saw the number was Sierra's. Maybe a break from this conversation would be nice. I held up a finger, as if to say "Just one minute" and then answered. I stepped off the dance floor, pulling Riley with me.

"Gabby? You'll never believe this."

"Believe what?" I raised my eyebrows at Riley and shrugged.

"Chad and I just got married."

"Married? I thought you'd broken up!"

"It's a long story. But we decided to elope. I'm sorry you guys couldn't be here. It was kind of last minute, though."

"Married?" I still couldn't believe it.

"Yeah, we want to go on our honeymoon. Are you still coming back this weekend? Because we can't leave Trauma Care without any employees."

"Married?" I had to stop asking that question.

She giggled on the other end. And Sierra hardly ever giggled. "Yes, married. I know it's crazy, but it just felt right. Why waste any more time?"

I glanced at Riley. That was right. Why should people waste any time if they loved each other? But what if their jobs were taking them thousands of miles apart?

"Congrats, Sierra. I'm really happy for you. And yes, we're leaving tomorrow, so you two can take your honeymoon. Where are you going?"

"Cancun. For two weeks. I know, it's kind of a long time. But five people in the area were shot last night, so I think it's going to get busy here in a few days."

"Of course I'll be there." How could I say no to Sierra? She'd been there for me countless times before.

Riley was staring at me with raised eyebrows when I hung up. "Did I just understand that correctly? Chad and Sierra eloped?"

I nodded. "I can't believe it." Riley and I were supposed to get married first. I mean, Chad and Sierra had only been dating for a couple of months. How could this have happened?

"Good for them. I hope they have a lifetime of happiness."

I glanced at Riley. A lifetime of happiness. That's what I was meant to have with him. So just how were we going to figure all of this out?

Riley stepped closer and lowered his lips over mine, softly and tenderly while humming, "The Street Where You Live." We swayed back and forth.

"*My Fair Lady*?"

He grinned. "You don't think I missed all of your references all week, did you?"

I shrugged. I definitely hadn't given him enough credit.

"You're no Eliza Doolittle, Gabby, but you do make me feel giddy whenever you're near. Like I'm several stories high, for that matter. And you're definitely a fair lady."

"That's just about the sweetest thing you've ever said to me, Henry Higgins—I mean, Riley Thomas." I grinned. "I've got to say, despite everything, I've really had the time of my life."

"*Dirty Dancing.* I picked up on those references, too."

I twisted my head as I looked up at him in admiration. "You're good."

"You wouldn't settle for anything less, would you?"

"Not on your life."

He grinned. "That might be a poor word choice considering how many times our lives have been on the line."

"Point taken."

"I love you, Gabby."

I wrapped my arms around his waist. "I love you, too, Riley."

And I did.

Whatever the future held.

###

Did you enjoy this book? Then check out the next book in the Squeaky Clean series: The Scum of All Fears!

Dear Reader,

Thank you so much for reading **Dirty Deeds**. I had a great time researching this book. Of course I *had* visit a fancy resort in the mountains of Virginia, just to make sure I got all of my details right. Research can be so tough sometimes. ;-) As I walked through the place, I imagined I was Gabby and thought about all the trouble she could get herself into!

Dirty Deeds is followed by **The Scum of All Fears.** In this book, Riley must confront a killer from his past who's determined to ruin him. Immediately following the that book is the next in the series, **To Love, Honor, and Perish.** These two books are intended to be read back to back, as the storylines connect.

Taking place at the same time as **Dirty Deeds** is the new novel about Sierra Nakamura, **Pounced**. Sierra finds a mystery of her own while Gabby and Riley are out of town, and of course her investigation involves animals! But Sierra not only finds trouble . . . could she find love as well?

Gabby's adventures continue in other books in this series, and her relationships—with friends, with Riley, with God—continue to bend and grow throughout. I hope you'll stick with Gabby and find out where all of her adventures lead.

Many blessings to you,
Christy Barritt
www.christybarritt.com

P.S. Please feel free to sign up for my infrequent newsletter. I send it approximately once a quarter, and it includes updates on my new and future releases. The link can be found on my website, at the bottom of the homepage: **www.christybarritt.com**.

P.S.S. If you enjoyed this book, I'd greatly appreciate a review! Here's a link to make it easier. Click **HERE**!

If you enjoyed this book, you may also enjoy these Squeaky Clean Mysteries:

Hazardous Duty (Book 1)

On her way to completing a degree in forensic science, Gabby St. Claire drops out of school and starts her own crime-scene cleaning business. When a routine cleaning job uncovers a murder weapon the police overlooked, she realizes that the wrong person is in jail. But the owner of the weapon is a powerful foe . . . and willing to do anything to keep Gabby quiet. With the help of her new neighbor, Riley Thomas, a man whose life and faith fascinate her, Gabby seeks to find the killer before another murder occurs.

Suspicious Minds (Book 2)

In this smart and suspenseful sequel to *Hazardous Duty*, crime-scene cleaner Gabby St. Claire finds herself stuck doing mold remediation to pay the bills. Her first day on the job, she uncovers a surprise in the crawlspace of a dilapidated home: Elvis, dead as a doornail and still wearing his blue-suede shoes. How could she possibly keep her nose out of a case like this?

It Came Upon a Midnight Crime (Book 2.5, a Novella)

Someone is intent on destroying the true meaning of Christmas—at least, destroying anything that hints of it. All around crime-scene cleaner Gabby St. Claire's hometown, anything pointing to Jesus as "the reason for the season" is being sabotaged. The crimes become more twisted as dismembered body parts are found at the vandalisms. Someone is determined to destroy Christmas . . . but Gabby is just as determined to find the Grinch and let peace on earth and goodwill prevail.

Organized Grime (Book 3)

Gabby St. Claire knows her best friend, Sierra, isn't guilty of killing three people in what appears to be an eco-terrorist attack. But Sierra has disappeared, her only contact a frantic phone call to Gabby proclaiming she's being hunted. Gabby is determined to prove her friend is innocent and to keep Sierra alive. While trying to track down the real perpetrator, Gabby notices a disturbing trend at the crime scenes she's cleaning, one that ties random crimes together—and points to Sierra as the guilty party. Just what has her friend gotten herself involved in?

Dirty Deeds (Book 4)

"Promise me one thing. No snooping. Just for one week." Gabby St. Claire knows that her fiancé's request is a simple one she should be able to honor. After all, Riley's law school reunion and attorneys' conference at a posh resort is a chance for them to get away from the mysteries Gabby often finds herself involved in as a crime-scene cleaner. Then an old friend of Riley's goes missing. Gabby suspects one of Riley's buddies might be behind the disappearance. When the missing woman's mom asks Gabby for help, how can she say no?

The Scum of All Fears (Book 5)

Gabby St. Claire is back to crime-scene cleaning and needs help after a weekend killing spree fills her work docket. A serial killer her fiancé put behind bars has escaped. His last words to Riley were: *I'll get out, and I'll get even.* Pictures of Gabby are found in the man's prison cell, messages are left for Gabby at crime scenes, someone keeps slipping in and out of her apartment, and her temporary assistant disappears. The search for answers becomes darker when Gabby realizes she's dealing with a criminal who is truly the scum of the earth. He will do anything to make Gabby's and Riley's lives a living nightmare.

To Love, Honor, and Perish (Book 6)
Just when Gabby St. Claire's life is on the right track, the unthinkable happens. Her fiancé, Riley Thomas, is shot and in life-threatening condition only a week before their wedding. Gabby is determined to figure out who pulled the trigger, even if investigating puts her own life at risk. As she digs deeper into the case, she discovers secrets better left alone. Doubts arise in her mind, and the one man with answers lies on death's doorstep. Then an old foe returns and tests everything Gabby is made of—physically, mentally, and spiritually. Will all she's worked for be destroyed?

Mucky Streak (Book 7)
Gabby St. Claire feels her life is smeared with the stain of tragedy. She takes a short-term gig as a private investigator—a cold case that's eluded detectives for ten years. The mass murder of a wealthy family seems impossible to solve, but Gabby brings more clues to light. Add to the mix a flirtatious client, travels to an exciting new city, and some quirky—albeit temporary—new sidekicks, and things get complicated. With every new development, Gabby prays that her "mucky streak" will end and the future will become clear. Yet every answer she uncovers leads her closer to danger—both for her life and for her heart.

Foul Play (Book 8)
Gabby St. Claire is crying "foul play" in every sense of the phrase. When the crime-scene cleaner agrees to go undercover at a local community theater, she discovers

more than backstage bickering, atrocious acting, and rotten writing. The female lead is dead, and an old classmate who has staked everything on the musical production's success is about to go under. In her dual role of investigator and star of the show, Gabby finds the stakes rising faster than the opening-night curtain. She must face her past and make monumental decisions, not just about the play but also concerning her future relationships and career. Will Gabby find the killer before the curtain goes down—not only on the play, but also on life as she knows it?

Broom and Gloom (Book 9)

Gabby St. Claire is determined to get back in the saddle again. While in Oklahoma for a forensic conference, she meets her soon-to-be stepbrother, Trace Ryan, an up-and-coming country singer. A woman he was dating has disappeared, and he suspects a crazy fan may be behind it. Gabby agrees to investigate, as she tries to juggle her conference, navigate being alone in a new place, and locate a woman who may not want to be found. She discovers that sometimes taking life by the horns means staring danger in the face, no matter the consequences.

Dust and Obey (Book 10)

When Gabby St. Claire's ex-fiancé, Riley Thomas, asks for her help in investigating a possible murder at a couples retreat, she knows she should say no. She knows she should run far, far away from the danger of both being around Riley and the crime. But her nosy instincts and determination take precedence over her logic. Gabby and Riley must work together to find the killer. In the process, they have to confront demons from their past and deal with their present relationship.

Thrill Squeaker **(Book 11)**
An abandoned theme park. An unsolved murder. A decision that will change Gabby's life forever. Restoring an old amusement park and turning it into a destination resort seems like a fun idea for former crime-scene cleaner Gabby St. Claire. The side job gives her the chance to spend time with her friends, something she's missed since beginning a new career. The job turns out to be more than Gabby bargained for when she finds a dead body on her first day. Add to the mix legends of Bigfoot, creepy clowns, and ghostlike remnants of happier times at the park, and her stay begins to feel like a rollercoaster ride. Someone doesn't want the decrepit Mythical Falls to open again, but just how far is this person willing to go to ensure this venture fails? As the stakes rise and danger creeps closer, will Gabby be able to restore things in her own life that time has destroyed—including broken relationships? Or is her future closer to the fate of the doomed Mythical Falls?

Swept Away, **a Honeymoon Novella (Book 11.5)**
Finding the perfect place for a honeymoon, away from any potential danger or mystery, is challenging. But Gabby's longtime love and newly minted husband, Riley Thomas, has done it. He has found a location with a nonexistent crime rate, a mostly retired population, and plenty of opportunities for relaxation in the warm sun. Within minutes of the newlyweds' arrival, a convoy of vehicles pulls up to a nearby house, and their honeymoon oasis is destroyed like a sandcastle in a storm. Despite Gabby's and Riley's determination to keep to themselves, trouble comes knocking at their door—literally—when a neighbor is abducted from the beach directly outside their rental. Will Gabby and Riley be swept away with each other

during their honeymoon . . . or will a tide of danger and mayhem pull them under?

Cunning Attractions (Book 12)
Coming soon

While You Were Sweeping, a Riley Thomas Novella
Riley Thomas is trying to come to terms with life after a traumatic brain injury turned his world upside down. Away from everything familiar—including his crime-scene-cleaning former fiancée and his career as a social-rights attorney—he's determined to prove himself and regain his old life. But when he claims he witnessed his neighbor shoot and kill someone, everyone thinks he's crazy. When all evidence of the crime disappears, even Riley has to wonder if he's losing his mind.

Note: *While You Were Sweeping* is a spin-off mystery written in conjunction with the Squeaky Clean series featuring crime-scene cleaner Gabby St. Claire.

The Sierra Files

Pounced (Book 1)
Animal-rights activist Sierra Nakamura never expected to stumble upon the dead body of a coworker while filming a project nor get involved in the investigation. But when someone threatens to kill her cats unless she hands over the "information," she becomes more bristly than an angry feline. Making matters worse is the fact that her cats—and the investigation—are driving a wedge between her and her boyfriend, Chad. With every answer she uncovers, old hurts rise to the surface and test her beliefs. Saving her cats might mean ruining everything else in her life. In the fight for survival, one thing is certain: either pounce or be pounced.

Hunted (Book 2)
Who knew a stray dog could cause so much trouble? Newlywed animal-rights activist Sierra Nakamura Davis must face her worst nightmare: breaking the news she eloped with Chad to her ultra-opinionated tiger mom. Her perfectionist parents have planned a vow-renewal ceremony at Sierra's lush childhood home, but a neighborhood dog ruins the rehearsal dinner when it shows up toting what appears to be a fresh human bone. While dealing with the dog, a nosy neighbor, and an old flame turning up at the wrong times, Sierra hunts for answers. Her journey of discovery leads to more than just who committed the crime.

Pranced (Book 2.5, a Christmas novella)
Sierra Nakamura Davis thinks spending Christmas with her husband's relatives will be a real Yuletide treat. But when

the animal-rights activist learns his family has a reindeer farm, she begins to feel more like the Grinch. Even worse, when Sierra arrives, she discovers the reindeer are missing. Sierra fears the animals might be suffering a worse fate than being used for entertainment purposes. Can Sierra set aside her dogmatic opinions to help get the reindeer home in time for the holidays? Or will secrets tear the family apart and ruin Sierra's dream of the perfect Christmas?

Rattled (Book 3)

"What do you mean a thirteen-foot lavender albino ball python is missing?" Tough-as-nails Sierra Nakamura Davis isn't one to get flustered. But trying to balance being a wife and a new mom with her crusade to help animals is proving harder than she imagined. Add a missing python, a high maintenance intern, and a dead body to the mix, and Sierra becomes the definition of rattled. Can she balance it all—and solve a possible murder—without losing her mind?

Holly Anna Paladin Mysteries

Random Acts of Murder (Book 1)
When Holly Anna Paladin is given a year to live, she embraces her final days doing what she loves most—random acts of kindness. But one of her extreme good deeds goes horribly wrong, implicating her in a string of murders. Holly is suddenly thrust into a different kind of fight for her life. Could it also be random that the detective assigned to the case is her old high school crush and present-day nemesis? Will Holly find the killer before he ruins what is left of her life? Or will she spend her final days alone and behind bars?

Random Acts of Deceit (Book 2)
"Break up with Chase Dexter, or I'll kill him." Holly Anna Paladin never expected such a gut-wrenching ultimatum. With home invasions, hidden cameras, and bomb threats, Holly must make some serious choices. Whatever she decides, the consequences will either break her heart or break her soul. She tries to match wits with the Shadow Man, but the more she fights, the deeper she's drawn into the perilous situation. With her sister's wedding problems and the riots in the city, Holly has nearly reached her breaking point. She must stop this mystery man before someone she loves dies. But the deceit is threatening to pull her under . . . six feet under.

Random Acts of Murder (Book 3)
When Holly Anna Paladin's boyfriend, police detective Chase Dexter, says he's leaving for two weeks and can't give any details, she wants to trust him. But when she discovers Chase may be involved in some unwise and

dangerous pursuits, she's compelled to intervene. Holly gets a run for her money as she's swept into the world of horseracing. The stakes turn deadly when a dead body surfaces and suspicion is cast on Chase. At every turn, more trouble emerges, making Holly question what she holds true about her relationship and her future. Just when she thinks she's on the homestretch, a dark horse arises. Holly might lose everything in a nail-biting fight to the finish.

Random Acts of Scrooge (Book 3.5)

Christmas is supposed to be the most wonderful time of the year, but a real-life Scrooge is threatening to ruin the season's good will. Holly Anna Paladin can't wait to celebrate Christmas with family and friends. She loves everything about the season—celebrating the birth of Jesus, singing carols, and baking Christmas treats, just to name a few. But when a local family needs help, how can she say no? Holly's community has come together to help raise funds to save the home of Greg and Babette Sullivan, but a Bah-Humburgler has snatched the canisters of cash. Holly and her boyfriend, police detective Chase Dexter, team up to catch the Christmas crook. Will they succeed in collecting enough cash to cover the Sullivans' overdue bills? Or will someone succeed in ruining Christmas for all those involved?

Random Acts of Guilt (Book 4)

Coming soon

Carolina Moon Series

Home Before Dark (Book 1)
Nothing good ever happens after dark. Country singer
Daleigh McDermott's father often repeated those words.
Now, her father is dead. As she's about to flee back to
Nashville, she finds his hidden journal with hints that his
death was no accident. Mechanic Ryan Shields is the only
one who seems to believe Daleigh. Her father trusted the
man, but her attraction to Ryan scares her. She knows her
life and career are back in Nashville and her time in the
sleepy North Carolina town is only temporary. As Daleigh
and Ryan work to unravel the mystery, it becomes obvious
that someone wants them dead. They must rely on each
other—and on God—if they hope to make it home before
the darkness swallows them.

Gone By Dark (Book 2)
Charity White can't forget what happened ten years earlier
when she and her best friend, Andrea, cut through the
woods on their way home from school. A man abducted
Andrea, who hasn't been seen since. Charity has tried to
outrun the memories and guilt. What if they hadn't taken
that shortcut? Why wasn't Charity kidnapped instead of
Andrea? And why weren't the police able to track down
the bad guy? When Charity receives a mysterious letter
that promises answers, she returns to North Carolina in
search of closure and the peace that has eluded her. With
the help of her new neighbor, Police Officer Joshua Haven,
Charity begins to track down mysterious clues. They soon
discover that they must work together or both of them will
be swallowed by the looming darkness.

Cape Thomas Mysteries:

Dubiosity (Book 1)

Savannah Harris vowed to leave behind her old life as an investigative reporter. But when two migrant workers go missing, her curiosity spikes. As more eerie incidents begin afflicting the area, each works to draw Savannah out of her seclusion and raise the stakes—for her and the surrounding community. Even as Savannah's new boarder, Clive Miller, makes her feel things she thought long forgotten, she suspects he's hiding something too, and he's not the only one. As secrets emerge and danger closes in, Savannah must choose between faith and uncertainty. One wrong decision might spell the end . . . not just for her but for everyone around her. Will she unravel the mystery in time, or will doubt get the best of her?

Disillusioned (Book 2) *coming soon*

Nikki Wright is desperate to help her brother, Bobby, who hasn't been the same since escaping from a detainment camp run by terrorists in Colombia. Rumor has it that he betrayed his navy brothers and conspired with those who held him hostage, and both the press and the military are hounding him for answers. All Nikki wants is to shield her brother so he has time to recover and heal. But soon they realize the paparazzi are the least of their worries. When a group of men try to abduct Nikki and her brother, Bobby insists that Kade Wheaton, another former SEAL, can keep them out of harm's way. But can Nikki trust Kade? After all, the man who broke her heart eight years ago is anything but safe...Hiding out in a farmhouse on the Chesapeake Bay, Nikki finds her loyalties—and the remnants of her long-held faith—tested as she and Kade put aside their differences to keep Bobby's increasingly erratic behavior under wraps. But when Bobby disappears, Nikki will have to trust Kade completely if she wants to uncover the truth about a rumored conspiracy. Nikki's life—and the fate of the nation—depends on it.

Standalones

The Good Girl

Tara Lancaster can sing "Amazing Grace" in three harmonies, two languages, and interpret it for the hearing impaired. She can list the Bible canon backward, forward, and alphabetized. The only time she ever missed church was when she had pneumonia and her mom made her stay home. Then her life shatters and her reputation is left in ruins. She flees halfway across the country to dog-sit, but the quiet anonymity she needs isn't waiting at her sister's house. Instead, she finds a knife with a threatening message, a fame-hungry friend, a too-hunky neighbor, and evidence of . . . a ghost? Following all the rules has gotten her nowhere. And nothing she learned in Sunday School can tell her where to go from there.

Death of the Couch Potato's Wife (Suburban Sleuth Mysteries)

You haven't seen desperate until you've met Laura Berry, a career-oriented city slicker turned suburbanite housewife. Well-trained in the big-city commandment, "mind your own business," Laura is persuaded by her spunky seventy-year-old neighbor, Babe, to check on another neighbor who hasn't been seen in days. She finds Candace Flynn, wife of the infamous "Couch King," dead, and at last has a reason to get up in the morning. Someone is determined to stop her from digging deeper into the death of her neighbor, but Laura is just as determined to figure out who is behind the death-by-poisoned-pork-rinds.

Imperfect

Since the death of her fiancé two years ago, novelist

Morgan Blake's life has been in a holding pattern. She has a major case of writer's block, and a book signing in the mountain town of Perfect sounds as perfect as its name. Her trip takes a wrong turn when she's involved in a hit-and-run: She hit a man, and he ran from the scene. Before fleeing, he mouthed the word "Help." First she must find him. In Perfect, she finds a small town that offers all she ever wanted. But is something sinister going on behind its cheery exterior? Was she invited as a guest of honor simply to do a book signing? Or was she lured to town for another purpose—a deadly purpose?

The Gabby St. Claire Diaries (a tween mystery series)

The Curtain Call Caper (Book 1)

Is a ghost haunting the Oceanside Middle School auditorium? What else could explain the disasters surrounding the play—everything from missing scripts to a falling spotlight and damaged props? Seventh-grader Gabby St. Claire has dreamed about being part of her school's musical, but a series of unfortunate events threatens to shut down the production. While trying to uncover the culprit and save her fifteen minutes of fame, she also has to manage impossible teachers, cliques, her dysfunctional family, and a secret she can't tell even her best friend. Will Gabby figure out who or what is sabotaging the show . . . or will it be curtains for her and the rest of the cast?

The Disappearing Dog Dilemma (Book 2)

Why are dogs disappearing around town? When two friends ask seventh-grader Gabby St. Claire for her help in finding their missing canines, Gabby decides to unleash her sleuthing skills to sniff out whoever is behind the act. But time management and relationships get tricky as worrisome weather, a part-time job, and a new crush interfere with Gabby's investigation. Will her determination crack the case? Or will shadowy villains, a penchant for overcommitting, and even her own heart put her in the doghouse?

The Bungled Bike Burglaries (Book 3)

Stolen bikes and a long-forgotten time capsule leave one amateur sleuth baffled and busy. Seventh-grader Gabby

St. Claire is determined to bring a bike burglar to justice—
and not just because mean girl Donabell Bullock is strong-
arming her. But each new clue brings its own set of
trouble. As if that's not enough, Gabby finds evidence of a
decades-old murder within the contents of the time
capsule, but no one seems to take her seriously. As her
investigation heats up, will Gabby's knack for being in the
wrong place at the wrong time with the wrong people
crack the case? Or will it prove hazardous to her health?

Complete Book List

Squeaky Clean Mysteries:
#1 Hazardous Duty
#2 Suspicious Minds
#2.5 It Came Upon a Midnight Crime
#3 Organized Grime
#4 Dirty Deeds
#5 The Scum of All Fears
#6 To Love, Honor, and Perish
#7 Mucky Streak
#8 Foul Play
#9 Broom and Gloom
#10 Dust and Obey
#11 Thrill Squeaker
#11.5 Swept Away (a novella)
#12 Cunning Attractions (coming soon)

Squeaky Clean Companion Novella:
While You Were Sweeping

The Sierra Files:
#1 Pounced
#2 Hunted
#2.5 Pranced (a Christmas novella)
#3 Rattled

The Gabby St. Claire Diaries (a Tween Mystery series):
#1 The Curtain Call Caper
#2 The Disappearing Dog Dilemma
#3 The Bungled Bike Burglaries

Holly Anna Paladin Mysteries:
#1 Random Acts of Murder

#2 Random Acts of Deceit
#3 Random Acts of Malice
#3.5 Random Acts of Scrooge
#4 Random Acts of Guilt (coming soon)

Carolina Moon Series:
Home Before Dark
Gone By Dark
Wait Until Dark

Suburban Sleuth Mysteries:
#1 Death of the Couch Potato's Wife

Stand-alone Romantic-Suspense:
Keeping Guard
The Last Target
Race Against Time
Ricochet
Key Witness
Lifeline
High-Stakes Holiday Reunion
Desperate Measures
Hidden Agenda
Mountain Hideaway
Dark Harbor

Cape Thomas Mysteries
Dubiosity
Disillusioned (coming soon)

Standalone Romantic Mystery:
The Good Girl

Suspense:

Imperfect

Nonfiction:
Changed: True Stories of Finding God through Christian Music
The Novel in Me: The Beginner's Guide to Writing and Publishing a Novel

About the Author:

USA Today has called Christy Barritt's books "scary, funny, passionate, and quirky."

Christy writes both mystery and romantic suspense novels that are clean with underlying messages of faith. Her books have won the Daphne du Maurier Award for Excellence in Suspense and Mystery, have been twice nominated for the Romantic Times Reviewers' Choice Award, and have finaled for both a Carol Award and Foreword Magazine's Book of the Year.

She is married to her Prince Charming, a man who thinks she's hilarious—but only when she's not trying to be. Christy is a self-proclaimed klutz, an avid music lover who's known for spontaneously bursting into song, and a road trip aficionado. When she's not working or spending time with her family, she enjoys singing, playing the guitar, and exploring small, unsuspecting towns where people have no idea how accident-prone she is.

Find Christy online at:
www.christybarritt.com
www.facebook.com/christybarritt
www.twitter.com/cbarritt

Sign up for Christy's newsletter to get information on all of her latest releases here: **www.christybarritt.com/newsletter-sign-up/**

If you enjoyed this book, please consider leaving a review.